SOOTHING THE BEAST

VIRGINIE MARCONATO

OLIVERHEBERBOOKS

PROLOGUE

He should have asked for her name.

As his feet pounded the sodden ground, Sigurd wondered at his surprising reserve in front of the girl. He was not renowned for his shyness, quite the contrary, nor was he usually tongue-tied in front of women he found attractive. With a smile and a suggestive comment he could win them around before they knew what was happening. But this had been different. He would have felt like a boor to accost the Saxon when she was here to see his friend, Wolf.

Men sought the Icelander's help for a variety of reasons. They had been attacked by a mob and needed protection, they wished to prove their innocence when accused of a crime by the local Saxons, they wanted advice about the best way to fit in their new country. But women... Women only came to Wolf for one reason.

Because they had been attacked and wanted retribution, and the last thing a woman who'd been hurt wanted was to find herself having to fend off advances from another menacing-looking Norseman.

He had not missed the way she kept glancing around the village as he led her to Wolf's hut. She was scared. Scared she would see the man who had assaulted her. In those circumstances, Sigurd could not have acted on the desire she'd provoked in him, he would only have frightened her further.

So he'd pretended not to notice her beautiful face, or her womanly curves, and left her with Merewen without a word.

Sigurd sent a stone flying into the undergrowth with a well-placed kick. Bloody hell, how many women would he have to rescue or see injured? Only the other day in town he had saved his friend's wife from a bastard intent on raping her. The man had only escaped with his life because Sigurd's priority had been ensuring Merewen was still breathing when she'd fainted from the shock. Mercifully, his intervention had prevented her attacker from actually taking her.

The blonde woman had probably not been so lucky. He knew his friend asked the women he helped to inform him of the possible consequences of the rape.

Had she come to tell him she had fallen with her attacker's child?

Another stone was sent flying against a tree. He'd make sure to ask Wolf who the bastard was. His friend had no doubt already punished him, but Sigurd could not help but feel this was personal, because this woman was... well, she was not like the others, even if he could not say why.

Her face kept floating in his mind. Heart-shaped, more delicate than a newly-unfurled flower, adorned with soulful brown eyes framed by thick gold lashes, he already knew it would haunt him for days. Why? Why did he have to be attracted to her of all women? Anyone else he could have pursued. Why did he have to fall for someone recovering from a rape and afraid of Norsemen?

He sighed and looked at the tree branches swaying overhead.

Damnation, as the Saxons said, he should at least have asked for her name!

CHAPTER ONE

EAST ANGLIA WINTER 1036

Feeling lighter than she had in days, Frigyth set off in the direction of the forest.

That morning she had bled. For a moment the relief of seeing the proof that her attacker had not gotten her with child had quite overwhelmed her. Then she had rushed out to Wolf, who'd asked to be informed about any new development. He'd shared her relief at the news and assured her she could rely on him if she needed anything else.

She didn't.

Now that she knew the attack wouldn't have consequences she might be able to put the whole ordeal behind her and start living her life.

Her lips trembled as the thought crossed her mind. Could such a thing ever be forgotten? She wasn't sure. But she would try. She had overcome enough misery in her life to know she was more resilient than most. At the death of her father a month ago, she'd thought she could finally start a life free of woe. Then, barely a fortnight later, she'd been attacked by one of the Norsemen living in the village beyond the lake, not a promising beginning to say the least.

Determined to push all grim thoughts from her mind, she walked on, only to come to a skidding halt almost immediately. A man was standing in the middle of the clearing. A tall, blond man with broad shoulders and a beard. A Norseman, unmistakably. Her heart almost jumped out of her chest. Was it Olaf, the one who—

Before she could finish the question already forming in her mind, the man moved and she saw his profile better.

It was only Wolf's friend, the one who had taken her to the hut earlier.

Frigyth let out a long exhale. Now that she knew he was not the man who'd raped her, her heartbeat should have returned to its normal rhythm. It did not, because at that precise moment, the Norseman moved into a shaft of sunlight and stretched. Captivated, she watched his long legs twist and tense under his skin-tight braies, his muscular chest bulge, his neck arch. The sun shining overheard caused his blond hair to gleam like a sheet of gold over his shoulders.

And then... Then he turned and saw her. The noises of the forest receded into the background as Frigyth stared at his face. Too busy looking around in case she spotted her attacker, she had not looked at him properly earlier. But now she certainly did, making the most of the winter sun's pale light .

He could have been Wolf's brother. If she'd had to describe the two men, the two descriptions would have been identical. And yet... His blond hair fell over his shoulders in a different way, his beard was shorter, his body leaner, the expression on his face different. His eyes were of a slightly less piercing blue, a warmer shade of ice.

Warm ice? Frigyth shook her head. What was she talking about? As if such a thing existed...

"Hello again." She had to say something, she could not just stand here looking at him, or he would take her for a ninny.

He tilted his head. "Hello. You've seen Wolf then?"

"Yes, I have." She flushed at the question. Did he know why she was here? She dearly hoped not. "Thank you for taking me to him."

"It's not a problem. Are you on your way back home?"

Unlike Wolf, he spoke with only the faintest trace of accent, as if he'd spent a long time in her country but had arrived too late to fully forget his origins. It gave his speech an entrancing quality. Not that she wouldn't have been entranced otherwise. She couldn't seem to tear her eyes from him, his nose and high cheekbones in particular. They seemed to have been carved out of stone. And yet the effect was not as forbidding as it could have been.

Just captivating.

"Yes, I'm going back home. I would like to get there before nightfall," she said, glancing up at the sky. It was probably already too late for that. In the winter night came early.

The man was still looking at her. The expression in his warm ice eyes was unfathomable. It was as if he made a conscious effort to hide his thoughts from her. Why? Usually she could tell what people thought when they looked at her. Compassion, like the woman in Wolf's hut, anger, like her father when he had drunk more than was wise, lust, like the man who had—

No. She would not think about that vile man now. Only moments ago she had decided to push the memory out of her mind. She could not stumble at the first hurdle.

"I should accompany you," the Norseman said eventually.

Frigyth's eyes darted around. Yes, perhaps. She had been attacked in the forest, after all, she knew what dangers lurked there... Still, she refused to live the rest of her life cowering.

"Thank you, but there is no need."

Sigurd would have insisted but the way the woman had stiffened told him he had better not. Evidently she was determined not to allow what had happened to her to frighten her. It was a brave decision and he should respect it. His only concession would be to follow her at a distance to ensure no harm befell her.

He had already resolved to ask Wolf later but here was the chance to do that himself. He would not let it pass a second time. "I never asked you your name earlier."

"No, you didn't."

He stared at her. He had not been after a confirmation, but an answer. "Well?"

"Well, what?"

"Will you tell me who you are now?"

"Why?"

Damn it all! Sigurd almost swore out loud. He had not imagined it would be so difficult to extract such simple information from anyone. "I don't know." He threw his hands up in a gesture of powerlessness. "Isn't it what people do when they meet?"

"People who intend to see each other again, yes. But we probably won't."

Something tightened in his chest at the notion. No, they probably wouldn't. Still, did she have to point this out so bluntly?

"Besides, I don't know your name either," she added.

Beast.

The word exploded in Sigurd's mind, as welcome as a blow to the skull. Why did the terrible nickname have to resurface at the worst possible moments? You would think after all this time he would have gotten over it! It had been more than ten years since anyone had called him that, but he still felt the sting of it too vividly for his liking.

"It's Sigurd," he growled. When the girl winced he understood he'd been too gruff by half. She'd only asked for a name, and he had almost bitten her head off, exactly like the beast he was trying not to be. "Forgive me, only it's... No one ever used my real name in Denmark, my country. They called me 'Beast' and it's rather..." He hesitated, looking for the best word to describe it. Demeaning? Hurtful? Cruel?

"Frigyth."

Sigurd blinked. Although he'd been in this country for more than a decade, occasionally there were words he didn't understand. Like this one. "I'm sorry, I don't know that word," he said, running a hand through his hair. What did that mean? Frightful? Humiliating? Or was it worse than that? Did she actually think it an appropriate nickname for him?

She gave a tentative smile. "It's not a word, it doesn't mean anything. It's just my name. You asked. It's Frigyth."

What an idiot! After barking at her and admitting that people called him a beast, now he had made it sound as if he thought the name too ridiculous to be a proper name. Which it wasn't. It was lovely, different. Just like her.

"Nice to meet you, Frigyth." Sigurd winced inwardly. Did he have to sound so ludicrously formal? Really, this was not going well at all. He had not felt this awkward with a woman since... Well, since ever. Either he'd been too young to think about seducing them or too determined not to be a failure to allow discomfort to stand in the way. Not a man used to feeling at a disadvantage in front of anyone, Sigurd was making a fool of himself in front of the little Saxon. The novelty was not a welcome one. "I was about to go and check the nest in that tree for eggs," he improvised, feeling completely at a loss.

She glanced at the tree he had indicated at random. "That one? Are you sure it is strong enough to hold your weight?"

Probably not, Sigurd thought, taking a better look at the oak.

There wasn't a nest that he could see either, but he had to do something. He could not stay here and look into Frigyth's soulful eyes or he would end up doing something even more stupid than snarling at her like a beast.

"It should be fine," he said levelly.

"Very well. I will leave you to it then."

She made no move to go, as if she had guessed he had only just made up the excuse and wanted to expose the lie. He could not retract it now. Grabbing the lowest branch, Sigurd hoisted himself up. As they'd feared, it felt barely strong enough to support him. The next two actually sagged under his weight. He paused and considered. The next branch up looked even more fragile. Still, it should hold if he placed his foot on the thicker part and wrapped his arms around the trunk while he pretended to look for the elusive nest. By now he was too high up for Frigyth to see what he was doing.

It all happened in quick succession, but not quick enough that he did not see it coming before it did. A crack split the silence, his foot slipped, his fingers had no choice but to loosen their grip on the flimsy branch they were holding. He fell, but by some miracle managed to land on his feet. The moment he felt his ankle twist on the sodden ground, Sigurd knew it might have been better if he'd landed on his backside after all. The mud made it impossible for him to stay upright. He collapsed like an empty sack of grain.

Frigyth was at his side in an instant.

"Are you all right? Dear me, you gave me the fright of my life! I thought you'd broken your neck."

"I'm fine," he said through gritted teeth. In truth he wasn't sure about the state of his ankle but he would never admit to it. He waited, tried to move it and barely repressed a grunt. It might not be broken, but it was definitely not right either.

"Why can you not stand? Did you twist your ankle?" She sounded suspicious now. Damnation, she had seen all was not as it should be.

"Of course, I can stand."

With tremendous effort, he did so, but as soon as he was up, he had to lean on the tree. His injured ankle could barely support his weight.

"You have sprained your ankle, and no wonder in this mud. Come, I will help you back to your hut," Frigyth decided. "Lean on me."

"No. I'm too heavy for you." She barely reached up to his shoulder. Damn it, she should not be exerting herself so!

She gave a small smile, not worried in the least. "You're too heavy for me to carry, certainly, but I think I can bear to have your arm wrapped around my shoulders."

The question was, how was he going to bear having her body pressed against his, and her scent filling his nostrils? When she seized his arm to force him to lean on to her, he shuddered. Despite her diminutive size, the woman was as stubborn as he was. He surrendered, knowing he had no choice. Whatever happened, he would *not* crawl back to his hut like an animal. There was a limit to his humiliation.

"This way." He nodded toward the edge of the clearing.

"See, I'm the perfect height to be your crutch."

He grunted. Crutch! Was she trying to hurt his dignity?

"You can lean in more. I'm not a flimsy oak branch, I won't break." There was laughter in her voice.

"Well, I'm not taking the risk," he snapped, not enjoying being the butt of her joke.

When she should have cowered at the growl, she giggled. "It is fortunate you hadn't collected the eggs yet or you would be covered in sticky goo right now, as well as in mud."

Sigurd groaned. Did she have to sound so amused? Did she have to point out what a humiliating situation this was for him? He was a man, he shouldn't have to rely on her to walk! He had wanted to impress her, and here he was, limping like an old man, and filthier than a pig in its bog.

What a shambles this had been.

CHAPTER TWO

"Here."

Frigyth helped Sigurd lie down on his pallet. She had expected him to protest, but he complied more readily than she had feared. He must really be in pain, she decided, or he would have made a show of not needing her assistance. It was not hard to guess that he hated being seen in such a vulnerable moment by someone he didn't know. But some things could not be helped and she did not think the less of him for being injured. It happened.

Besides, she was grateful for the distraction. Without him she would now be walking through the forest, doing her best to keep panic at bay at the idea of a man pouncing on her from behind a bush.

Anything was better than that, even tending an irritated giant.

"We will need to elevate your leg to reduce the swelling," she declared, taking charge. Before he could say anything she turned around to grab the three-legged stool from behind her. Then she placed a small sack of flour on it. Taking care not to jolt his leg too much, she placed his calf on it. Perfect. This would be as comfortable as could be.

"How do you know what to do?" Sigurd asked just as gruffly as before.

"I've had my ankle twisted more than once," she answered, looking at his leather boot pensively. It was enormous. My. His foot had to be twice as big as her own. "I know what to do by now. I will need to remove your shoe to assess the damage. I don't think the ankle is broken, for if it was, you would have howled in pain when you landed on the ground."

"I don't howl!" He sounded mightily aggrieved at the idea. She chided herself for the ill-chosen word.

"No, of course, you don't. You're not a beast. But if it was broken, you would likely not be able to put any weight on it at all, is what I mean. I hear it's awfully painful. Now let me see what we're dealing with."

He rolled his eyes and Frigyth smiled to herself. He looked like a disgruntled bear but at least he was heeding her instructions and he had not refused to have his foot examined. With slow, careful gestures she started to unlace his boot. Taking it off was not easy but by proceeding slowly, she managed not to inflict more pain than necessary. Checking his face for signs of discomfort she knew he would never allow himself to show, she then peeled away the woolen sock.

As she revealed more and more of his foot, her heart started to beat faster and faster. It was not only big, it was long, elegant, with well-trimmed nails, and clean, nothing like those of the men she had seen. The inexplicable urge to stroke it to see if it was as soft as it appeared to be seized her. Perhaps she could do it, but just imagining running her fingers over the pale skin caused excitement to flutter in her chest.

How odd... She had never before thought of feet as enticing and, after what had happened to her, she should be wary of being alone with a man she didn't know. If Olaf had pounced on her in the forest, where everyone could see him, would this man, Sigurd, not think of making the most of the protection of the hut to have his way with her?

No. What was she thinking? Not only was he injured, but he was Wolf's friend. She felt certain she could trust a friend of the Icelander's.

Sigurd cleared his throat and she realized she had been lost in contemplation for far too long. What would he be thinking? And what was she doing, staring at his foot thus? She had to stop being so silly. This man was not her lover, and this was hardly a sensual moment. He had twisted his ankle and she was supposed to help him get better.

"I will have to bandage your ankle," she whispered. "It will help with the pain and the swelling as well."

Sigurd clenched his teeth. Having Frigyth bent over his prone form and brushing his naked skin with delicate fingers would not help with the swelling in another part of his anatomy. He could already feel it stirring to life at the thought. But there was no choice, he could tell she wouldn't leave until she had set him to rights and, in truth, he didn't want her to leave. He would just have to let her swaddle him like a babe and be happy about it.

There was one thing he needed to do before that, though.

He took the blanket next to him and threw it over his body to hide the effect her proximity would have on him. She arched a brow and he saw her lip quiver in amusement. Oh, wonderful, now she thought he was a weakling. Could this get any worse? She would leave the hut thinking him as masculine as a old woman, as resilient as a kitten and as strong as an invalid, *not* the impression he wanted to give her.

"I'm more comfortable like this," he grumbled. His self-esteem demanded he said something to justify himself. He could not bring himself to lie and say he was cold, and he could not admit to the real reason for his gesture for fear of frightening her. Besides, it was not a lie. He *was* more comfortable like that, knowing she wouldn't be able to see the effect she had on him.

To his relief, she didn't comment and asked instead where she could find pieces of cloth to bandage his ankle. He nodded toward the chest by the door and braced himself for what was to come. When she brushed a light finger over the top of his foot, he closed his eyes. This was going to be torture.

"Am I hurting you?" she asked, sounding self-conscious.

Pain was the last thing in his mind right now. No one, perhaps not even himself, had stroked that part of his body before. His lovers usually focused on another part of his anatomy. He had not minded, but he was surprised to discover how sensitive the skin around his ankle was and how pleasurable it was to have small fingers brush along the top of his foot. If it felt good even when he was hurt, he could not begin to imagine how it would feel on the other foot, where she would be able to apply more pressure.

Then he remembered she had asked him a question.

"No, you're not hurting me," he said rather huskily, imagining what he would do if she started to stroke him in a different place. Not that she would of course...

Nodding, she carried on with her maddeningly arousing ministrations, taking care not to cause him any unnecessary pain. She needn't have bothered. Looking at her perfect profile was distraction enough and anyway, all his bodily sensations seemed to have fled to the part of him covered with the blanket. He would not have noticed anything unless she started to hit his foot with a hammer.

After an eternity that somehow seemed too short, she stepped back, taking her fresh, forest scent with her. Sigurd started to breathe again. Outside it had started raining, and the light had dimmed significantly. He saw Frigyth bite her bottom lip in consternation.

A consternation he shared.

"You cannot walk back home now. It will be too dangerous," he said, voicing out loud what she was clearly thinking. "Night has already started to fall."

She didn't even think of protesting. "No. I could go to Wolf, perhaps?"

His whole body recoiled in protest. She was not going anywhere. If she was to stay in the village, she would stay here. With him. Nevertheless, he tried to sound accommodating. Better she made the decision herself than he forced it on her.

"Yes, you could go to him," he agreed through clenched teeth. "But I think his wife might object."

"Wolf is married?" Did he imagine the hint of dismay in her voice? Probably not. He knew all too well women lusted after the mighty Icelander whom many saw as the savior of the community, but he would have liked at least this one not to fall under his charm. "To the dark-haired woman I saw in his hut?"

"Yes. Merewen. Didn't she say she was his wife?" He frowned. Why the secrecy?

"Oh no! Oh, I'm so stupid!"

Clearly she *was* disappointed. "Why are you stupid?" Great. Now it seemed he was the one asking her awkward questions...

"Because I thought she was his slave, I even told her as much. Now I know why she was put out." Frigyth shook her head. "Well. In any case, I am happy for Wolf. It was about time he found someone who will look after him for a change. He deserves it, after all he's done for others."

Oh. Maybe she was not disappointed after all. Maybe he'd found the one woman who did not lust after his friend. Blood started to flow back in Sigurd's veins. Maybe despite a disastrous beginning all was not lost.

"Stay here." The words were out of his mouth before he could think, and in far too abrupt a manner. Damn, did he have to be such a forceful boor? "I mean, I will be happy to provide you with shelter for the night, to thank you for your help, you know." He glanced at his bandaged ankle.

She hesitated. "I don't know you..."

"No, but Wolf can vouch for me. Go to his hut now, ask him whatever you want. He will tell you that you have nothing to fear from me." Willing her to trust him, he kept his voice even, his gaze steady—and his lap covered. At the thought of having her sleeping next to him he had gone as hard as an untried youth. It would not do for her to see it, now less than ever. "I swear I won't hurt you. You've seen I cannot walk unaided anyway. A kick to the ankle will be enough to send me to my knees if I decided to make a fool of myself and inconvenience you." Seeing that she already thought him a pathetic weakling, he might as well use it to make her see he was no threat to her. The damage was already done.

But in reality, thanks to her care of him, it was not as bad as he had feared at first. Of course, now was not the time to point out that an injured ankle would not stand in the way of his desire if he thought she was willing... Hell, he wasn't sure a severed arm would if by some miracle she demanded to be bedded.

"I can't think of many things that could send a man like you to his knees," Frigyth whispered.

I can't either. I never kneel for anything. Except... When I want to pleasure a woman.

Bloody hell, where had that thought come from? Imagining himself at Frigyth's feet with his head buried under her skirts wasn't going to help soften parts of him that should never have been allowed to manifest themselves in the first place.

Heart beating hard, he waited for her decision.

"Very well," she said eventually "If it's really no bother, then I'm grateful for your invitation."

"It's not. Now. Are you hungry?" he asked, desperate to push away the lewd images crowding his mind. "I don't have much in the hut but you're welcome to have a look, see what you can find."

"Thank you, yes, I am hungry."

She explored her surroundings, taking her time, and then turned to him with a smile. A smile that caused his chest to expand.

"There is enough for me to make griddle cakes. I could have made some fried eggs to go with them if you had not been so clumsy earlier but I guess we'll just have to do without." She pinched her lips together as if to stop herself from laughing. Sigurd groaned. She was never going to let him forget the incident.

"I'm not clumsy, I'm heavy. It's not the same," he couldn't help but retort. "I can promise you I know how to use my fingers in normal circumstances."

The words hung in the air, more suggestive than he had intended. What was wrong with him? Could he not behave?

Frigyth flushed a deep red but, to his relief, did not seem frightened. "Fortunately, there is some honey. It will give flavor to the cakes. I will start cooking now."

THE CAKES WERE the best he had ever eaten. Crumbly, delicately charred, slightly sweetened with the honey, they melted in Sigurd's mouth.

"How on earth did you manage to make something so delicious with just a bit of flour and some water?" he asked, staring at the half-eaten cake in his hand. "I've tried many times to make these and I always end up burning them. And the dough is not as light as this, more like something I could use to smash someone's skull."

She smiled. "I guess you're not as nimble with your fingers as you like to think. The secret is to not overwork the dough. It's all about delicacy and knowing when to stop."

Was he reading too much into her words or was she flirting with him? His groin, mercifully still covered by the blanket, leapt to life. Again. Bloody hell. It was going to be a long night if he stirred every time she said or did anything...

"I do know about delicacy and I can tell when to stop or when to be more forceful. Only, I don't apply those skills to cooking."

Sigurd groaned when Frigyth's mouth opened in shock. Had he really said that? What was *wrong* with him? For the second time that evening he had alluded to his skill in bed to a woman who had every right to fear men like him.

To his relief though, she ignored his ill-considered comment, merely clearing her throat before standing up. "I will go wash the dishes."

He could tell she was only looking for an excuse to avoid having to look at him so he didn't offer to help. It was already more than he could have hoped for that she had not fled in panic after what he'd just said. He finished the second half of his cake and watched her, trying not to dwell on the way her dress hugged her in all the right places, in all the places he longed to explore with his hands and mouth. She truly was exquisite. Perfectly formed, delicate yet surprisingly strong, with a thick mane of hair and velvety eyes, this woman was a man's dream.

Yes... So much so that one of the men who lived in the

village had not been able to keep a clear head around her. The last mouthful of cake turned to dust in his mouth. A swig of ale made little difference. One of the villagers, perhaps someone he knew well, had attacked her. Who? He tried hard to put the question to the back of his mind. Could not. He just had to know.

When she turned to face him again, he spoke.

"I assume you came to see Wolf today because of what happened with a man."

There it was. The question he had been itching to ask since the moment she had arrived in the clearing. He braced himself for her protest. Would she balk? Perhaps not. Perhaps the darkness wrapping around them would help her to open up.

She swallowed and averted her eyes, providing him with the confirmation he hardly needed. Instead of answering, she started to tidy the remnants of their meal.

"I'm afraid there's hardly any honey left," she observed, placing the lid back on the pot.

"Don't worry about it. I know where to get some more."

She nodded. "That's good. I often thought I would like to live in a village. In town, most of the food we eat has to be bought and the quality is not always the best. You're lucky to have access to such a supply of good food."

He took in a deep breath. She had evaded his question but he couldn't let it go. "Who?"

"Who what?" she repeated as if she had already forgotten they had been talking about something more important than food a moment ago.

"Who is your aggressor? I imagine he lives in the village if Wolf helped you. So who is it?" He gritted his teeth.

"Why would you want to know that?"

She'd asked him the same question when he'd enquired

about her name. And just like then, he was at a loss. What could he say?

So I can skewer the bastard. So I can rip his balls off and make him eat them while you watch.

Of course, he could not say that. He might think these things and even wish to do them, but he could not tell her as much. He would only frighten her.

"He might be a friend of yours," she said in a whisper, as if that was a valid reason for her to protect the man's identity. It wasn't.

"All the more reasons for you to tell me. I can't bear the idea that I might see this man every day, drink his mead, jest with him, not knowing what a monster he really is."

"What good would it do for you to know?"

He stared at her and this time could not help but give her the honest answer. "So I know who to beat to a pulp the next time I see him."

She opened wide eyes at the violence in his tone. "I don't want you to hurt anyone. Not on my behalf. And there is no need to do anything, Wolf already dealt with him. From what I saw, I doubt he was able to walk for a few days after. So it's all over now."

Unable to walk properly.

Olaf.

The other day Sigurd had pointed out to him that he seemed to be limping. The man had mumbled something about having gotten involved in a tavern brawl in town. At the time Sigurd had thought nothing of the plausible explanation. Now he knew he'd gotten a beating for having raped Frigyth.

He shot to his feet before he could blink and turned to the door. He was going to kill the bastard.

Understanding his intent, Frigyth whimpered and grabbed his arm. "No! Please, don't. You're already hurt!"

It was only when she spoke that he remembered his injured ankle. As soon as he did, pain slashed through him. Oh, yes, it hurt but it would not be enough to stop him! "I'm going to kill him," he said through gritted teeth. "Let me pass." She was blocking the door and he didn't want to have to push her out of the way.

She didn't move, only paled further.

"Please. I can't stand the idea of you or anyone becoming a murderer for me. And I don't... I don't want to talk about it. It's all over. Wolf avenged me, and I know now there is not going to be any consequence so I-I just want to forget," she stammered, clutching at his arm desperately.

"You mean you came to tell Wolf you have not fallen with child?" he clarified, momentarily distracted. She swallowed at the very personal question but he had to know. If she was pregnant he would definitely not let Olaf get away with it.

"Yes. It's the important thing. Do you understand? At the moment, only Wolf knows what happened to me. If you hurt someone out of the blue, people will ask why, and then I will have my shame spread all over the village. Please don't do this."

Huge brown eyes were looking at him in supplication. She was still holding his arm. Sigurd felt something inside him harden. Never before had he been so blinded by fury. People who preyed on innocent women and children were the scum of this earth but fortunately, he was strong enough to punish them. He never let remorse stand in the way of what was right, never listened to their mangled explanations, or allowed himself to be swayed once he had established facts. Let the bastards face the consequences of their actions with someone who was able to give them what they deserved and to hell with the rest. They should have thought about the risks before they hurt anyone.

Nevertheless, he could not leave Frigyth here in the hut on her own while he went to murder a man in cold blood. And she was right. At the moment, Wolf was the only one aware of what had happened to her, so she was able to hold her head high in the village. This was not about him but about her and the privacy she was trying to preserve. He had to respect her wishes, put her dignity above his preferences, even if he didn't like it. It was not his decision to make.

Taking a deep breath, he nodded once. "Very well. I will not confront Olaf if you stop considering what happened as your shame. The shame is every bit his, do you hear?" he spat. "Every bit. I will not have you thinking you did anything wrong when *he* is the bastard."

He stared at her until she nodded her agreement. Eventually, she did.

Since she was already touching him, he didn't try to resist his need to draw her into his arms. He had been aching to do so from the moment he had understood why she had come to the village. To his relief, she melted against him and buried her face into his chest in search of comfort. They stayed locked in a tender embrace for a long time. Then Frigyth seemed to realize they should not be touching so intimately and drew back.

Some color had returned to her cheeks, he was pleased to see, perhaps due to their unexpected intimacy.

"Better?" he asked.

"Better. But I'm tired now."

Frigyth cast a nervous glance toward the pallet in the corner of the hut. It was the only bed she could see. Where was she supposed to sleep? Surely not... in it? With him?

Her heart started thumping hard in her chest. She should have thought of that before she accepted Sigurd's offer. But what other option did she have? It was too cold to sleep in a ditch, too dangerous for her to be on her own outside, especially after dark. She knew it all too well. The last time she'd found herself alone in the forest Olaf had seen it as permission to satisfy his urges. No, she could not leave the village now. But the only other person who might offer her shelter was Wolf, and they had already established that it would be awkward for him to welcome her under his roof. She didn't want his wife to think there was anything dishonorable between them.

Sigurd saw her hesitation and gestured at the fur-covered nest.

"You will sleep on the pallet, of course. I will find another place."

"I can't!" she protested. "It's your bed and you're injured."

"It's only my ankle, I haven't exactly been flayed alive," he growled. She might have to stop alluding to his injury, she realized. He seemed genuinely put out to be reminded about it. "I will sleep on a blanket by the fire pit. Unless you preferred I left the hut altogether? It's not a problem, I could always go to Wolf, or Magnus."

Did she want him to leave? No. The answer left no doubt in her mind. Not only was it not fair to ask him to leave his house, but she would feel safer with him next to her, ready defend her against ill-intentioned villagers. He had proven he would not let anyone touch her.

"Please, stay here. It would make me feel better."

His shoulders relaxed, as if she had given the answer he wanted. Hers relaxed as well. She would be safe with this man, she was certain of it, even if she'd known him for less than half a day. He would not try to take advantage of the fact she was sleeping in his bed.

He cleared his throat, visibly ill-at-ease. "There is just one more thing I will ask, if I may. You do not have to answer me if you don't want to, but forgive me, I cannot let it go. Had you known a man before Olaf touched you?"

Frigyth brought a hand to her trembling mouth. No, she had not. She had been a virgin up until that day. Would it have made a significant difference if she had not been? She had asked herself that question a hundred times. She still wasn't sure of the answer. In any case, it was hardly worth speculating about now.

"No," she said in a whisper.

Sigurd roared. "I'm going to—"

"No," she repeated before he could finish the sentence or hop to the door. "You promised me you would not do anything."

There was a pause, during which he seemed to grow even larger, even more menacing. In that moment, she could see why he might have been called 'Beast', and her heart fluttered in her chest. Had she been too hasty in thinking it was safe to stay alone with him?

"So I did," he said eventually, the words little less than a snarl.

Sigurd bunched his fists, willing himself to stay calm. Frigyth clearly had no idea of the effort it cost him not to storm out of the hut, axe in hand, to go hack at the man who had not only raped her, but taken her maidenhead. Yes, he had sworn not to hurt Olaf, but it didn't mean he found it easy to stick to a promise he already regretted. Damn it all, it was not as if he had promised her not to eat the last oatcake! This was an altogether more portentous decision, one which could have disastrous consequences. His every instinct told him he should not have made such a foolish promise. He was not a violent man, even if he was impulsive, but never had his control been more sorely tested.

This woman was rousing his protective instinct like never before and, in the same way that he did not understand why she should appeal to him so, he wasn't sure why the idea of her being hurt bothered him so much.

Only the other day he had rescued Wolf's wife from assault but, although he'd been outraged at the man's actions, he had not felt the urge to shred him to ribbons for daring to touch her. It seemed that it was as he'd told his friend . Once you met the perfect woman, all your resolutions flew out of the window. Yes... And so did all sense of restraint and the ability to think, apparently. He gave a grim smile. The boys who had called him 'Beast' for so long would no doubt be delighted to see him rip a man limb from limb.

But Frigyth would not. She had told him as much only a moment ago, and she needed his reassurance right now.

Without thinking, he drew her into his arms again. He might just about manage to stop himself from gutting a man who deserved nothing more, but he would not be denied the need to hold her. Mercifully, she didn't draw back. Just like before, she nuzzled against him, like a little animal burrowing in the undergrowth in search of a safe place. The image made him smile but then bile rose in his throat. She shouldn't need to look for a safe place.

"I'm sorry," he said with his mouth in her hair. "No one should have to find out what sex is in that awful way." Would she ever recover from the ordeal and allow a man near her? It was far from certain. Olaf might well have taken more than her innocence that day; he might have taken away her trust in men and the ability to feel pleasure in their arms.

"I have been kissed, of course," she said tentatively, as if she didn't want him to think her a silly child. He did not. "A few times, by one of my childhood friends. We used to hide from my sisters and exchange kisses under the moonlight. It was sweet and gentle. And I always thought..." The words ended up in a sob but Sigurd could imagine all too well what she meant.

He screwed his eyes shut and tightened his hold around her. She had always thought men would touch her reverently, not throw her to the ground and skewer her for their selfish plea-sure, regardless of whether she wanted it or not. She had imagined she would gift her maidenhead to the man of her choice, not be robbed of it in such a violent manner.

"Of course, you did. And this friend of yours is a lucky man." What wouldn't he have given to be the first one to taste her lips, to be allowed to kiss her now!

"Thank you." She stayed in his arms a moment more and finally drew away, looking as self-conscious as after their first embrace. "I will go to bed now, if I may. I would like to leave at first light tomorrow morning."

He only nodded because if it were up to him, she would never leave at all.

CHAPTER THREE

Dawn rose on a misty, gray morning.

"There are a couple of griddle cakes left if you're hungry," Sigurd told Frigyth, gesturing at the plate she had covered with a cloth the evening before. His mouth started watering at the idea of biting into one of the crumbly, sweet cakes. Frigyth might have seen it because one corner of her mouth curled up.

"You eat them. Once I'm gone, you will have to go back to lumpy, dry, burnt cakes. Make the most of mine while you can."

Oh. If only he could make the most of her in other ways...

"Thank you. I will."

She started to gather the furs from the pallet with the obvious intention of shaking them outside. He stood up to help her and winced when he put all his weight on his ankle. He had not felt it too much in the night, but then he'd been lying down, and asleep most of the time. Now the pain was back with a vengeance.

"This is ridiculous. I should not be incapacitated thus!" he grumbled, falling back down on the stool.

Frigyth didn't answer. Instead she placed a hand over her

hip and looked wonderingly through the narrow window. "It's so dark today compared to yesterday. Do you think the sun lost its brilliance during the night and will never shine again?"

Sigurd blinked. What sort of a question was this? "No," he said slowly, not sure how to hide his disbelief, not even sure he was required to answer.

"I don't either. It's merely hiding behind the clouds." Next she turned her attention to the dying fire at her feet. "Do you think you will be able to revive these embers?"

"Of course, I will." He bristled. Did she think him so inept? The embers were still glowing, it would be child's play to revive that fire. And even if it had not been, he could always start a new one. "It will be roaring in no time."

"Well. We are agreed. A little mist cannot dim the brightness of the sun, and a fire cannot die so easily." She stared pointedly at him. "So how could a mountain of a man feel in any way diminished by something as trivial as a sprained ankle? You tell me."

He stared back at her, lost for words. This woman had the knack for asking the most improbable questions. Before he could think of anything to say, she exited the door with the bundle of furs. When she came back a moment later he still hadn't moved a muscle. He watched her rearrange the pallet in silence and suddenly stood up, sprained ankle all forgotten.

"Now *you* tell *me*," he said, planting himself in front of her. "How can a marvel of a woman be in any way diminished by what was done to her without her consent?" Unable to resist, he brushed her cheek with a light finger. "The sun will come back tomorrow, the fire will roar back to life and spring will be back in a few weeks. It is the way of the world. Time is all that's needed."

Frigyth gave a little sob and leaned into the caress. She

didn't even appear conscious of having done so. "I'd like to believe you."

"Do. I've never been more certain of anything in my life." She was strong, she would get over what had happened to her. If only he could be the one to benefit from it...

She lifted her head and he stopped himself before he could lean in and kiss her. The intention to do so must have shown on his face because her eyes became as round as newly-minted coins.

"I should go now," she murmured.

He didn't move. The last thing he wanted was for her to go. But what could he say to stop her? He had no reason to detain her any further.

"Do you have anyone waiting for you at home?" Was that why she was in such a hurry to leave? An unpleasant thought popped into his head. Was she married perhaps? He had never considered it a possibility before, but after all, why wouldn't she be? She was old enough. No. He shook his head. She wouldn't have been a virgin if she'd been married.

"I live alone," she confirmed. "My sisters are now married and Father died a few weeks ago."

"I'm sorry."

Seeing as, in all honesty, Frigyth was not sorry her father had passed, she did not answer. Sigurd must have thought her lack of reaction odd but, thankfully, he didn't pass any comment. For a moment she had the inexplicable urge to confide in him, explain why she felt that way, then thought the better it. There was little point in it. He'd only offered his condolences because it was the done thing, nothing more. He didn't want to hear all about the life of a woman he didn't know and who was about to walk out of his life.

"Goodbye, Sigurd. Thank you for offering me shelter for the night."

Though she did not have to rush back home, since no one was waiting for her, she sensed she had better leave. She had spent an agitated night, tossing and turning on the furs, fighting the impulse to go lie next to the virile man sleeping so close to her.

"I should be the one thanking you for not abandoning me to my fate last night," Sigurd said softly. "You chose to help me when you could have left me lying in the mud, as powerless as a bug on its back, unable to right itself."

A powerless bug indeed. Frigyth gave a small smile at the image. How could such a forbidding man be so... mischievous at times? She started to the door then hesitated. There was one last thing she needed to do to put her mind at ease.

"Promise me you won't hurt the man once I'm gone."

Though she knew her attacker's name, she refused to use it. The less she thought of him as a normal person with an identity, the easier it would be to forget him. She would not forget what he'd done but in time she might forget what he looked like, what he'd told her, the way he'd moved, the way he smelled, everything that made him a man. He would become a nameless, faceless creature of evil, almost imaginary.

At least that was the hope.

Sigurd straightened to his full height. "Just so we are clear, you're asking me to allow him to get away with what he did to you?"

"He's already been punished, I told you." Though he had sworn not to hurt him last night, she had the awful impression he would forget all about his promise the moment she was gone.

"He was beaten to a pulp, something that will have happened to him a dozen times already. That's hardly fitting punishment for what he did."

Frigyth didn't dare ask what he would consider fitting, as

she wasn't sure she had the stomach to hear it. "Just... Please. Promise me."

"Very well." The two words sounded as if they had been wrenched from his gut. "If you insist, I promise I won't give him what he deserves. But know that I will only be doing it for you, and nothing else. If it were up to me I would—"

A knock on the door mercifully interrupted the confession she had been trying to avoid. Frigyth gave a little gasp and retreated to the corner of the hut, fearing being seen too close to Sigurd. For a moment, engrossed in their conversation they had been standing perilously close to each other, as only people about to kiss could be.

"Enter."

The door opened on a tall, curvy woman with long, blonde hair braided in an intricate pattern. A Norsewoman, evidently, one who knew Sigurd well, judging from the smile she threw him. She appeared to be just a few years older than him. His sister maybe? Or...

Frigyth wavered on her feet as realization slammed into her. How naïve could one be? Women did not smile at their brothers as if they wanted to tumble into bed with them. Nor did they lick their lips invitingly when they looked at them.

The woman was not his sister but his *lover*.

Sigurd's stomach lurched when he saw Edith walk into the hut as if she owned the place. No, not now!

"Well. You're here." Edith cocked her head.

"So you see." He racked his brain for a way to get rid of her before she saw Frigyth. The confrontation between the two women was one he wanted to avoid at all costs.

"I thought you'd have been detained in town or something of the sort, seeing as you didn't come visit last night." She made a face she probably imagined to be irresistible. It was not. "I was so put out I had to pleasure myself instead. Not as satisfying as it could have been, not by a long shot. I much prefer to feel you surge between my legs—or in the other place."

Sigurd gave an inward groan. His eyes flicked over to where Frigyth was standing, shock painted on her face. It was clear she had no idea what they were talking about and dreaded to think up a possible explanation. With some effort, he tore his gaze away from her.

"Edith..." he started, before closing his mouth. What could he tell her?

Stop talking about what we do in bed in front of Frigyth! She is the last person I would like to know how crudely I can behave with my lovers.

This was excruciating. But the woman didn't seem to see his discomfort or notice they weren't alone. Before he could tell her as much, she spoke.

"Why didn't you come last night, as agreed?"

"I twisted my ankle in the afternoon, climbing a tree." What had galled him yesterday now pointedly came to his rescue. He couldn't just say that he had forgotten all about their agreement because of the little Saxon huddling in the corner. "I couldn't walk."

"Oh, poor you," Edith crooned, taking a few steps forward. "Is it very painful? Shouldn't you be lying down? I could take care of you. I know just the thing to distract you."

Her hand landed on his chest, her intent clear. He had to stop her before she pushed him onto his pallet and started to tear at his clothes. The comely widow had been a regular bedmate over the years but today he could not summon an ounce of interest for her.

He cleared his throat and stared pointedly to where Frigyth was standing. Edith followed the direction of his gaze and stiffened.

"You're not alone?" She sounded distinctively unimpressed.

It was not hard to guess she had assumed he'd spent the night with another woman and was only using the twisted ankle as an excuse. But he cared not. All he cared about was preserving Frigyth's good opinion of him. If it wasn't already too late. After what she'd heard, it was far from certain she would ever want to be alone with him again.

He lifted Edith's hand from his chest.

Damnation, he knew he was not her only lover, why couldn't she have gone to Magnus if she was in need of a man? Unlike him, the blacksmith was actually considering marrying her. He'd told him as much only the other week. Why persist with him when a good man was willing to make an honest woman out of her?

"I should be going," Frigyth whispered, keeping her gaze to the floor.

"No," Sigurd answered before he could think. Not so soon, not like this.

"Yes."

Without a word she ran to the door. He set off after her and cried out when his swaddled ankle felt as if it were breaking in half. Standing up propped against the table was one thing, going off at a run, quite another.

Damn it all to hell, he would not be able to get to her with that ankle. She was already at the edge of the forest.

Sigurd watched, powerless, as Frigyth disappeared through the trees—and out of his life.

CHAPTER FOUR

The weather was grim and the offering at the market particularly poor this morning. Frigyth sighed. It was always the same toward the end of winter, every year she started to long for the arrival of spring. But this morning she found herself longing not for a time, but for a *place*. If she'd still been at the Norsemen village, she could have gone and found fresh, tempting food, instead of having to make do with the pitiful choices available to her here. Except... She had no idea how to recognize edible mushrooms or berries, how to catch fish, or where to get honey. True, she could cook, but what good did that do if all she had were shriveled old turnips and moldy oats? Nothing tempting could be made with that.

The only thing of quality she could have bought was salted fish and this, unfortunately, was not an option. Shuddering at the mere thought, she started for home, feeling more glum than ever. She would just have to make oatcakes. Again. And eat them on her own, again.

It was then that it hit her. She wasn't longing for a place at all, but for a *person*.

Shaking her head, she turned the corner to her house.

It was no use thinking like that. Really, what choice had she had but to leave Sigurd's hut? She could not have stayed with him at the village. What reason would she have given? That she felt lonely in her empty house? That she had enjoyed cooking for someone who had liked what she'd made? That her heart started to flutter every time she looked at him? She would have liked the opportunity to see where it could all lead because it was a new, heady sensation.

Of course, not. She just would have to make do with uninspiring food until spring, and learn to live on her own. In all probability, Sigurd had forgotten all about her already, too busy attending to his beautiful, demanding lover.

"Frigyth. Is that you?"

The deep voice made her start so much she almost dropped her basket. Slowly, she turned to face the man she had never thought to see again.

Heavens! He'd grown even taller since she'd last seen him, or so it seemed.

"I... What are you doing here?" she asked stupidly.

"Good morning to you, too." He laughed the sunny laugh she remembered, one of the few happy memories of her childhood. "A charming welcome, that is!"

Frigyth reddened. "I'm sorry, I meant—"

"Don't worry. I know what you meant. I did set off for London with no intention of returning, after all. But..." The look in Caedmon's eyes suddenly shifted, and his voice became softer. "I found that I had to come back. And I think you might know why."

Something fell to the bottom of her stomach. Indeed she could guess why her childhood friend had come back before starting his new life in earnest.

Because he wanted her to be a part of it.

"Let us go inside. It's too cold to stay here," she murmured. This would be a difficult conversation, better held in private.

As she poured Caedmon some ale, she wondered how best to approach this. Because, as much as she liked him, she didn't want to marry him, and she feared this was where they were headed.

She'd suspected for months that he harbored feelings for her, feelings she could not return, no matter how much she tried. He was a personable, handsome man, and a good friend, and she had enjoyed his kisses, but she did not wish for more. She had never imagined being married to him, even when he'd held her in his arms like a lover, even when he had hinted she should go with him to London all those months ago. Perhaps naively, she had hoped he would forget about his intention during his stay in the city, or meet a woman there, one who would make him realize that what he felt for her was not really love, but merely a deep affection and a desire to protect her.

Apparently, he had not.

She sat down next to him. There was no sense in dragging this out. Better to nip his hopes in the bud without further delay. He didn't deserve to be led on a merry chase. "I'm sorry, Caedmon."

He covered her hand with his, ever the attentive friend. "Why are you sorry, Frig?"

"Because I think I know what you are going to ask me. But I cannot marry you."

Caedmon stilled. It was clear he had not expected the blunt statement and she wished she had not hurt him but she couldn't let him hope in vain. It would only be more cruel in the long run.

When he spoke, it was as if he had not heard her. "I know you want to leave this town, and the bad memories behind and now you can. I heard from the neighbors your father is dead.

With him gone, no one can stop you. A new life in London is just the new beginning you need."

Her heart seized in her chest. His friend had traveled hundreds of miles to offer her the life she had never thought to have. How could she tell him she didn't want him? She could not. Her best option was to make him see that *he* did not truly want *her*.

"I'm sorry, but I always saw you as a brother." This was true at least, and no man would want a wife who had only fraternal feelings for him.

His eyes gleamed. "Come, Frig. We were never like brother and sister you and I. We would not have kissed if we had been, would we? And I never kissed Dunne or Birgit, only you."

She flushed. Yes, at one point she might have looked at the tall, handsome Saxon as a potential husband, but she didn't anymore. Faced with his dark eyes, all she could think of was a pair of crystal blue irises. She'd once thought Caedmon the epitome of masculine strength, she now knew he was more about graceful elegance.

And elegance was not what made her body hum in desire.

Letting go of her fingers, Caedmon placed a gentle hand over her cheek. "I gave you your first kiss. And I look forward to showing you what can be shared between a man and a woman."

Oh, but she already knew about that. The awful pain, the rough handling, the shame. Of course, she knew, deep down, that it did not have to be like that, that men and women could come together in desire and respect but the assault was still too fresh in her mind for her to envisage being in a man's arms with anything than dread.

Tears filled her eyes and before she could stop herself she threw herself into her friend's arms.

"Frig?" He sounded understandably alarmed. "What is it?"

"You can never be the first. While you were away, I-I was... attacked."

A deathly silence followed her words but Caedmon did not let go of her in disgust, as she had half-expected. Instead, his hold around her tightened. Then he growled.

"Who?"

It was the same question Sigurd had asked her, the same loathing in his voice. She shook her head. "You don't know him. It's not important. What I'm saying is that you cannot want me now."

He flared up at this and pushed her away so as to have a better look at her. His dark eyes were ablaze. "Do you think all I care about is your maidenhead? Well, I don't. I care about you. Do you think I would be ashamed of you because of the attack you suffered? Horrified at the idea of taking a soiled woman for a wife? Well, I'm not. I'm not ashamed because you're not soiled, do you hear?" Again, the same thing Sigurd had told her. "What happened to you was not your fault, and now you're a grown woman, you need a protector now more than ever."

"I already have one. The Norseman who rescued me. He punished my attacker, and beat him severely."

"That's all very well, and I am grateful he was here for you, but you need someone who can look after you properly, night and day. As your husband, I will be that man."

Oh, Lord. She had thought he would finally see that she was not the woman for him but he was more determined than ever to marry her. And all for the wrong reasons. It was imperative that they married so he could protect her, he'd claimed.

As proposals went, this was not quite what she had hoped for.

She had no choice but to resort to lies. "When he saw I was on my own, the man offered to marry me. Not knowing when or if you would come back, I accepted his offer. I felt it was my only option. So you see, I can never be your wife."

There. It couldn't be any clearer than this. He could not marry a woman who was already married.

His eyes narrowed. "I want to meet this husband of yours, who leaves you wandering the town on your own when dawn has barely broken. Some protector he makes! And why is he not here in the house with you?"

Frigyth bit her lip. She had not expected Caedmon to insist. But now he wanted to see her supposed husband. He was a stubborn man. If she didn't show him someone, he would not give up until she admitted she was not truly married and free to accept his offer of protection.

But she could not go to Wolf and pretend to be married to him when he already had a wife! Not only would it not be fair to Merewen, it would be too easy for Caedmon to expose her lie. She needed someone who was unmistakably Norse, and looked strong enough to have beaten up a man, who knew her and what had happened to her, who would not ask awkward questions, someone who was unmarried and willing to help her.

The name was in her mind before she could even think.

Sigurd.

He fit the role perfectly. She knew where he lived and he had proven himself reliable and helpful. He was a Norseman and would understand what she was talking about when she alluded to the attack. Yes... He might very well agree to pose as her husband and convince Caedmon she was lost to him if she was persuasive enough.

"Very well. I was on my way back to the village anyway. I only came into town because it is market day. Come with me. You can meet him then."

During the journey she became more and more tense. What if Sigurd wasn't home? What if he gave her away by looking surprised to see her? What if he agreed with Caedmon that she needed someone to protect her day and night and advised her to marry her friend?

What if...

What if he was in bed with Edith right now, plunging between her thighs or in 'the other place', wherever that may be?

She cursed her foolishness. Going to Sigurd had seemed a good idea at the time but she was fast regretting her decision. As soon as Caedmon started asking questions, the truth would come out, and then she would have two irate men in front of her demanding explanations.

But how could she turn back now? She could hardly claim she had been mistaken and she was not married after all... She would just have to hope Sigurd was both able to lie his way out of a hole and willing to do so for a woman he barely knew.

All too soon they were at the hut.

There, Frigyth hesitated again. Should she knock on the door? No. It would appear too suspicious as she was supposed to live there. But she could not burst in either, precisely because she *didn't* live there, especially if Sigurd was entertaining a lover!

Just as she was wondering how she should proceed, he came out of the hut. He arched a brow when he saw her but at least he was alone—and dressed. It was the best she could have hoped for. She took a step forward before he could say a word and looked at him straight in the eye.

"I'm back, husband."

Sigurd blinked.

Husband. Had he heard that right? Had Frigyth really called him husband?

He'd been shocked enough to see her standing in front of the hut, looking lovelier than ever in a green gown that made her eyes appear almost amber but this...

He run a hand through his hair. "Erm..."

Before he could add anything, Frigyth started to talk hurriedly. "I'm sorry, I could not find the tools you wanted in town. But I bumped into an old friend at the market. Caedmon."

She gestured toward the tall Saxon standing behind her. Instantly Sigurd's hackles rose. Before he knew what he was doing, he had drawn her to his side. "Did you? And why did you bring him back home?"

With his arm around her shoulders, he knew he looked like a possessive husband, or an animal who did not like seeing another male sniffing around his female. But to his surprise, she molded herself against him, as if she didn't mind. As if she were grateful, even. He straightened further, alarm spiking through his gut. Who was this man and why had Frigyth thought to find refuge in his hut?

"Caedmon wanted to meet you, you see." She wrapped an arm around his waist. Although he knew she was only acting the part of his wife, he relished the contact. His hand tightened over her shoulder. They fit together so perfectly it was hard to think it was not the hundredth time they had ended up in that position. "Because I told him all about what happened, about me being assaulted and you rescuing me. And then marrying me."

The arm around his waist tightened in warning. She was urging him to go along with the lie. No need. He would do whatever was necessary to help her. Posing as her husband was hardly a sacrifice.

"Mm. I still don't understand why that would be any of his business?" he grunted.

There was an uncomfortable pause. "Caedmon once thought he might marry me."

"I still do."

The man had the gall to take a step forward and thrust himself into the conversation. This time it was Sigurd who tightened his hold around Frigyth. "Well you can't marry her. She's mine."

He didn't say 'we're married'. That would have been a lie. But it did feel as if she were his. And she would marry that man she obviously didn't want over his dead body.

"I thank you for what you did, for stepping up to avenge her. I wish I had been there to do it myself. But as I understand, you only wed her to offer her the protection she needed, in a Norse ceremony." The arrogant pup looked at Frigyth as he carried on. "I am back now, I can offer you that protection, and marry you in a proper ceremony. We can easily have this uni—"

"We are not having this union cancelled, annulled, dismissed, ignored or whatever else you are planning to do," Sigurd snapped. "Frigyth is staying here with me and that's all there is to it."

The man did not even glance his way, ignoring the ice in his voice. "Frig. You do not have to stay with a man you don't want just because you feel threatened on your own, is all I'm saying. You can walk away with me now and we can get married before we go to London together. The choice is yours."

Sigurd let go of Frigyth to plant himself in front of the sod. He was not going to be ignored any longer. He'd been impressed despite himself to see that the man did not cower in front of him. Not many people dared stand up to him when he meant to intimidate them. But enough was enough.

"Who the hell are you, telling Frigyth she can put me aside?" Really, the nerve of the man!

"Sigurd, please, Caedmon is a friend." Frigyth intervened, placing a hand over his forearm as if she feared he was about to jump at the man's throat, not an unreasonable assumption, he had to admit, considering he was fighting the urge to do just that.

"Oh, a friend, is he? A friend who wants you to leave your husband to go with him!" In that moment he had quite forgotten they were not truly married. "A friend who wants to marry you and get you into his bed, no doubt! Well *that's* not going to happen!"

On this, at least, he was adamant. No one was going to get between this woman's legs if he had anything to say about it.

The two men glared at each other for a long moment. Then the Saxon took a step back. Sigurd drew Frigyth against his flank once more.

"It seems to me that the Norseman might well be the protector you need," the man said eventually, eyeing them together, as if to assess the link between them. "Will you swear to me you are not here against your will?"

Frigyth felt bad for lying to her friend about being already married but she didn't want to become his wife and this was the least painful way of telling him as much. He wouldn't be able to take it personally. He'd believe she had married a man who had been of assistance to her in his absence, because she thought him gone for good. He could not object to that. Besides, she could not rid herself of the notion that he didn't really want to marry her either, that he was only doing what he felt was right by her. He had always wanted to alleviate her suffering and make her life easier. She loved him for the intention, but he deserved a chance to meet a woman he loved and who loved him and build a family with her.

With her out of the way, he might allow himself to look for such a woman.

"I swear it I am here of my own free will. And Sigurd will not harm me."

This she knew instinctively to be true.

Caedmon nodded. "I am leaving with a convoy of merchants in a fortnight. Before my departure, I will come back and ask you one last time. If you find life in the Norsemen village not to your taste after all, then I *will* take you away, husband or no husband."

"Now, listen here, you—"

"Thank you, Caedmon," she cut in hastily, coming to stand between the two men. Her pretend husband would never harm her but she wasn't sure he would not gut her only true friend in front of her eyes. Though their acquaintance was short, she knew Sigurd had a fierce temper. "Your friendship means the world to me."

With her blocking the way, the two men had no other choice but to glare at each other over her head. Finally, Caedmon nodded and left.

CHAPTER FIVE

"**W**ould you care to explain?"

Frigyth let out a sigh. She had fully expected Sigurd to have questions and she could not blame him for wanting to understand what had just happened. He had helped her to get rid of Caedmon by pretending to be married to her but he had no idea why he should have been required to when it was obvious the man posed no danger to her. Still, without knowing, he had played his role to perfection. In fact, she had been surprised by his vehemence. It had truly looked as if he wouldn't hear of her going to another man. She had done her best to suppress the flutter of emotion this had provoked inside her because deep down she knew he didn't care who she married, he just wanted to have the upper hand on a man he seemed to have taken an immediate aversion to.

"It is as I told you. I happened upon him on my way back from the market this morning. I hadn't seen him in months and thought he was now living in London."

Sigurd grunted. "And you just happened to blurt out that you had been raped and were now married to a Norseman?"

She bit her bottom lip. He was right to be dubious. Indeed, that was not how the conversation would have gone if she had not consciously steered it that way. She would have to explain everything from the start. After what he'd done to help her, Sigurd deserved to understand.

"Caedmon's family lived on the same road as mine when we were growing up, and he has always been very protective of me and my sisters." The same age as she was, he had been a constant support for her. "I saw him as a big brother, and he saw me as the sister he never had, but as we grew up, I think he started to see me differently."

"Yes. He now sees you as a woman he wants to bed." Sigurd was not trying to be delicate, which did not surprise her. He could be dreadfully blunt. But she could not let him think this of Caedmon.

"There is more to it than that. He genuinely means to help me, the way he always has." She shook her head. "I think he mistook the deep affection we feel for each other for something more meaningful. I had hoped that while he was away he would realize what was between us was not really love but evidently he did not."

Sigurd frowned and crossed his arms over his chest. He had not missed that she was skirting around the real issue. She braced herself for his next question. "But why did you tell him about what Olaf did to you? It's hardly something you would mention in passing to someone you haven't seen in a while, no matter how close you were as children."

She flushed. Trust him to come to the heart of the matter. She had not meant to reveal the whole of her discussion with Caedmon but it was obvious Sigurd would not let her get away with half-truths. She would have to bare it all.

"He started to explain that he had come back because of me, to offer me the life I deserved away from the town I grew up in and I didn't want him to get ideas into his head because, as much as I like him, I do not wish to marry him. But I didn't want to hurt his feelings by refusing his offer. I thought the less painful way would be to make him change his mind about me." She flushed. This had not been her proudest moment but she had truly meant to preserve Caedmon's pride. "So when he started hinting at a union between us, I told him what had happened to me in his absence, thinking it would put him off the idea of making me his wife."

Something flashed in Sigurd's eyes. Anger. Unmistakable. The blue eyes had almost become black.

"I thought we'd discussed this only the other day and you'd agreed you would not see what happened as your fault or think it makes you less worthy in any way?" The fierceness in his voice almost frightened her. She nodded slowly and watched him struggle to contain his fury.

"I don't really think I am less worthy than I was before..." She was surprised to see that she meant it. "I only thought he might prefer not to ally himself with a... soiled woman."

She could tell Sigurd did not like the use of that word but he let it pass because he wanted to hear the rest of her explanation. "I take it that didn't work, if he still insists on marrying you?"

"No. He was appalled on my behalf, but he said it didn't change a thing, or rather, it only made it more imperative that I should have a husband to protect me."

"Humpf, at least the man has some honor," Sigurd grunted.

Frigyth nodded. Caedmon had stood by her and she'd been moved. "I panicked and said that my rescuer had thought the same thing and married me the following day. I really thought it would be enough to placate him, but somehow he concluded that I had only accepted that man's offer out of desperation, for want of a better alternative, because I was afraid of being on my own. He wanted to make sure I was happy with my choice, not trapped in a union imposed on me as some sort of reward by a man taking advantage of the situation."

"Humpf," Sigurd said again. "Perhaps you should stop talking. You're making it more and more difficult for me to hate the man."

"Good! I don't want you to hate him! He's a good man." When there was no answer, she carried on. "He asked to see my supposed husband but I could not take him to Wolf, who's already married. I had to think quickly. Fortunately, I had not named my rescuer, only mentioned the fact that he was a Norseman."

"I see. So it could have been anyone in the village." He didn't seem best pleased by the notion.

"No. It needed to be someone who was aware of what had happened to me and would want to help me without question. Someone I knew and could trust." She lifted her gaze to him. "It could only be you."

The words were a blow to Sigurd's chest.

It could only be you.

Though Frigyth didn't mean them in that way, it felt like the most meaningful compliment anyone had ever paid him. A lonely orphan, a 'beast,' he had never been anyone's first choice.

This woman he was inexplicably drawn to had chosen him to be her fake husband. It felt hugely significant.

He cleared his throat, trying to focus on their conversation. "Do you think it worked?"

Frigyth made a face. "He didn't seem too happy about it, but he did say it would be my decision in the end. And if he really means to leave again in a fortnight, this time for good, then I guess all I have to do is hold on to the pretence for another few days. So yes, it might work."

"You will need to remain here then, with me, until he goes to London. Since we are supposedly married, it would be odd for you to do otherwise. Besides, he said he would come back here looking for you. You cannot go back into town now. Your friend only agreed to let you choose me because he thinks I can protect you adequately."

Sigurd had not missed the assessing look the man had thrown him, and the way he'd narrowed his eyes when he'd seen Frigyth pressing herself against him. He had concluded that with such a man she would be safe.

It seemed that looking like a beast had its advantages after all.

Sigurd lifted a brow. "Well? Don't you agree you had better stay here?"

"I-I supposed so," Frigyth stammered. "I hadn't thought about it."

But he had. He had thought of little else since she'd called him husband, since she'd nestled herself into his arms in search of help and support. It felt so right, so obvious that they should live under the same roof.

Not being on his own had been his goal, his dearest wish, his ambition from as far as he could remember. As a child he'd had no way of making it happen. Everywhere he'd been rejected. As a youth, he'd not been in a position to entice anyone or support a family, so he had consciously avoided thinking about it. As a man he could have finally made it happen, taken a lover, made her his wife and built a life with her.

But when the moment had come to make his dream come true, he'd balked. He felt like a hunter fed on heroic stories about to enter the lair of the legendary beast he'd spent his life pursuing. Was he as ready as he thought, capable of mastering it? Would the reality live up to the impossibly high expectations?

He could not be sure.

What if he hated family life? What if he'd been on his own

for so long that it annoyed him to have another person to take into account? What if he got tired of having to justify himself, of having to accommodate someone else's preferences?

With Frigyth under his roof, pretending to be his wife, he could have a taste of companionship without any of the pressure. If it was awful then it mattered not, she would simply leave at the end of the appointed time with no hard feelings. And if it was as fulfilling as he had always imagined, then, he might well have won the prize he had hankered for all this time.

It was a perfect way to find out if what he craved could bring him the peace he had always dreamed of, an opportunity he was not going to let pass.

"If you really want to convince him we are married, then there is no other alternative," he declared. "You will have to spend the next two weeks here, as my wife."

He was right. Frigyth bit her lip. She would have to stay here. Doing anything else was out of the question. It would give either Caedmon the impression that she was not happy with her choice of husband or worse, expose her lie. *Then* he would be irremediably hurt.

"Do you think we should tell the whole village we are married as well? In case he asks around?"

Sigurd seemed to mull on this for a while. "I don't think he will. And even if he does, they will confirm that we live together."

Yes. It would be enough. Besides, Caedmon would spent the next two weeks in town, not in the village. "Very well. If it's really no—"

"It's not. I have only one condition."

Her heart started to thump hard in her chest. Of course he would want for some sort of compensation, it was only to be expected. Would he ask her to behave in all ways as his wife would? In other words, share his bed at night? Would she accept if he demanded it of her? Would he even be so crass? What little she had seen from him seemed to indicate he would not be so indelicate. He had been outraged at the idea of a man forcing himself on her, surely he would not now coerce her into giving him her favors in exchange for his help?

"What is that?" she asked, barely managing to get the words out.

"I would like it if you cooked for us while you're here."

Relief flooded Frigyth's veins. He wanted her to cook, that was all. Well, she could do that with her eyes closed and without compunction. "I will. It's the least I can do."

"I have more food in the hut than the last time you were here."

"I'm glad to hear it. How is your ankle by the way?"

He winced, as if he didn't like to be reminded of his moment of weakness and a smile came to tease her lips. Sigurd looked like a disgruntled bear again and she found it just as irresistible as she had a fortnight ago. As to why such a thing should appeal to her, she was none the wiser. It did not make sense. After a chaotic childhood, she needed peace and quiet in her life. Shouldn't she be drawn to even-tempered people, especially men? Probably.

And yet... yet she was undeniably attracted to this forbidding, hot-headed Norseman.

"My ankle's fine. It was never a serious injury. Forget about it. I know I have." He paused. "And by the way, Edith didn't stay the other day."

The change of topic threw her. "Who is Edith?"

Sigurd realized only then Frigyth might not remember the widow's name, might even have forgotten all about the incident. Why did he have to bring it up? Why should she care who he bedded anyway? They were not really married. But he wanted to set things straight with her, he needed her to know he had not just watched her run away and tumbled another woman into bed a moment later, as if he didn't care she'd gone.

He had cared. More than cared.

"The woman who came to visit the morning you left." He saw from the gleam in her eyes that she hadn't forgotten, even if she was surprised he would bring the topic up. "I didn't run after you because of my ankle that morning. I should have but I could not. In any case, I wanted you to know that I did not bed her. That day or since."

Frigyth reddened and he cursed himself for embarrassing her. "There was no need to tell me as much. What you do in that regard is no concern of mine."

"I know."

Unfortunately, it wasn't. But he would like it very much for it to be her concern, wanted her to be the one gracing his bed, wanted her to mind who he slept with, wanted her to be jealous, possessive, as jealous and possessive as he was where she was concerned. Why was he being so foolish? She had only come to him to keep an unwanted suitor at bay and for want of a better alternative, because the man she had originally thought of, Wolf, was not available.

She was not jealous of Edith or the others, she did not care. This was all pretense, nothing more.

"I haven't gone to Olaf either," he added, balling his fingers into fists. Resisting Edith's advances had been easy, as she had lost the appeal she'd held overnight, but that particular promise had been excruciating to keep. Only the day before, the bastard had walked past as he was cutting wood outside his hut and nodded in greeting. Sigurd had reduced the log to kindling in an effort to contain his fury, knowing it wouldn't do to chop the man to bits in the middle of the village. The next time he might not be so reasonable. To think Olaf owed his life to the woman he had so sorely misused!

"Is Coldman the friend you kissed a few times?" he asked Frigyth, even though he could all too well guess he would be.

The way she reddened told him all he needed to know. He was.

"Yes. And his name is Caedmon."

"Same thing. All these Saxon names sound similar to me." Sigurd frowned. Of course, they didn't. Why was he being so petulant, so ridiculous? "And why does he call you 'Frig' anyway?"

She shrugged. "He always has. It's rather an obvious nickname for me, don't you think?"

He could not help a smile. "In my country Frigg is a goddess. Is that what you mean by it being an obvious choice for you? If so, I agree."

"Oh." She blushed a delicious color. "No, of course not. I didn't mean that. I only... Well, i-if I were called Odella, for example, then Caedmon would call me Od."

"*Odd*? He wouldn't dare, surely? There's nothing odd about you."

He smirked, causing her to blush even further. "That's a bad example, but you know what I mean..."

Sigurd watched her, enjoying himself immensely. She was adorable when she was flustered. Then he decided to put an end to her embarrassment. "All I'm saying is that he's not very imaginative."

"Maybe he's not. Why is that problem, exactly?"

It wasn't. Damn. It seemed she'd won that argument with a simple question. He walked over to the fire pit and made a great show of stirring the fire back to life. He might want to avoid getting in an argument with the diminutive Saxon woman if he were to survive the next fortnight. A formidable opponent, she knew where to hit with her questions.

"A goddess, you say."

He turned round, a log in his hands. "Pardon me?"

"You said Frigg was a goddess."

He dropped the log into the fire. "Yes. The goddess of marriage, amongst other things. How apt."

She didn't comment. Then she licked her lips. His groin instantly tightened. Damn, forget arguments, he would have to bring his body to heel if he wanted to survive the next few weeks.

"I will see what I can find to eat, seeing that I am to cook," Frigyth whispered.

"Yes. I will get some more wood."

Later that night they sat down to a meal of cabbage soup, eggs fried with nettles and wild garlic followed by spiced honey tarts. Sigurd licked his fingers and declared it the best meal he had ever eaten.

"Well. You are certainly holding your side of the bargain. Be careful. If you carry on treating me like this, I might never let you go."

Warmth suffused Frigyth. He sounded so genuine... "Be careful. If you carry on complimenting me like this, I might never want to leave."

As soon as the words left her mouth she regretted them. What had possessed her to say such a thing? She didn't want to give Sigurd the impression she thought this would lead anywhere. Asking him to pose as her husband had been a spur of the moment thing, motivated by her desire to spare her friend's feelings, not a ploy to entice him. She certainly didn't think anything could—or should—come out of it.

Silence stretched between them, only punctuated by the crackling of the flames. Then Sigurd stood up. In his haste, he knocked over the jug of ale. Thankfully, it was almost empty and he managed to catch it before it fell to the floor.

"Bloody hell!" he swore, shaking his wet hand.

Frigyth could not help a smile. She was quickly getting used to his dirty mouth.

"Why do you always swear in my language?" she asked as he placed the jug back on the table.

"What do you mean?"

"You always swear, more than the average person, I would say, and you always swear in my language." Sigurd looked caught out and she berated herself for making him think she thought him uncouth. She didn't. All the same she could not help but think there had to be a reason behind it, precisely *because* he was not uncouth. "I don't mind, only I thought you might do it in your language. It might be more natural."

There was a long pause. She could tell he wanted to be honest but had never thought before about the reason why he used a foreign language when he swore. Why hadn't she kept her mouth shut? Did she have to be so curious all the time? What had been an innocent question had clearly awoken some hidden demons in him.

"Don't worry about it," she said hurriedly. "It was a stupid question."

He didn't say anything, or even acknowledge she had spoken. He just stared straight ahead, deep in thought. "I... I suppose it started because I wanted to fit in," he said eventually.

Just like that Frigyth was drawn back into the conversation. "Fit in? How so?"

"When I arrived from Denmark, I was sixteen summers. I did not speak a word of your language. I had to learn everything here. It suited me fine, as I wanted to shed my identity, melt into the background. I wanted to become someone else." He shrugged. "The lads who taught me to speak were still young, trying to prove to themselves they were men. They swore a lot. I suppose I picked it up, not realizing at first that it was not the normal way of talking. And then the habit stuck."

"Why did you want to become someone else?"

His blue eyes clouded over. "I told you when we met. In Denmark I was called 'Beast'."

She guffawed. And he'd thought 'Frig' was uninspired! Whoever thought it clever to call a big hulking man 'beast' was clearly even less original then Caedmon. Then the laughter got stuck in her throat when she saw he was not jesting. "Why?"

He shook his head but this time there was a small smile floating on his lips. "Of course, you would ask why..." he murmured. "You always do."

Oh, no. He'd noticed her curious nature. Not that it was hard to spot...

Instead of answering, he began to tug at his shirt. Frigyth swallowed hard. They were in the middle of a conversation, why was he undressing?

"I was called Beast because of this."

He turned and lowered the waistband of his hose to expose a mark in the middle of his lower back, just between the two dimples bracketing the curve of his spine. Her throat went dry. This was such an intimate part of his body to see... and so beautiful. Hard muscles rippled under a skin that looked smooth and inviting. Her fingers itched to caress it and she thought it prudent to cross her arms over her chest to resist temptation.

"I have this mark in the shape of a monster's head," she heard Sigurd explain in a gruff voice. "Of course, I have never seen it myself, placed where it is, but I've been told enough times about it. One day when I was about ten I went swimming in the fjord with other boys and they saw it. They started to scream and jeer, saying that I was marked by a beast. The nickname stuck."

Frigyth stared at the purplish mark on his impossibly muscular back and suddenly her lips started to itch. She was shocked to find that she would like nothing more than to kiss the mark and trace its ragged contours with her tongue.

"It looks nothing like a beast to me," she breathed.

Sigurd stiffened in shock when the lightest finger brushed over his lower back. Then, all too quicky, shock morphed into desire. How many times had he wished to feel Frigyth's hands on him since the day she had stroked his foot? Too many.

He closed his eyes. That the first thing she should touch was the reviled beast mark seemed significant somehow.

"It doesn't look like a beast?" he whispered back. He'd thought she would be disgusted.

"No. And if you could see it, I'm sure you would agree with me. The only thing I can think of is that the boys wanted to mock you because they knew you couldn't see it. Either that or the shape changed when you grew into a man. In any case it's nothing to be worried about." The fingers landed on his back again. Sigurd shivered.

"You should stop touching me," he growled.

He didn't want her to ever stop but he was perilously close to acting like the beast he was named after. If she carried on he would turn around and take her mouth. And he would not be gentle.

"I'm sorry."

"No. It is I who is sorry. I didn't mean to snarl at you. I guess, once a beast, always a beast."

"Please. You are no more a beast than I am a turnip!"

Sigurd blinked and turned to face her. "What are you talking about?" A turnip? Had she lost her mind? He had never seen anyone look less like a rotund vegetable than the woman in front of him.

"This."

She lowered the left sleeve of her dress, revealing a perfect, round shoulder that looked good enough to eat. His heart leapt in alarm at the same time as his groin tightened. Surely she wasn't going to bare herself to him? Not now, when he was already on the edge of madness? He would not be able to withstand it.

"If you think seeing you naked will convince me to call 'turnip', I can stop you right there. I already know it won't."

She shook her head and turned to the side, revealing a small, dainty birthmark the color of crushed berries on the top of her creamy shoulder. A turnip. Or rather, what a mean-spirited idiot would have called a turnip if he'd been of a mind to tease her. Unable to resist, he did as she had done and brushed a finger over it. So soft... He lingered over the gesture and heard her inhale sharply.

"It looks nothing like a turnip," he said, glad she was staring at the fire pit, for there was a distinctive bulge at the front of his hose now. "I think it looks more like a... bird," he improvised. It didn't, not really, but he refused to even think of it as a turnip.

She let out an incredulous snort, not fooled for a moment. "You must have strange birds in your country!"

He smiled. "We do. Birds so fat and round they are sometimes mistaken for root vegetables. It's only because they fly that we can tell the difference."

"Stop talking nonsense." Frigyth's mouth was quivering when she faced him again. "What I'm trying to say is that a mark placed on your body doesn't define who you are."

"No. Maybe not." His jaw clenched as he became serious once more. "But a nickname people give you can influence the way others see you. When you are introduced to someone new as 'Beast', it is not innocent. You might get away with it as a child. When you grow up and you start towering over people, they take fright."

"Yes. I can see that." Her eyes had softened.

"The other boys delighted in spreading the word, saying

that all sorts of evil beasts had placed their mark on my body to claim me as one of them."

"Mmm." Frigyth sounded pensive. "Maybe they were just jealous."

"Jealous?" He was incredulous. "Whatever for?"

"Come, you are taller, fitter, smarter, more handsome than most, of course, people are going to be jealous of you! The men, at least. The women will just lust after you, beast mark or not."

A silence followed the words. Sigurd was stunned. Frigyth thought him smart? Handsome? And, as a woman she... lusted after him? His heart leapt at the same time as his shaft.

"I-I should go to bed. It's been a long day," Frigyth stammered, turning toward the pallet.

What had possessed her to say such a thing? Not that it was a lie, but now Sigurd would think she lusted after him like that Edith. She didn't, did she? Of course, she thought him handsome, but who wouldn't? He was a stunning man. And, of course, she'd been affected by the sight of his naked back. How could it have been any different? It was not something you saw every day.

She hugged herself and strode over to the other end of the hut. It had been a mistake to get involved in such an intimate conversation, to show him the mark on her shoulder. If she had just mentioned it, the same point would have been made. Baring herself to him had been too intimate. Thank God her mark was on her shoulder, not her hip or breast.

She settled on the furs without asking, knowing he wouldn't hear of her sleeping anywhere else, just like on the first night she had spent at his hut.

"Good night, Sigurd. Thank you for letting me stay."

He was still in the middle of the hut, looking at her, an undecipherable expression on his face.

"Good night, *birdie*. You're welcome."

CHAPTER SIX

"You will need some clothes."

"Yes," Frigyth agreed, chewing on her piece of bread. If she was to stay a fortnight in the village, she would need something to change into at some point. At the moment, she only had the clothes on her back. Merewen, who might be prevailed upon to lend her some, was not here at the moment. Sigurd had just explained that she and Wolf were in hiding right now. The Icelander had sent word to him that they would stay away from the village for a few days, in case a man called Alaric, who was after Merewen, came looking for her.

The day before yesterday Sigurd had answered to tell him it was safe to return but there was no knowing how long they would choose to stay away.

"We'll go to town to get whatever you need from your house," he decided, before emptying his cup of ale.

"We?"

"I'm coming with you. I won't risk Coldman seeing you on your own and abducting you."

She sighed. "He would never do such a thing. And for the last time, his name is Caedmon."

Sigurd grunted as if he had no idea why she should remind him when he couldn't care less and a corner of her mouth lifted despite herself. *Why* did she like it so much when he acted so unreasonable? It didn't make sense.

They set off without further ado. Outside, the sun was trying to make an appearance but in spite of it, the day was bitterly cold. Frigyth wrapped her cloak more tightly around her and shivered.

"We'll take the boat," Sigurd announced, veering to the right when she was already taking the path to the forest.

"The boat?" She blinked. Had she heard him right?

"The town is just across the lake, is it not? Much quicker to cross it than go around it."

Yes, it would be... except for one detail. "I can't swim." She looked at Sigurd. It sounded ridiculous to admit as much to a man who'd crossed the seas to come to her country.

"It's all right, there will be no need to. You'd be hard-pressed to do it anyway, in such a small, *dry* boat." He cocked his head when she opened her mouth and then closed it again. "I sense another objection coming," he added calmly.

"I can't row either."

"Ah. There goes my plan of watching you kill yourself at the task while I recline in the winter sunshine. Oh, well."

She could not stop a giggle. "I believe you're mocking me."

"I believe I am." He gave her a smile that reduced her insides to warm honey. "Come, there's nothing to fear. You won't have to either swim or row. Just make the most of the sunshine, such as it is, and watch me."

Her heart skipped a beat. It sounded like the most scandalous temptation to watch a man of his stature exert himself. "I suppose I don't have a choice?"

"No. The mighty beast has spoken. The little bird better beware."

She followed him to the lakeshore where half a dozen boats were moored. He stopped in front of the one tied up on the far end.

"This one? Are you sure?" Somehow it seemed too small for him and her.

"Yes. It will be fine."

He held out his hand and there was no choice but to step into the frail vessel. She couldn't prevent a yelp when it wobbled dangerously. Was this supposed to happen? Surely not.

"It's all right. Just sit down carefully." She did as she was told and Sigurd stepped aboard, barely causing the skiff to move. You would have thought he weighed no more than a child, which was ridiculous. He had to weigh twice as much as she did. "Ready?"

"Yes." After all, she was in it now.

Sigurd pulled on the oars once, twice, and slowly the boat left the shore. He made it look easy but she suspected it required enormous strength to make the boat move at all. She swallowed, realizing they were now completely surrounded by water. It was unnerving, there was no denying it. Raised in town, she had never placed a foot on a boat or learned to swim.

As Sigurd obviously knew what he was doing, however, she soon forgot her anguish and just made the most of the way the pale sun gleamed on his golden hair, of how the muscles rippled on his forearms with each pull on the oars. In spite of the cold, he had rolled his tunic and shirt to the elbow and the dusting of blond hairs on the tanned skin fascinated her. Did he have other marks on his body, she wondered, before chiding herself. Mentally undressing him was not going to help her keep hold of her composure.

Eventually, they reached the other side of the lake.

Frigyth blinked, shocked to see that they were outside the

town gates by the south door. Indeed it was faster to travel by boat... The walk would have taken them most of the morning.

She accepted Sigurd's hand to disembark and led the way to the road where she'd spent her whole life. Never had it looked narrower or more grim. That the sun had now been swallowed up by enormous gray clouds did not help. Steeling herself, she reached for her key in her cloak pocket.

The smell of the house as she opened the door hit her almost like a physical blow. She knew then that she would have to move sooner or later. Too many bad memories were associated with the place. Caedmon was right. She should leave the house, make her life elsewhere. Just... Not in London. Not with him.

She stepped inside, determined to be brave, and closed the door behind Sigurd.

Seeing him, so tall and assured, in the place where she had been so miserable, was odd, but comforting. It was as if his mere presence chased the ghosts away. If he noticed her uneasiness, he did not comment on it.

"Do you need help?"

"No. Thank you. I won't be long."

With those words, she disappeared into the room at the back where the beds were. Although her family had by no means been rich, the house boasted three rooms and even a tiny store room at the back. Her father and mother had been neighbors and so the two families had decided to knock an opening into the wall connecting the two houses after they got married, making it the largest house in the area.

Without looking around she gathered her best woolen dress, another, more serviceable one, a spare shift and some stockings, as well as her second cloak. All this was rolled into a bundle and fastened with twine. When she brought it back into the main room Sigurd took it from her as if doing so were only natural.

"I will carry this for you."

"I am perfectly capable of doing so myself," she protested, knowing it would be to no avail. If he'd set his mind on it, he would not budge.

"Of course, you are, but it will inconvenience me far less than it will you."

There was no point insisting, she would never win. Instead, she poured them each a drink of ale and asked Sigurd if he wanted anything to eat. As if he'd sensed her discomfort, he refused.

"No, we'll eat something when we get back. Let's go, make the most of the light."

As they reached the end of the road they were stopped by Gedla, one of her neighbors, who was getting home with her children. The last thing Frigyth wanted to do in this cold was to linger, but the meeting with the woman was providential, so she returned the greeting with more enthusiasm than she might otherwise have done.

"Will you tell my sister, Dunne, if she comes calling for me, that I will be staying at the Norsemen village for the next few weeks?" she asked the woman. "I promised to go see her before the babe is born, but I'm not sure when I will be able to."

"Of course. The Norsemen village, hey?" Gedla kept throwing meaningful glances in Sigurd's direction. Tall, with blue eyes and golden hair, he stood out in the town, and she had evidently identified him as one of the Norsemen—one who appealed to her tastes.

"Yes." Before she knew what she was doing Frigyth edged closer to him. It was not a conscious decision, and in truth, she could not quite make sense of it. Still, Sigurd did not appear to mind. With a smile he drew her to his side and wrapped his free arm around her waist.

"You're right. Better to have her think we are together in

case your faithful watchdog comes sniffing around," he murmured in her ear while the woman turned to address an argument between the two boys behind her.

Frigyth shook her head. Thankfully he'd thought she was merely trying to appear as if they were the married couple they were posing as and did not think it odd that she had snuggled close to him. "Caedmon doesn't care for her. There is little chance she will be in a position to tell him she saw us together."

"Maybe not. But she's eyeing me up like a cat eyeing up its next meal and I don't fancy being the next thing she... eats."

"No." Frigyth gritted her teeth and nestled even closer to him. She didn't fancy it either.

Sigurd let out a low chuckle. "I thank you for looking after me, birdie. You make quite the fierce protector."

Warmth invaded her cheeks at the use of the affectionate nickname and the look in his eyes but she was prevented from answering when Gedla turned her attention back to them.

"Why on earth are you—" The question got stuck in her throat when she saw them entwined together. She blanched and then went red when she considered her question answered. "I see."

"If you'll excuse us, we had better get going. It will be dark before too long and I fear it will start snowing soon. You go get your children warm, and I will do the same with my woman," Sigurd said in his best commanding voice before leading Frigyth away from the bemused woman.

"Do you have bad memories from your childhood?" Sigurd couldn't help but ask Frigyth once they were settled in the boat, the bundle of clothes between them. He'd noticed how she'd hurried around the house, as if she didn't want to linger any longer than necessary.

She stilled, proving his intuition had been correct.

"Yes," she said tersely. So tersely that he didn't press further. He knew all about the suffering an unhappy childhood could bring and would not make her share something that was evidently painful.

He pulled on the oars, cursing Frigyth's neighbor for having delayed them on their way to the lake. It was a lot colder than it had been that morning and the light was fading fast. Even worse, a nasty wind had started to blow and was doing its best to steer him off course. Sigurd did not comment on the waves coursing along the surface of the lake but he was starting to worry. It was taking all his strength to fight the current and keep them out of the zone where he knew rocks were hidden under the water.

He did his best to behave naturally but he could see Frigyth's eyes darting around wildly. She was no fool, she knew all was not quite as it should be. That morning she had been able to relax but now she appeared tense, even if she did her best not to let it show. To distract her, he asked her a question about her neighbor.

"The woman you talked to earlier. Is she married?"

"Gedla? Yes, she's married. Why do you ask? Because you are thinking of making the most of her invitation?" She shook her head. "For shame, it was as you said, she ogled you as a cat would ogle its next meal. Do you find that sort of behavior appealing, perchance? I can't see why. Well yes, in any case, she is married, so don't be getting any ideas, do you hear? Her husband is a good man."

Well... Sigurd hadn't expected such a tirade. Was she jealous? The idea pleased him.

"I'm not getting any ideas," he answered, pulling harder

than ever on the oars. Damn it, they were getting too close to the forbidden part of the lake for comfort. The shore was not so far now, but he was not certain he would manage to avoid the rocks altogether. "A woman so openly fickle is hardly tempting. I'm sure she...*ogles* all the men passing through town."

"She does, actually." Frigyth made a face he was at pains to identify. Pity for the husband perhaps? "But I'm sure she—"

He would never know what she meant to tell him because at that moment the noise he'd been dreading to hear split the air.

Crack.

CHAPTER SEVEN

A jolt. A cry from Frigyth. "What was that?"

That had been a jagged rock piercing the hull of the boat from underneath, the very thing he'd been desperate to avoid. Sigurd forced himself to calm. They weren't too far from the shore, and he knew how to swim better than most. With the wind's help, he would easily be able to take Frigyth back to shore.

Yes, he trusted in his ability to keep her from drowning. But that didn't mean they were not in trouble for all that. For one thing, the water would be ice cold and for another, the rocks looming under the surface could tear them to shreds.

Damnation, he had promised her earlier that she would be safe and here they were, in a sinking boat in the middle of a freezing lake. In a moment, it would be dark, and it might well start to snow.

He pulled on the oars with renewed determination. The nearer he got them to the shore, the less time they would spend in the water. All too soon, though, he had to admit defeat. The skiff was sinking fast. He took hold of her bundle of clothes and threw it overboard. With luck, the wind would push it toward the shore and it would wash up there, ready for them to pick up tomorrow.

"What are you doing?" Frigyth shrieked.

"Listen to me," he said, working very hard to sound matter-of-fact, as if what he was about to announce was not a disaster. "The boat is going to sink, it is inevitable." There were already several inches of water at their feet so this could hardly come as a shock to her. She would have guessed what was going to happen by now.

"The... *what*?" she croaked. Mm. Maybe she had not.

"I will row for as long as I can, keep us out of the water but we will end up in the lake at some point." He paused before delivering the blow. "The water will be freezing. I need you to be prepared for it."

She ignored his comment completely. "But I can't swim!"

"I know." Didn't she remember telling him as much earlier? Maybe not. It was clear she was fighting crippling panic. "Please, listen. The shore is not so far. I will get you there, I promise. I won't let you drown. Just stay calm and allow me to carry you. The calmer you are, the better it will be for me. Just breathe and go limp in my arms. I will easily carry you. Do you trust me?" In the near darkness, all he could see were her eyes, huge with fright. Her teeth were chattering already. He took her hands and she nodded. "I will keep you safe. I'm a Dane, remember? We are more fish than men."

She nodded back. "I trust you."

"Good. Now, let's try to get as near the shore as possible."

While he rowed, Frigyth did what she could to scoop out water in her joined hands. Their combined efforts made little difference but at least it got them warm. Soon their feet were completely submerged in icy water. There was no point battling the elements any longer and using up all his strength rowing. He would need it to swim later.

"We need to go now."

Sigurd slid into the water, doing his best not to betray the shock at the temperature and held out his arms to Frigyth. After a brief hesitation, she leaned in toward him.

"Argh!"

Hundreds of daggers attacked Frigyth's body at once, stealing all the air from her lungs. Sigurd had warned her about the temperature of the water but, fool that she was, she had ignored it, too preoccupied by the fear of drowning. Right now, though, she was more worried about her heart giving out than her head sinking under the water surface.

Doing her best to relax, she closed her eyes. They had to get out of here, fast, before they froze to death.

Sigurd started swimming. His breath was coming in short bursts in her ear. She guessed this was due to the temperature of the water rather than exertion because, as he'd promised, he seemed to have no difficulty keeping her afloat.

A moment later, pain exploded in her hip. A jagged rock hidden under the surface had ripped through her skin. Frigyth bit her lip so hard she tasted blood. There was no use in worrying Sigurd by crying out in pain. At least by being the one smashed against the rock, she had protected him from injury. He was the one who needed the use of his legs to swim, not her.

At long last, he hoisted her onto a gravel beach and crawled next to her. They lay panting side by side, with their hands entwined, for what seemed like an eternity. Frigyth stared at the moon burning bright overhead, unable to believe she was alive. Frozen to the marrow, exhausted, in pain, but alive.

Just then it started to snow, the soft, fluffy flakes hitting her frozen skin like tiny pinpricks.

Eventually, Sigurd looked at her. His eyes were glinting in the moonlight, the color of liquid crystal. If she was exhausted, she could not imagine how he must feel. He'd been battling the wind with the oars, then holding her afloat and swimming for their lives in the freezing water.

He sighed, then bolted to his feet when he saw that her dress was stained red. "You're bleeding!"

It was hardly surprising, considering the way she'd been slammed against the rocks. "Yes. It's nothing," she rasped.

And truly, it was. Considering she could have been drowned, crushed against the rocks, or had to watch as Sigurd was swept away by the currents, she could not help but feel lucky to have gotten away with a cut and a few bruises. Besides, the cold from the lake had numbed the worst of the throbbing. But when she accepted Sigurd's hand and made to get back up, she could not help a yelp of pain. When she started to walk it was even worse. The whole right side of her body felt as if it had been beaten to a pulp by a blacksmith's hammer. The best she could manage was a pathetic limp.

"Forgive me, but I won't be able to carry you," Sigurd said, anger in his voice.

"Of course, not," Frigyth answered. There probably wasn't a single functioning muscle left in his arms. "It's no issue."

"Lean on me, at least."

She wanted to refuse but quickly saw she had better do as he suggested. Not only would it prevent her from putting too much weight on her damaged leg, but that way they would also share some much needed body warmth.

They set off, as slow as a pair of plodding heifers. The wind had mercifully dropped, but the snow was falling steadily now, covering the land in white. Frigyth had never been so cold in all her life. She lost track of where they were, focusing on placing one foot in front of the other. Sigurd talked to her all the way, urging her on, holding her close against him.

In the clearing next to the village, they happened upon Ingrid, the brewer's daughter, who was gathering wood. Sigurd groaned. The meeting was providential. He hadn't thought to meet anyone in this weather.

"What happened to you?" she exclaimed, her eyes darting in panic from him to Frigyth, whom she would have seen around the village. "You're limping. You're soaked. You're *bleeding*! You can't walk! You need help." She looked to the clearing behind her. "There is a group of us gathering wood yonder. Let me go get my father or Olaf to—"

"No!" He and Frigyth snapped at the same time, causing Ingrid to recoil.

"We'll manage," Sigurd said more amenably, regretting snapping at the girl. It was not her fault Olaf was the last person he would allow near Frigyth. "Just... If you really want to help, run ahead to the village and tell someone to get a fire running in my hut."

He had to get Frigyth warm as soon as possible, but he would not have her being carried in Olaf's arms. That was more than either of them could bear. He looked at her in concern. In the silver light, her lips appeared almost black. By the gods, it would be a miracle if she didn't catch a fever after tonight's ordeal.

"Do you want me to ask Wolf?" Ingrid asked.

"Oh, he's back?" That was the best news he'd had all day.

"He arrived this afternoon, just before we left."

"Then yes, please ask him to get the hut ready for us."

Without a word, Ingrid ran to the village.

They walked on, Frigyth limping more and more with each step. Just as they reached the edge of the forest, Wolf burst in from behind a clump of trees. Without a word he swept Frigyth into his arms. Sigurd gave a sigh of relief. Though she had not uttered a word of complaint, he had not missed that she was about to collapse. He didn't want Olaf to come anywhere near her, but Wolf was another matter. He didn't have any qualms about him holding Frigyth in his arms.

"What happened?" the Icelander asked in Norse.

"I'll tell you later. Just get her back to the hut as fast as you can. Careful not to jolt her too much, she's injured."

He could tell Frigyth was about to protest, but Wolf nodded and turned toward the village before she could. Sigurd followed at a more sedate pace. His whole body was stiff with cold and aching from his exertions, but he had no choice but to plod on. When he finally made it back to the hut, Wolf was waiting for him outside the door.

"Frigyth is changing out of her wet clothes," he explained. "As she doesn't have any spare clothes, I instructed her to get under the covers to get warm. That's why I'm here."

The thought of Frigyth being naked just a few feet away sent a welcome burst of heat through Sigurd's body. "Thanks, my friend. How is she?"

"Cold, in pain, and somewhat shaken, I think, but she will be fine. I left ale, cheese and bread on the table. And some of Helga's ointment."

"That's perfect. I will need to see to her injuries."

"You need to get out of these wet clothes first and get warm yourself."

Sigurd only grunted and walked up to the door, effectively dismissing Wolf. He knocked cautiously. "Can I enter?"

A timid voice answered. "Yes."

Thanks to Wolf, the hut was pleasantly warm. He let out a sigh of relief when the heat of the fire wrapped around his frozen limbs, breathing life back into his veins. Finally, the worst was over.

He found Frigyth buried up to her nose under the fur covers. He cleared his throat when he imagined her naked, her skin softer than the animal pelts, her cheeks rosy, her nipples puckered by the cold. The urge to join her under the covers and share his body warmth with her was overwhelming.

"I will give you one of my shirts to put on while your clothes dry," he said gruffly. "It will be more comfortable under the furs and should be long enough to cover your thighs."

"Thank you." Frigyth reddened at the thought of putting on a garment that belonged to Sigurd. Yes, it would definitely be long enough to cover her. It would also smell of him. She could not resist the temptation.

He rummaged around in the chest by the door until he found a long linen undergarment. "I will turn around while you put it on, unless you want me to leave the hut?"

"Of course not. It's still snowing outside," she replied. Was he being serious? "And you're already wet through. You need to get out of your clothes."

The words sounded more evocative than she had intended. Mercifully, Sigurd seemed oblivious to it. Perhaps he was just too cold to worry about anything else. He'd been outside longer than her after all, and was still wearing dripping wet, icy cold clothes.

She quickly darted out of the covers and donned the shirt he'd placed on the table before turning his back to her. Wearing such a piece of clothing was just as intimate as she had imagined it would be. Though it was indeed long enough to reach her knees, the collar gaped over her chest, revealing her breasts almost to the nipples. She could not allow anyone to see her in such a state of undress, much less a strapping, virile Norseman, especially when the idea caused her whole body to heat up.

She rushed back to the safety of the furs. Once she was covered, she called out to Sigurd. "You can get changed now. I will close my eyes."

"I need to see to your injuries first."

"No. Not before you get out of those wet clothes."

She was adamant. He had done enough for her already. Now he had to take care of himself. Besides, the wound had stopped bleeding. There was nothing to be done, save wash the blood away. That could wait.

When Sigurd informed her he was dressed, she was still shivering. "I can't s-seem to get warm enough," she stammered, answering the silent question in his eyes.

"Me neither," he grunted, which was hardly surprising. If she, under the furs, was still too cold, she could well imagine he would fare even worse. "What we really need is to share our body warmth under the covers." He spoke slowly, as if fearing she would misunderstand the suggestion for a lewd offer. She did not. He was right. It was the easiest, most efficient way to get them both warm. In fact, she should have suggested it herself.

She nodded. "Yes. Come here."

And just like that, Sigurd wasn't cold any more. Frigyth was welcoming him in her bed. How many times had he fantasized about that moment?

"Here." Careful to choose the side that was not cut, he lay next to her. "Drape yourself over me," he instructed as levelly as he could, tucking her tight against his flank, lifting one slender thigh to bring it in contact with his and resting her arm across his chest. The more of his body she touched, the better it would be for both of them.

"Mmm, yes, that's better," she sighed. After a while, she stopped shivering and he felt her whole body relax. "You're so warm..."

No wonder. He was burning with desire. How could it be any different? The woman he craved above all others was half naked and sprawled all over him. That she was wearing his shirt, such a masculine yet intimate garment, was oddly erotic.

"I'm so sorry about what happened," he said, his mouth at her temple. "I told you you would be safe and—"

The hand at his chest gave a light squeeze, silencing him. "Stop. You saved me. There was nothing you could have done to prevent the storm."

"No. But we could have walked back to the village instead of taking the boat, or stayed in town for the night, in your house, we didn't have to—"

"Sigurd. It's done." Oh, his name in her mouth! "Stop worrying about it. It's over, and now we're both warm. I just want to sleep." Her words were already slurred. "I'm so comfortable here next to you."

The weight in his chest eased marginally. Even if he would never forgive himself for the sinking of the boat, at least she didn't seem to resent him for almost killing her. He buried his face into her hair, which was only very slightly damp.

"Then sleep. It will all be better in the morning."

CHAPTER EIGHT

The pallet was empty when Frigyth woke up.

She opened an eye to find Sigurd stoking up the fire. How long had she slept? Guilt swept through her. She should be helping him, instead of languishing in bed! The sun was already high in the sky. Remembering at the last moment the way the shirt gaped over her breasts, she wrapped a fur around her shoulders before extracting herself from the warm nest. All her muscles protested at the move, but she ignored them.

"Good morning."

"Yes. Good morning," Sigurd said briskly, not glancing her way. "Don't worry. It will be plenty warm in a moment."

She frowned. It was already more than comfortable in the hut. If she, with her legs bare and her throat exposed could think so, surely Sigurd, who was dressed in his normal clothes, should not feel cold? Or perhaps he had seen the way she was clutching at the fur and hadn't understood she was only protecting her modesty.

"I'm all right. I don't think we need any more wood," she said, going to help herself to a cup of ale. "I'm thirsty, though."

"Yes, me, too," he said, joining her by the table. She poured him a cup and he finally looked at her when he accepted it.

She frowned. His eyes were unusually bright. Had he... been crying? The thought was preposterous but she could not help but wonder. "Are you all right?"

"I didn't sleep too well," he observed, staring into his empty cup.

Oh. That would explain it. She, on the contrary, had slept with the sleep of the dead in the comfort of his embrace.

"Wolf came to ask about you earlier, so I sent him to the lake to see if he could retrieve your clothes," Sigurd told her, helping himself of another cup of ale. "With any luck, the wind will have pushed them to the shore and he can find them."

"Thank you." She glanced at her shift and dress, draped over the stool. They looked still damp but they might be dry before the evening. "Are you hungry?" she asked, wondering what she could make if he was.

"No," he surprised her by saying. She'd have thought he would be starving after the previous day's exertions. "You can have the rest of the honey tarts if you want."

"What honey tarts?" The ones she had made the other day were long gone. Didn't he remember finishing them before setting off for town yesterday morning? He must indeed be tired after a sleepless night if he did not.

Just then there was a knock at the door. "Sigurd? Are you in here? I found Frigyth's clothes."

"Don't come inside!" Sigurd barked in Norse. With a nod of apology to Frigyth he joined his friend outside.

Wolf looked alarmed by his urgency. "What's the matter?"

"Nothing. But Frigyth is wearing only my shirt."

"So? I assume it's big enough to cover her adequately? She is not exactly the biggest of women..." Wolf sounded amused, but Sigurd did not return the smile. True, the garment was long enough, but it revealed far more of her throat and chest than he was comfortable with. The idea of anyone, even a friend he could trust, seeing as much as her naked shoulder was enough to make his blood boil.

"Do you remember how you dismissed me like a dog the day I brought the ointment for Merewen?" he replied, looking Wolf straight in the eye. "She was covered as well, if I remember correctly, and yet you sent me away before I could get a glimpse of the nail on her little finger."

Wolf grunted and kicked a stone into the wall of the hut. "Point taken."

Sigurd wondered why he was feeling so possessive. Pointlessly possessive, he might add. After all, it was not as if Wolf would take advantage of Frigyth. His friend was no lecher. He would have averted his eyes of his own accord once he had seen how the shirt gaped over Frigyth's breasts.

And it was not as if Sigurd had any right to consider her his anyway.

He blinked, and shook his head. He seemed to have difficulty thinking straight this morning. All he wanted was to get back into the warmth of the hut and catch up on his sleep, preferably with Frigyth tucked tight against him. No wonder he had not been able to fall asleep last night, with a warm woman pressed against him. He'd been throbbing all night, the pulsing in his groin slowly creeping up into his skull until he'd had no choice but to get up.

Desperate to get out of the cold and snow, he took the soaked bundle of clothes from his friend. He knew he should ask him about what had happened with Alaric but he just could not summon the energy right now. Tomorrow, once he'd had some sleep, he would.

"Thank you. I should have gone to retrieve the clothes myself but I—"

"It's no bother," Wolf cut in. "Are you sure you're all right? You don't look too well, my friend."

Sigurd didn't feel too well, in truth. "I'll be fine," he said nonetheless. "I expect a dunking in freezing water in this weather would not do many people good, even Danes used to the cold. Now, let me find a rope to hang these so they can start to dry out."

He placed Frigyth's clothes on the makeshift clothesline with trembling fingers. By the time he entered the hut, he was shivering all over. Damn, this might well be more than just tiredness.

Frigyth watched Sigurd stagger back inside the hut, her wet stockings in his hands. His face was pale and drawn and dark circles made his eyes appear sunken in his skull. He had never looked more wretched.

"Sigurd?" He mumbled something unintelligible, stumbled and crashed into the table as if he had not seen it.

She screamed and ran to him. "Are you sure you're all—?"

Before she could finish the question, he sagged against the table. Forgetting modesty, she let go of the fur to grab him under one arm and guide him to the pallet. Let him see her breasts, she cared not. She was sure he would not have noticed if she'd been stark naked in this moment, anyway. His eyes were not focused and his face, so pale a moment ago, was now alarmingly flushed. As soon as she placed her hand on his forehead, she recoiled.

He was boiling hot.

"Oh, Lord," she muttered to herself, pulling at his clothes to undress him while he was still half-conscious. Once he had collapsed, it would be impossible to move him and he needed to cool down. "Please, no!"

Sigurd mumbled something in Norse, probably an injunction to leave him be. She ignored it. The important thing was to do what was right by him, not what he wanted. Should she call for Wolf? He would be able to move the big Dane about more efficiently than she could. But then she remembered she hadn't heard his voice in a while. He was probably already back in his hut.

She would have to do this on her own.

Pushing and pulling, shoving and lifting, she managed to strip Sigurd down to his braies. By the time she was finished, they were both sweating and out of breath, though she knew in a moment she would be back to her normal state. The same could not be said of Sigurd. His chest was as hot as if someone had lit a fire underneath the skin. How long had he been like this? No wonder he'd spent a restless night. Why had he not said anything before?

Oh, the wretched man!

As she stared at the lifeless body in front of her, Frigyth took in a sharp inhale, feeling on the edge of tears. She hadn't caught a chill from her dunking in the frozen lake, but Sigurd had.

And now she feared he would die from it.

"Is he any better?"

Frigyth shook her head and started to worry her bottom lip. The Icelander had brought another cupful of old Helga's potion for Sigurd to drink. She was grateful for the attention, but she was starting to doubt it would work. "Not really. He just cannot lie calmly and he keeps muttering to himself in Norse. It seems to me that he says the same thing over and over again."

As if on cue, Sigurd started mumbling. Wolf listened, his head cocked. After a while, he nodded to himself. "Alone, all alone."

"I beg your pardon?"

The big man crossed his arms over his chest. "That's what he keeps saying. That he's all alone."

"But he's not alone. I've been here the whole time!" For the past two days she had been at his side day and night, forcing feverfew potion through his lips, washing his body with a cool cloth to bring the temperature down, worrying herself sick. As a result, she was exhausted. And now Wolf was telling her all her efforts had gone unnoticed! She felt about to cry.

Wolf sighed and placed a hand over her shoulder. "He doesn't mean now, I don't think. I can see your care of him has been exemplary." He hesitated, then seemed to decide she deserved his honesty, and after all she had been through, she could only agree. "Sigurd was orphaned at a very young age. He spent his childhood in the woods by himself, fighting for survival. He never had anywhere he could call home, no one to care for him. I know it still haunts him, even though he would deny it most forcefully. That's what he's talking about, I think."

"Oh, no." Frigyth's heart broke in two. An orphan... Her gaze wandered over to Sigurd behind her, thrashing on the pallet. It was hard to imagine this strapping, confident, protective mountain of a man as a child, all alone, scared and starving. "I had no idea."

"No, I guess he will not have told you. It's not something he likes to talk about. He might well knock me unconscious if he ever finds out I told you." There was a silence. "You need to sleep, Frigyth, you look worn out. Do you want me to stay the—"

"No," she cut in. That was not an option. This man had saved her life, kept her afloat in the freezing water, swam her to safety, forgotten his own discomfort to make sure she was warm and had wanted to tend to her injuries before seeing to his own needs. The least she could do was repay the favor, even if she was admittedly exhausted. "I'm staying."

"Have you eaten, at least?" Wolf asked, understanding she

would not relent. "I could bring you some of the salted fish Merewen prepared—"

"It's fine. I'm not hungry, anyway," she said as levelly as she could. The mere thought of salted fish when she was already feeling queasy from the lack of sleep was too much. "I made some bread earlier."

"Very well."

Once Wolf was gone, assuring her he would call again in the morning to check on them both, she lay on the pallet next to Sigurd. He was thrashing on the furs like a man in prey to a nightmare, much like he had for the past two days. Now she knew for certain he was having nightmares, reliving the loneliness of his childhood.

Her heart broke anew. No child should have to go through that.

"Sigurd. I'm here, it's all right. You're not alone anymore," she whispered in his ear, her hand poised over his chest. It was so soft, matted with short, golden hair, that she could not resist stroking him. "You're not alone. Feel me. I'm here. You're not alone. I'm right here. I'm not leaving you. You're not alone."

She kept repeating this, over and over again, hoping he could hear her, hoping he could derive some reassurance from it. After a while, he quieted down and tightened his hold around her, like a man holding on to a branch to avoid being swept away by the currents. She let him hold her, relishing the notion that she had brought him the comfort he desperately needed.

Once he was calm, she raised herself onto her elbow to look at him.

He was so... impossibly compelling.

Beautiful.

Unable to resist, she placed her lips on his. For two long, agonizing days she had watched him writhe in pain and anguish. She wanted to comfort him, wanted to allow herself this small reward.

As soon as their mouths touched he raised his hands to cup her face. She started, having thought him asleep, then relaxed under the caress. His fingers were strong and callused, but his hold was gentle, reverent. Frigyth moaned at the delicious contact. In this instant, it was as if she had finally become a woman. It was an odd thought, perhaps, but that was what it felt like.

"Sigurd," she whimpered, "please, kiss me. Kiss me as if you loved me."

With a grunt, Sigurd rolled her under him and started devouring her. There was no other word for it. This was nothing like Caedmon's kisses. Comparing the two was like comparing a babbling stream and a gushing waterfall, a pleasant breeze and a raging storm. Caedmon had tickled her senses, Sigurd over-whelmed them, turned her nerves endings inside out and upside down. Already knowing she would never be kissed like this ever again, Frigyth gave herself over to the most wonderful moment of her life, weaving her fingers into Sigurd's hair, grinding her hips against his, moaning into his mouth.

He didn't know what he was doing anyway, so she might as well make the most of it.

And she did, allowing her fingers to roam along his naked, muscular back, feeling the slight raise where his 'beast' mark was, reveling in the way his muscles bunched and twisted under her palms, grinding her hips against the hard rod pressing between her legs. My... This felt like more than kissing, like a prelude to lovemaking. And she felt... She felt ready for it.

What would she do if he asked her to spread her legs and let him take her? She might well agree.

All too soon, Sigurd broke the kiss, leaving her panting for air and more confused than ever.

He rubbed his nose into her hair, nuzzled his face against her neck as if trying to cover himself with her smell. Then he opened his eyes and said something in Norse, looking at her through blurry eyes. Frigyth would have given ten years of her life to know what that sentence meant. All she knew was that this time he had not mentioned how alone he was. Her eyes filled with tears.

This was the most intense, the most emotional moment of her life.

"Me, too," she said, hoping this was an appropriate response.

Slowly, she felt Sigurd relax against her and finally, blessedly, fall into the deep, restorative sleep he needed.

CHAPTER NINE

I n the morning, two things were clear. One, Sigurd was well on the road to recovery. The fever had broken in the night and when he opened his eyes, his gaze was as sharp as it had always been, blue as a clear summer sky.

Stunning.

Two, he had absolutely no recollection of having kissed her last night. No glint in his eyes, no curve of the lip, no questioning look betrayed any knowledge of what had transpired between them under the cover of darkness. There was only one conclusion to be drawn from this. He had no idea that for a brief, heady moment, they had shared a passionate kiss, that he had held her as if she were the most precious thing he had ever held in his hands and devoured her as if he wanted to make her his in every way.

It was better that way, she told herself sternly, because what would she say to justify what she had done? He would know from the fact he had been almost unconscious that she had been the one taking the initiative for the kiss. How would she explain the impulse? She could not. All she'd known was that, at the time, it had seemed right, the only thing to do.

"I see you're better," she said, bringing him a cup of water. After days of fever, he would be thirsty.

"Thank you. How long was I unconscious?"

"Three days," she said, knowing he would hate to hear it, but unable to lie to him. Wolf would only tell him the truth later on, anyway.

"Three days! Bloody hell! I wonder what you will think of me," he grumbled, looking as put out as he had been the day she had tended to his ankle. The tall Dane really didn't like being seen in a position of vulnerability. Her mouth twitched. It *was* adorable, say what she might. "First you tend to my ankle, and now this..."

She waved the protests away. "I'm glad I could help, and I don't think any less of you for being ill."

"Don't you? Well, perhaps you should. You must think we Danes are weaklings."

Frigyth opened wide eyes. Weakling? Had he seen himself? Surely he didn't really think he had a weak constitution? "Sigurd. You had to swim in freezing water with a dead weight in tow and then walk in the snow with dripping wet clothes. Once you were back at the hut, you refused to change and get warm until you had made sure I was comfortable. If after that you had not caught a chill, I would seriously wonder if you were human."

"Oh, I am human. You told me yourself I was no beast and I was starting to believe it, fool that I am. So don't go changing your mind now."

"I won't." Her lips quivered. He must really feel better if he started to make jokes. Her whole body relaxed in relief. He was fine, he was not going to die.

But he had forgotten the kiss. She was not special to him any longer.

She sat on the stool and looked at him, oddly intimidated all of a sudden. For days she had lain next to him, stroked his long body tenderly, spoken to him in the night, kissed him to within an inch of her life only the day before. And now... Now she didn't know how to behave in front of him.

"I'm sorry I was such a burden to you."

"You weren't," she assured him.

But he must have been, Sigurd knew. Frigyth looked exhausted, he could guess all too well that she had spent the last three days tending him. On the table were various potions, a basin of water, heaps of clean and dirty linen, and the remnants of a loaf of bread. It was obvious she had worked ceaselessly to bring him back to health, barely taking the time to eat or sleep.

And all this time no one had been there for her.

"Who saw to your injuries in the end?" he asked in a low voice. He had not forgotten she had been cut at the hip.

Please don't say Wolf.

The idea that another man could have seen a part of her body, and such an intimate part as well, was enough to send his blood racing through his veins.

She shook her head. "No one. I did it myself."

"I should have helped you." Instead he'd been lying on the pallet, weak as a kitten. He shook his head in disgust.

"There really was no need. All I had to do was wipe the dried blood away."

The image caused Sigurd to swallow hard. Her tender flesh torn, bruised and cut, covered in dried blood. It should never have happened.

"How do you feel now?" He'd noticed as she moved about that she had a slight limp, even though it had been three days since their near-drowning.

"I feel fine. It seems it is my turn to limp now, though," she murmured. Then she lowered her gaze to her fingers. They were tugging nervously at the hem of her sleeve. "I never thanked you for saving my life." To his horror, tears had pooled in her eyes, tears he wanted to wipe away. Or even better, *lick* away. "You didn't—"

"Please. You don't need to thank me," Sigurd grunted. Not when he had been the one endangering her in the first place. He should never have put her on the boat in that weather. But damn it all, he just could not think straight when she was around. "You never asked to go to town by boat."

"We only went because I needed clothes," she pointed out, undeterred. "None of this would have happened if I hadn't come to you, and needed new clothes for my stay. I think—"

"You don't need to think. Please. And, in any case, I do believe you repaid the debt by saving my life in turn."

She made a face. "It was the least I could do. As I said, your life was only endangered because we went to get the clothes for me."

"There's no point arguing about all this now. It's done, and it's over. I feel restored to my usual self."

This was the truth. Oddly, considering how he'd been in bed for days, he felt good. He'd gone through dark moments, though. In his delirium he'd relived the awful solitude of his childhood. He'd been cold, hungry, alone, despised once again. *Beast* he'd kept hearing. *You're nothing but a beast. Go back to the woods where you belong.*

But then all of a sudden... all of a sudden he'd been warm, safe, loved. He'd even—

Sigurd blinked. He'd kissed Frigyth. Or at least, a woman who looked and smelled an awful lot like her. That was why he felt so good, he realized, because his befuddled mind had allowed him to do what he could not do in real life. He remembered a clean, forest scent and running his fingers into soft, blonde hair that flowed though his fingers like water. Her body had been soft, small, and warm underneath his, her lips sweet, her tongue daring and hot.

He had thought then that he didn't want to wake up if in his dreams he was kissing her.

What would she think if she knew what they had done in his heated imagination? Unfortunately, he knew the answer to that question only too well. She would be horrified to know he fantasized about plundering her mouth and possessing her body and he couldn't blame her.

"I was thinking of making oatcakes this morning," she said, rising from the stool. "Would you like some?"

He growled when his stomach manifested its approval. "Please. I feel like I haven't eaten in days."

"Well, you haven't," Frigyth pointed out with a smile. "Maybe that's why."

"Mm." He stared at her smile. Her mouth. Yes. He was starving. "Maybe that's why."

THE RUSTLING WOULDN'T STOP.

"Is anything the matter?" Sigurd enquired softly in case Frigyth wasn't truly awake. "Can't you sleep? Is the pallet uncomfortable?" He didn't think so, piled as it was with furs. She had not complained about it before, but tonight something was clearly wrong.

"Forgive me," she answered just as softly. "I woke you."

"No, don't worry. I wasn't sleeping either." After so many days doing nothing but sleep, he wasn't tired. "What is it?"

"I'm not used to sleeping alone," she said in a small voice.

He frowned. Who did she usually sleep with? Not a husband, he knew. A lover then? Caedmon? The notion of another man sleeping with her in his arms caused his jaw to clench so much he feared he might crack a tooth.

Thankful it was dark and she was too far away to see the murderous expression on his face, he raised himself onto one elbow, intent on asking her who she was used to sleeping with. But she spoke before he could.

"I hate it."

His heart skipped a beat. Was she saying what he thought she was saying? Did she want to sleep next to him? Now? His heart resumed its beating, twice as fast as usual, and blood raced to his lower body at the prospect.

Of course, they had slept together before he fell prey to the fever, but that was different. There had been no other choice, they had needed the warmth. Still, he remembered how soundly she had slept in his arms. There had been no tossing and turning then.

"My sister Birgit and I always slept together. I don't remember a time when I did not share a bed with her. Dunne, my elder sister, slept with my mother."

Sigurd could not help a grunt. "And your father didn't object to that arrangement?" With a child in his bed, the man would not have been able to indulge his senses whenever the mood took him.

There was a pause and he realized he had embarrassed Frigyth with his question. What a boor he really was! No one wanted to imagine their parents rutting.

"My father spent most of nights away. When he did come home, sometimes Dunne would join us in the second bed." There was another pause, as if she was remembering what happened on those nights. In the darkness, he couldn't see her but he thought he heard her inhale sharply. Her father clearly made up for lost time on those nights, and his daughters had been able to hear everything. "Anyway, what I'm trying to say is that I find it odd to be on my own. I feel cold."

"Are you saying..." He could scarce believe what he was hearing—or what he was about to suggest. "Would you like me to join you on the pallet?"

Her answer was a mere whisper. "Yes. I slept next to you during your fever and it helped. I didn't think you'd object, since you were not conscious... But now perhaps you would rather—"

"No." He was up before she could finish her sentence. "I can sleep with you, it's not a problem. You need your sleep."

Without further ado, Sigurd settled next to her on the pallet. Frigyth had moved to the side to make space for him. The furs were warm, and smelled of her. He closed his eyes. This was perfection. Well, it would be if she allowed him to take her into his arms the way he had the other day. He stayed still. She just wanted a body next to her, to remind her of her sister, not a lover. She doubted Birgit had let her drape herself over her.

Once he was settled, she made a sound that shot straight to his heart. She seemed to think order had been restored. And in a way, it was.

"Birgit got married a few weeks ago, just before my father died. I still haven't grown used to sleeping on my own. It's ridiculous, I know."

"It's not." Sigurd felt her arm brush against his and he clenched his teeth. "I spent my whole childhood wishing I had someone to sleep next to."

Of course. Frigyth bit her lip. How could she have been so insensitive as to talk about being alone to an orphan? She knew about Sigurd's lonely childhood. Should she tell him Wolf had confided in her? No. He would hate it. If he ever told her about his past, it would have to be because he chose to. Still, she could not resist giving him the opportunity.

"You never had brothers or sisters?"

"No." The word was little more than a whisper.

Her heart constricted. If he'd been orphaned at a young age and had had no siblings, then he'd truly been all alone, as Wolf had said. No wonder he'd relived the painful moments in his delirium. It seemed she was not the only one who'd had a difficult childhood, if for entirely different reasons.

"Thank you for coming to lie next to me, I think I will be able to sleep now."

"You're welcome." She heard a soft snort. "The pallet is more comfortable than the fur on the floor anyway."

Indeed, it would be. "You should have asked to come before!" She was horrified he had been lying on the hard floor while she enjoyed the pallet.

"And risk frightening you? I think not. But you asked me yourself, so I know you must trust me to behave as I should."

Frigyth's chest suddenly felt too tight. Had he been waiting for her invitation all this time? "I do trust you. I trusted you from the start."

"I know. Sleep now, birdie. You've earned it."

CHAPTER TEN

F rigyth spent the best night she had in weeks. Every time she woke up, there was the warmth of a body by her side, its comforting presence allowing her to drift back to sleep.

She stretched and looked around. The pallet was cold and the hut was empty. Where was Sigurd? It looked to be mid-morning at least. Of course after the few nights spent looking after him she had needed the sleep but she could not remember ever sleeping so late, even after her near drowning.

With regret, she left the pallet and got dressed in the warm woolen gown that was now dry. A lively fire was dancing in the pit. Heavens. She must have been sleeping soundly if she'd not heard Sigurd stoke it with logs and stir it back to life. He was surprisingly discreet for a man of his bulk, but still...

Just then, a grunt had her rush out of the hut.

Frigyth's heart flew into her throat when she saw Sigurd and Wolf locked in a tight embrace over by the well, each evidently trying to throw the other one to the ground. What was happening now?

Then she saw Merewen watching with her back against the

nearest hut and a smile on her face. Evidently, she was not worried by the outcome of the fight. Was she so certain her husband would win? The thought did little to reassure Frigyth. She didn't want to see Sigurd pummel anyone to the ground, but she did not wish to see him injured either. He was by no means a weakling but Wolf was enormous, perhaps as much as an inch taller than him, and even heavier. Muscles rippled under his exposed skin.

"Aren't you worried?" she asked her friend, rushing to her side.

"Worried? Hum, no. Seeing my husband sparring whilst half-naked with another handsome man never fails to provoke feelings in me but worry is not one of them."

Frigyth blushed and averted her eyes from Wolf's chest. She would *not* leer at her friend's husband, even if he was, admittedly, beautiful in his own way. As for Sigurd... She spent enough time ogling him up already.

"But I thought they were friends!" she cried out. What could have sparked the argument? She could not fathom what would possess two men who thought so highly of each other to want to come to blows. Just then, Wolf threw Sigurd to the ground, sending him sprawling in a tangle of limbs on the frozen ground. She gasped. "They're going to kill each other!

"Oh, Frigyth, they are not going to kill, or even hurt each other," Merewen assured her, her eyes still glued to her husband. "This is no real fight, just practice. They are simply doing what they can to stay in shape. Look carefully. If they really meant to hurt each other, Wolf wouldn't be waiting for Sigurd to get up before finishing him off, believe me."

Indeed, the Icelander was not trying to take advantage of his move, instead running his hand through his long hair. Now that the beatings of her heart had subsided, Frigyth could see he was smiling.

"Am I supposed to be impressed by this pathetic display, Dane? Your fever has left you weaker than a lamb. I swear a child could have sent you to the ground."

With a curse, Sigurd jumped back to his feet, lithe as a sprite. "Damn shirt! Let's see how you fare when you can't grab at my clothes, you mongrel!"

He threw his shirt over the fence in an angry gesture—and all the air left Frigyth's lungs.

Heavens, but the man was truly magnificent. Unlike Wolf, who was all about raw power, he was sculpted and lean, graceful and taut. Transfixed, she watched the muscles on his back twist and cord when he lifted both arms to smooth his long hair away from his face. The reddish mark in the middle of his back drew her eye. The Beast. It called out to her, irresistibly.

Just like it had the other day, her mouth started to water at the idea of licking it.

"I see you're not worried anymore..." Merewen let out a tinkling laugh and winked at her.

"I-I'm not lusting after your husband, if that's what you mean," Frigyth stammered, caught out. Dear me, how embarrassing. What if her friend thought she had intentions toward her husband? Merewen's answer both reassured her and caused her to flush a deep red.

"Oh, no, I didn't think you were. Rather it seems to me you are lusting after his opponent. Watch, and enjoy. I wonder who will come up on top today because they are equally matched, whatever my husband says. Wolf is perhaps stronger but Sigurd is quicker."

The men fought without tiring for what seemed like an eternity. Frigyth could not believe it, Sigurd was barely two days recovered from his fever. Where he found the stamina and strength needed to hold his own against the Icelander, she could not fathom. It was as Merewen had said, they were evenly matched, and because they were not actually trying to kill each other, they never resorted to underhanded methods. As a result, she wondered how there could ever be a winner.

And then Sigurd sent Wolf down with a graceful sweep of his leg. It looked so smooth and easy you would have thought he hadn't applied any force. Of course, Frigyth knew different. One doesn't fell a tree with a flick of the fingers. As soon as the big man hit the ground, Sigurd was on his back, immobilizing him in an iron-hold. Frigyth winced. That looked painful.

"Enough! You win!" Wolf growled. With his arm bent in such an awkward position, there was no way he could free himself, not when his opponent was using all his weight against him.

Sigurd released his friend out of the arm lock and helped him up. It had been a good fight, and he'd been pleased to see that his illness had not impacted his skill or stamina much. In fact he felt full of energy.

Wolf wrapped an arm around his shoulder and whispered in his ear. "You can thank me for this later, my friend."

Thank him? His eyes narrowed. "Are you saying you only pretended to be beaten?"

"Your little wife is watching. Don't tell me you hadn't noticed." The Icelander nodded toward the two women standing by the hut. Indeed, Sigurd had not missed the way Frigyth could not seem to detach her gaze from him. It had infused strength in his veins. "Why else do you think I let you get the better of me for the first time in months?"

"It's the second time I beat you this week, actually."

"Is it?"

"Yes. Contrary to you, old man, my memory doesn't fail me!"

"Mm, I must be growing soft." Wolf laughed and patted his stomach. His body was that of a warrior in his prime, there was nothing soft about it. "I'll be looking forward to that cask of mead, friend."

Sigurd shook his head. Arrogant sod. But he couldn't deny he was pleased to have won the fight in front of Frigyth. After the humiliating incident with his ankle and then the fever, he didn't want her to think him a ridiculous wimp who could not take care of himself.

He glanced at her as he put his shirt back on. In that moment, she didn't appear to think him weak or ridiculous. If he had not known any better, he might have thought she was aroused. The notion sent blood rushing to his groin and he twisted his body to the side to hide the sight.

"I dearly hope you have some energy left, husband, and you didn't spend it all on Sigurd," Merewen purred, coming to them.

"For you, little one, always."

With those words, Wolf lifted his wife into his arms and they disappeared into the hut. There was little doubt about what they would do once the door was closed. Sigurd rolled his eyes when he saw Frigyth go bright red. Couldn't they be more subtle?

He cleared his throat, trying to ignore the pang of jealousy. What wouldn't he give to sweep her into his arms and take her straight to bed as well.

"Well, that was just what I needed," he declared, rubbing the side of his neck.

Frigyth didn't look impressed. "May I remind you that you were at death's door only a few days ago?"

He groaned. No, she may not, he had not forgotten that for the second time in a fortnight, she had seen him in a position of weakness. "I'm fine," he snapped.

"Why did you have to fight your friend?"

The corner of his mouth lifted. There it was. Frigyth was questioning him again. It hadn't taken her long.

"We have to practice and hone our combat skills. Those muscles did not appear by magic, you know, and they would vanish all to easily if we just sat on our... er... backs all day. I need to rebuild my strength after being at death's door and Wolf wants to be able to defend his wife if need be."

She harrumphed. "Still, isn't there a better way to stay in shape than to half kill a friend?"

An image tore through his mind. Him, holding a certain Saxon woman up against the wall while he pumped into her relentlessly. Yes, that would certainly help maintain his upper body strength. "There is a better, more pleasurable way, you're right, and I think that's what Wolf is doing right now," he purred, leaning in toward her. "But he prefers to do it with Merewen rather than with me. I am only good enough for rough handling."

Frigyth's eyes narrowed, making her appear about as menacing as a kitten. He fought very hard not to laugh. "I meant swimming or lifting tree trunks, or whatever else it is you men do."

This time he laughed out loud. "Lifting tree trunks, is that what you think men do? Why on earth would we do such a thing? I can honestly say I have never lifted a single dead tree in my life."

"No. You'd much rather try to climb them and then fall on your... er... back."

Oh, that was a low blow. And as if to make his humiliation more complete, his manhood jerked. The wretched thing liked her teasing, just as much as it would like a lewd glance or a brazen caress! What the hell? This was unprecedented. Women did not usually make him hard by mocking him.

Well, apparently, this one did.

"I need a wash," he said gruffly.

"Yes, you do." An arched brow made her realize she had just

all but called him dirty. She reddened again. My, she *was* flustered today... His manhood jerked again. Soon it would start to lengthen if he was not careful. Sigurd wondered if he should not use the excuse of a wash to bring his body some welcome relief.

"I-I didn't mean to suggest that you repel me," Frigyth stammered, "only that you—"

"Oh, I know I don't repel you. Don't think I missed the way you eyed me up earlier." Her eyes had been positively ablaze with longing, something she might not have noticed, and he should definitely not mention to her. Well, too late.

She threw her arms into the air in defeat. "I give up. I will go and gather more wood for the fire while you wash."

As she turned and walked away he could not resist one last taunt. "Call me if you need any tree trunks lifted, birdie. It's a man's job, apparently."

FRIGYTH DROPPED the whole pile of branches to the floor in shock.

"You're washing!" she accused, making it sound as if it was the worst thing a man could do.

Sigurd seized a piece of cloth and covered his groin. That this was entirely for her benefit was clear from the lack of urgency in his moves. He was not bothered in the slightest by his nudity, only trying to protect her sensibility.

"Yes. I told you I needed a wash. Why are you so surprised?"

"I thought you would go to the river, not bathe here! I would have waited outside otherwise, not barged in on you in... in such a state."

He chuckled and started rubbing at himself. "You truly have odd ideas about what men do, you know. It's the middle of winter. Why would I go to the freezing river when I can heat some water in my home and wash with warm water?"

She made a helpless gesture. "I don't know!"

So I don't have to see you naked! she almost screamed. How was she going to forget the sight? It had been bad enough to see him bare-chested earlier, now she would have to deal with the memory of his glistening wet naked body, including a part of him she should never have seen.

A part he was still rubbing. Surely he didn't need so long to dry it? Surely she should not keep staring at it?

Time seemed to come to a standstill. Frigyth's mouth was dry and she realized that she should have turned around as soon as she'd seen Sigurd was naked, or even better, rushed back out of the hut. She should *not* have stayed there ogling him.

What was the matter with her? Could she not spend a whole day without wanting to touch, smell, kiss or lick this man? Apparently not.

"Birdie, not that I'm not enjoying the way you're looking at me but it's cold. I'm going to need to get dressed in a moment. Which means I'm going to have to drop the cloth. You can stay or you can go. I don't mind either way. I'm just warning you."

The wretched man. How could he tease her so? As if she would want to stay!

"I-I'll go get some herbs for the pottage."

A grunt was all the answer she got.

CHAPTER ELEVEN

L ater that evening, they sat down to a pot of pottage that could have fed an entire army. Desperate to ensure she did not see an inch of Sigurd she wasn't supposed to see, Frigyth had gathered as many herbs as her arms could carry, which turned out to be a lot more than they needed.

"You can look at me, you know. I'm not naked anymore."

Oh, she knew he wasn't. Unfortunately.

Frigyth started. Unfortunately? Where had that scandalous thought come from? Surely she didn't want him to eat his meal naked?

Well, her treacherous mind answered for her, *would you really object?*

Yes, of course, she would!

She bit into her piece of bread and chewed. Things were getting out of hand. She was only supposed to pretend to be married to Sigurd to convince Caedmon she could not be his wife. She wasn't supposed to lust after him, or melt when he called her 'birdie', or want to see him naked, or imagine running her tongue over his beast mark, or steal kisses from him, or do any of the things she was doing. She wasn't supposed to get ideas into her head. In a week at the most, she would be gone. The less she thought of Sigurd as a virile man who could take her to bed, the better.

He was only a friend, someone who was helping her temporarily.

"Is something wrong?" he asked, his voice even deeper than usual.

"No." Somehow she found the strength to meet his gaze. He had stopped eating and was looking at her intently. In the light of the fire his eyes appeared darker, nothing like their usual blue. "I was thinking about the best way to peel and clean leeks. They are a pain to prepare, you know."

This was a lie, of course. She was thinking of him, of his body, taut and lean, smooth and strong, muscular and altogether too tempting. Of the kiss they had shared the other night, of the softness of his mouth, the heat of his touch, the taste of his tongue.

Oh, this was torture!

"Leeks." Sigurd grunted, as if he'd guessed the best way to prepare vegetables had been the furthest thing from her mind. Then he said the last thing she expected him to say. "We need to teach you how to swim."

She recoiled in terror. "You're not... You don't mean to take me back to that freezing lake, do you?" The idea was enough to turn her blood to ice. She'd not known how to swim but she'd never been afraid of the water. Now she was wondering how she would feel standing on the shore with the memory of their ordeal fresh in her mind. Not comfortable, to say the least.

"Knowing how to swim could save your life," Sigurd argued, piercing a piece of cheese with his dagger.

Perhaps. But only if she found herself neck deep in water, which hopefully would never happen again. "Don't worry. I don't intend to go on a boat any time soon."

"You never know when you might have to."

"I'm sure I—"

"You can't be sure of anything. Everyone should know how to swim."

Seeing he was not to be deterred, she pleaded. "Let us wait for the summer at least."

The summer... She swallowed hard. Of course, she would long be gone by then.

After a long moment, Sigurd nodded and helped himself to more pottage. Grateful for the reprieve, she finished her meal in silence.

The next day, after another night by his side, she went to Merewen's hut. While they made bread together, her new friend told her all about what had happened to her in the last few days. She had been abducted by one of her former neighbors, almost raped and killed, only to be rescued at the last moment by Wolf, who had been after the man for months. It made for horrific hearing but Merewen talked as if her abduction had been the best thing that had ever happened to her.

"I knew when I saw Wolf standing in front of me that I loved him and he loved me. He had come for me, and we would be able to give our marriage a chance. The rest did not matter."

Frigyth walked back to the hut more pensive than ever. Before she could go in, she stopped to watch the sun go down below the horizon. Never had the sunset been more beautiful than here, at the village. At home, nighttime was always to be dreaded and, anyway, the view was obscured by the jumble of houses. Here, nothing came to spoil the vast expanse of sky.

Crimson ribbons, slate-gray stripes and golden streaks competed for prominence on the pale blue horizon. It was a spectacular sight, one she wished she could see every day.

"Beautiful."

She started and turned around, feeling absurdly caught out

doing something forbidden. Sigurd was leaning against the hut, his arms crossed over his chest. He was looking at her, she noticed, and not at the sky. Could he mean...? She pushed the treacherous thought away before it could fully take form.

"Yes. Beautiful." She wasn't talking about the sunset, though. She meant *Sigurd* was beautiful, with his face lit up by the dying sun and his eyes shining like gems. It was enough to take her breath away.

"I will never get tired of gazing upon such beauty." Once again, she had the unsettling impression he was not talking about the view but about... Well, about her. But how could he? She was not what she would call a beauty. Or... Was she?

She frowned. After all, she had never seen herself as clearly as she saw others. What did she really look like? She knew she had blonde hair, because she could see it when she brushed it, she had been told her eyes were brown, but no one had described them to her in any more detail. The reflection she could glimpse on puddles after a storm was never clear enough for her to discern much. Her nose did not appear to be crooked or overly long, her mouth seemed ordinary, with lips neither too thin nor distractingly full. But could she be called a beauty merely because of the absence of a glaring problem? Surely not. She was too small, for one thing, and did not feel particularly feminine.

"You seem lost in thought, birdie."

"I was wondering..." She stopped. No, she could not say what she wondering and ask Sigurd if *he* thought her beautiful. He would understandably misinterpret the question and think she was after a compliment, or worse trying to entice him.

"Let me guess." His lips quivered. "You were wondering about the best way to boil turnips? I'm afraid I can't help you there. You're the cook."

Frigyth giggled. This man... He could always make her

laugh, even when laughing was the last thing she felt like doing. "No, I was wondering... Is the sunset here very different than the one in your country?" He shot her a piercing stare, as if he would have preferred her to be honest and tell him what she had truly been thinking about. But now she thought about it, she did wonder. "I'm sorry, it's probably a stupid question."

"It's not stupid, and yes, it is different, in the same way a woman can be very similar to other women and yet be like no other."

Indeed. Or a man. Sigurd was tall, blond and strong like most men in the village and yet he was uniquely beautiful. Did he know it? In the same way she had no real idea what she looked like, he might be unaware that he possessed the most striking features. Had anyone told him his eyes were not only of the deepest blue but wide and expressive as well, framed by velvety gold lashes? Did he know that his nose and square jaw lent his face masculine authority? Was he aware that his mouth... Oh, that his mouth was sin personified. It was impossible to look at it and not want to kiss him.

As she knew all too well.

Yes, she mused, he must have seen that he appealed to women. Wasn't he being pursued by Edith in his own home? A thought suddenly crossed her mind. Had he been to see a woman this afternoon while she was making bread with Merewen? It was not impossible. After all, why should he change his lifestyle just because he was helping her? There would be no reason to.

"Let's go back in," she mumbled, suddenly chilled. "It's getting cold."

The following morning, a group of women came to ask her if she wanted to help them clean and card wool. Frigyth agreed readily. It felt good to feel she had friends in the village. Merewen had been invited, too, as she was learning the skill as well. Like her, Wolf's wife had been raised in town, in a family of rich landowners. This life was new to her.

Time flew by and it was already mid-afternoon by the time Frigyth made her way back to the hut, exhausted, hungry, but happy.

A smile curled the corner of Sigurd's lips when he spotted a small figure through the window. Then he frowned. How was it that that the mere sight of Frigyth caused his heart to lift? No one had ever had that effect on him.

No, because he'd never lived with anyone, and had never had anyone walking back to be with him after their day's activities, cook for him or sleep in his bed at night. Really it was no wonder she should stir unprecedented feelings within him.

Except... except that she'd had that effect on him from the start, when he could not have imagined she would ever come and live with him. He'd instantly been attracted to that woman, without knowing why. It was as if they were two halves of a whole. When they were together he was at peace, when she was away, he missed her. He wanted to see her laugh at things he said, wanted her to question everything he did, wanted her to look at him the way she had looked at him the day he'd been fighting—and then washing.

Wanted her to touch him.

With each passing moment the urge to draw her into his arms and kiss that provoking bow-shaped mouth grew more and more pressing. That problem might well have to be addressed soon.

Frigyth entered, stopped dead in the doorway, looked at him for a moment, panic flaring in her eyes—and promptly ran back outside.

Sigurd followed, puzzled and not a little bit worried by her reaction. What now? Last night he'd been dripping wet and stark naked when she'd entered the hut; understandably she'd been shocked and yet she had stayed. So what was it about his dry, dressed self that had scared her to the point of making her flee?

"Frigyth?" he called out.

Retching noises answered him. He darted to the back of the hut, and found her leaning against the wall, panting hard.

"Are you all right?" What a stupid question. Of course, she wasn't. People who were all right did not throw their accounts on the ground. They did not look as pale as buttermilk.

She took in a deep breath and raised her head. "I'm sorry. The fish..."

He frowned. "What fish?"

"You... You're cooking salted fish, are you not?"

"Yes." He could not help being hurt by her reaction. They both knew he was not as good a cook as she was, but never had he sent anyone retching before. It was an unwelcome first. Especially given the fact that he had wanted to surprise her by cooking for once. "Is it that bad?"

"Forgive me. I didn't mean to insult you. But salted fish..." She shook her head. "I cannot stand it. The taste, the smell."

There was something odd in the way she said it. He sensed it was not just the taste or smell she couldn't stand. Nevertheless, he didn't press her. At least, it wasn't personal. He'd simply chosen the wrong thing to make. He pursed his lips, wondering what to do.

"I'm afraid it's all we have to eat for tonight and the hut might keep the smell for a while. But wait here."

Frigyth watched as Sigurd exited the hut a moment later, the pot of stew in hand. Holding it as if it might shatter at any moment, he walked over to Wolf and Merewen's hut. When he came back, he gestured that she should remain outside while he disappeared into the hut again.

It didn't take him long to reappear, a smile on his face.

"We are going camping in the woods."

"We are?" She eyed the enormous bundle he had slung over his shoulder. It looked as if he had gathered all the furs covering the pallet and rolled them together. Excitement bubbled in her chest at the idea. She had always dreamed of sleeping outside in the woods. She would never have dared doing it on her own, of course, but with Sigurd, she knew she had nothing to fear.

It was a perfect idea.

"I swapped my salted fish for some of Wolf's bread and cheese so we won't starve even if I don't catch anything. And with those furs we will be quite cozy." He looked up at the sky, which had gone a deep purple color. "It's cloudy, so it's mild tonight. I thought you would rather smell pine than fish as you try to go to sleep?"

Tears welled in her eyes at his thoughtfulness. This man...

"I would. Thank you."

CHAPTER TWELVE

A lively fire burned in the middle of the clearing, filling the night with its light, its warmth and its comforting crackling noise.

Sigurd had been right. Snuggled under the furs, she couldn't feel the cold. A sigh of contentment escaped Frigyth's lips. This was just as perfect as she had imagined it would be. Next to her, a rabbit was roasting on a makeshift spit, its skin popping and bubbling as it cooked. Sigurd had placed a snare as soon as they had arrived and by the time they had lit a fire and settled the furs under an overhanging branch, the animal had been caught, ensuring they would eat their fill tonight. She could tell Sigurd was at home in the woods in a way only someone who had grown up in the wild could be. It was obvious that he, unlike her, had not spent his childhood in a town.

But alone.

"It smells good," she said, smiling at him. So good she was salivating.

"Better than salted fish?"

She bit her bottom lip. "I'm sorry for that, really. I didn't mean to offend you. Whenever I smell salted fish, I heave, it's uncontrollable, ever since—"

"It's all right, I think I've understood it was nothing personal. You don't need to tell me why if you don't want to."

But she did want to. She wanted to confide in him, sensing he would not judge or mock her. Besides, she felt bad knowing about his miserable childhood. Perhaps sharing hers might help her get over the guilt. Then they would be on a more equal footing. And perhaps he might, in turn, tell her about his.

"That smell brings back bad memories," she explained. "I hear shouting, I feel fear, like I did that night..."

The words hit Sigurd with the force of a charging bull slamming into him. Who had been shouting at Frigyth, frightening her so much that she heaved when she thought about it years later? A husband she had fled? For the second time, he wondered if she was married. But this time, he wondered if she was married to a violent man. Was that why she couldn't stomach the idea of him going to Olaf? Because she knew what it was to live with a brutal man and did not want to have to deal with it again?

She must have seen the questions flash in his eyes because she started to speak, her voice muffled by the furs she had drawn up to her nose. Either she was cold or she wanted to hide. He suspected it was the latter since she had not complained about the cold before now. The idea that she might be ashamed or embarrassed tugged at his heart.

"My father was a drunkard, an unpredictable, hot-headed man. All the family suffered as a consequence."

Suffered. Sigurd clenched his fists. "Did he hit you?" Or... worse? She had told him she'd been a virgin when that bastard Olaf had raped her, but that didn't mean her drunkard of a father had not used her to satisfy his lust in ways that would not damage her maidenhead. The idea made him sick.

To his relief, she shook her head. "He never touched me... in that way. But that didn't make the situation much better. We never knew when he would fly into a rage, whether he would be home with us at night or out drinking with friends, fighting or whoring. I've lost count of the amount of times he came back home bruised and bloodied from a brawl at the tavern. My mother had to stitch his wounds time and time again, all the while enduring his foul cursing and ranting. And my sisters..."

"What about them?" Had the man touched them, if not her?

"They both ended up married to men like that, older and unreliable. I don't want to be the next one." Her fingers tightened on the furs she was holding in front of her face. "At my father's death I swore to myself I would not let anyone else ruin my life. It was too painful. I don't want to be like my mother, and live the rest of my life in the same dread, having to deal with a husband who cannot control himself whether he's had a drink or not, coming back home bruised and battered on a weekly basis. I need peace and reassurance. I need security, I need calm..."

I need love.

Frigyth didn't say the words out loud but he heard them all the same. His chest tightened. Wasn't that what he wanted, too? He pushed the thought aside. Now was not the time to worry about what *he* wanted.

"And the salted fish?" he asked softly. "I'm guessing it has something to do with it all?"

She nodded. "Most days it was all we had to eat, so much so that I got sick of it. One evening, I refused to eat. I must have been nine or ten. My father came back home while my mother was urging me to try it, as there wouldn't be anything else. He went mad, shouting that if I didn't like what he provided for us, what my mother had cooked for me, I would have to eat it as it came. He stuffed a piece of the dry, salted cod into my mouth and held me tight against him until I'd swallowed it. I was sick all night. I haven't been able to eat it or even smell it since."

"No. Of course, not." Sigurd was appalled. What a horrid story. He had the sudden urge to punch the nearest tree to alleviate some of the tension in his body. "I'm sorry."

"You weren't to know." She gave him a tentative smile. "How could you have guessed that the mere smell of the fish would send me running?"

"Still." He'd never felt worse.

"Sigurd, please don't worry, not now." She looked around, wonder in her eyes. The flames of the fire made them sparkle even more than usual. By the gods, he had never seen a more entrancing woman. "You made my dream come true, you know."

His breath caught in his throat. The confession sounded so impossibly intimate. He could almost hear *you're the answer to all my dreams.*

"How so?"

"In our bed at night, while we waited to see whether my father would come back or not, Birgit and I used to dream we could take refuge in the forest, and sleep by a fire under the trees, just like I'm doing tonight. We thought we would be safe, away from home, hidden from the world."

Sigurd shook his head. She'd wanted to escape the warmth of her home, when he'd been shivering alone in the woods... The irony was not lost on him.

"Well, you are. You're safe here with me."

Her answer, and the way she didn't even hesitate before answering, shot straight to his heart.

"I know I am."

Frigyth realized that she did feel safe, cherished even, with Sigurd. As far back as she remembered, she had never felt wanted, needed, much less loved. Her mother had been too busy trying to live with her father to worry overmuch about her, her youngest child, her sisters had had their own fears to deal with. Her father, of course, had been incapable of any feeling toward the children he had sired in a drunken romp and regularly hit.

Only Caedmon had brought some light, some affection in her life. But what she'd felt in his arms was not the same as what she felt when next to Sigurd, in the same way that their kisses had been radically different. One had been sweet, one was devastating, and had the power to sweep through her.

At long last, she removed the furs from her face. Being out in the forest was just as enchanting as she had imagined it would be as a child. Of course, then, she had not thought she would be guarded by a strapping Norseman who could make her heart flutter. It only added to the pleasure of the moment.

Silence stretched in the clearing. Then Sigurd cleared his throat. "I think the meat is cooked. Would you like a drink before we eat?"

"Yes, thank you." She accepted the cup of ale he was handing her.

The rabbit was delicious, succulent and cooked to perfection. Frigyth ate her portion with relish, stripping the bones clean before licking her fingers. "You said you were a bad cook," she observed, settling back into the nest of furs. "But this was excellent."

Sigurd gave a rueful smile. "I had no choice but to fend for myself growing up, so I became quite proficient at making the most of what nature had to offer. Being able to roast meat is not the same as being a cook, though. Left to my own devices, I would never starve, it is true, but I would never eat any delicacies either. I already told you I'm hopeless at making dough. I never had anyone to show me."

Frigyth's throat tightened. As bad as her childhood had

been, at least she'd had a home and some company. She'd not had to worry about where to sleep, how to get warm or what to eat. As unhappy as her mother had been, at least she had looked after her daughters and taught them what little she knew. By all accounts, Sigurd's early years had been even more miserable than hers.

"I can make bread and sweet tarts once I have all the ingredients, but as I grew up in town, I would be hopeless in the wild," she admitted. "Left to my own devices, *I* might well starve. It seems we make quite a good team between us."

"Yes, it seems so."

Was it the flames making his eyes appear so intense? Had she not known they were the deepest blue, she would have thought them amber in this moment, burning from within.

"Time to sleep, I think," he drawled.

"Yes."

Time to lay beside him, which had already become her favorite time of day.

As SOON AS she woke up, Frigyth knew something was different.

It was not that they were outside that made her heart leap, even though that was certainly unusual. It was waking to find herself in Sigurd's arms. Usually, they slept side by side, but they did not really touch. The occasional brushing of her hand against his arm was inevitable, but this was different. They were entwined, as only lovers could be. In the middle of the night she'd woken up to a dying fire and an impression of cold. She remembered burrowing closer to him in search of warmth and hearing an indistinct rumble as he drew her into his arms as naturally as if they had slept in such a position a hundred times before. It had been impossible to resist the lure of his embrace and she had fallen back to sleep with a smile on her face.

And now Sigurd was draped over her, with his front molded to her back, his strong arm wrapped over her waist, his hand splayed over her stomach, possessively. She stayed where she was, relishing the comfort of feeling surrounded by so much virile maleness.

Sigurd moved and she felt him poke her with... A furious blush invaded Frigyth's cheeks. He was poking her with a part of his anatomy only men possessed. With a part of him that she had never felt before, only seen and been unable to forget. With a part she should *not* want to take in her hand and stroke.

Just then, he groaned and nudged at her more insistently, as if he'd guessed what she was thinking and gave his agreement. Heat invaded her loins, a most disconcerting reaction. The last time a man had pressed against her thus she had frozen in panic at the idea of him plunging his shaft into her, not melted in anticipation. But the last time it had not been a man she trusted, and he had trapped her under him, not held her in a cocoon. The last time she had wanted to escape, not rub herself against the hot rod poking at her.

Frigyth cleared her throat. Was this an invitation? Should she accept it? It shocked her to realize that she wanted to.

He moved again and rumbled something in her ear. He sounded only half awake—or gruff with desire, she wasn't sure. She wasn't even sure in which language he had spoken. Unable to stand it any longer, she opened her mouth.

"Do you want... erm..." She wasn't quite sure how to word her question.

Do you want me? Are you about to jump on me?

Her words seemed to shake him out of his dazed state. "Bloody hell! Frigyth, I'm so sorry."

Sigurd moved as fast as if he'd been burnt, leaping away

from her. Bemoaning the loss of warmth, she turned to face him. In the morning light, he looked devastated.

"Don't be sorry. Please."

Not for making me feel wanted and yet in control of what would happen. For making me feel like a real woman.

Sigurd didn't seem appeased by her reassurance. It was clear that he had been more than half asleep when he'd rubbed himself against her and not fully conscious of his actions. She could not help a pang of disappointment. He had not wanted her. Mayhap he had been dreaming about holding someone else, a woman he really desired.

"It's not what you think. I didn't mean to touch you like that. This has nothing to do with you. Men always wake up like this, regardless of who they sleep with, regardless of where they are," he explained hurriedly, making sure their bodies were not touching in any way.

"You mean you have woken up... er... like this every morning when we slept together?" she could not help but ask.

He rubbed a hand over his bearded jaw, clearly wondering if he should be honest with her. She tilted her head, indicating that he should. "Yes. Unless they are old enough not to want to do anything about it, men wake up hard."

Frigyth's eyes widened in surprise. Men woke up ready to take women... She'd had no idea. Sigurd had slept next to her for a few nights and yet she had not noticed it before. Her heart sank. No, she had not, because he had not acted on it. Because he didn't want her. He wasn't about to jump on her, now or ever. She was a fool for having even entertained the possibility. He had Edith and no doubt others to go to when the need for a woman arose.

"I see."

By the gods! Sigurd was horrified. He'd woken up hard as a poker, which was admittedly not his fault, but instead of rolling away from the sweet-smelling woman nestled in his arms, he'd pressed himself against her in clear invitation, rubbing his shaft between her legs as if to demand entry. That he'd only been half-awake and she had not protested was no excuse. He should never have frightened a woman who'd already been assaulted. She would have thought for a moment that he was about to pounce on her.

It didn't bear thinking about.

He'd made clear he did not and this state of affairs had nothing to do with her but he could see she didn't quite believe him. There was an odd expression on her face. Not fear, though... If he didn't know better he might have thought it was disappointment. But it was most likely disbelief. Frigyth was not stupid, she had felt him nudge at her and known he'd been ready to possess her, however much he might say to the contrary.

He had to reassure her.

"I promise this means nothing. You need not fear I will attack you in any way."

"No. I know that." To his relief, she didn't even hesitate. "We're only pretending to be married. You're not interested in me in that way."

Oh, if only that were true! But what could he say? He could not admit to the ugly truth. She needed to be confident in his ability to control his urges, or she would refuse to stay in the hut, for fear he tried something with her. She needed to believe he had no intention of bedding her or she would not ask him to share the pallet with her again.

This idea was too dire to contemplate.

"Don't worry. I didn't agree to pose as your husband so I could have my way with you."

That, at least, was true. But it did not mean he did not fantasize about having her in his arms day and night, of kissing her senseless, of seeing her naked and panting under him. He wanted to know everything there was to know about this woman's body, the color of her nipples, of her folds, of her intimate fur, of her toenails, even. She would be all shades of pinks and reds and gold and coral. She would smell of cut flowers and he would bury his nose in her intimate hair. She would taste of fresh cream and he would lap it all up while she moaned and begged him to take her, which he would do with all the passion he was capable of.

He cleared his throat. Such thoughts were not helping him to gain mastery over his body.

"Let us make our way back to the hut," he suggested, leaving the warm nest of furs. Perhaps the cold breeze blowing in the clearing would help bring his throbbing shaft to heel.

She nodded and started to gather the furs.

There was nothing else to say.

CHAPTER THIRTEEN

For a long, excruciating moment they walked side by side in silence. Then, as they left the meadow, a bird took flight from a nest in the tree right ahead. Frigyth turned to Sigurd, excitement lighting her face. What now? He smiled inwardly at her irrepressible spirit. At least the awkwardness of the moment had passed.

"Wait. I will go and gather some eggs!" she announced as naturally as if she had done such a thing all her life. "You said there was nothing to eat in the house save from the salted fish, so we will need something for today. You liked the eggs fried with nettles and wild garlic the other day, did you not?"

"I did. But it is my responsibility to find food, not yours." He would not have her climb a tree at the risk of breaking her neck. If *he*, who was used to doing it, had fallen and broken his ankle, anything was possible. She was, as she'd pointed out several times, not used to life in the wild.

"Yes, and you did catch the rabbit yesterday, but you're too heavy to climb trees, as well we know." She stared pointedly at his ankle.

"I can't believe you would dare to throw this into my face," he grumbled. Would she ever let it go?

Frigyth let out a small tinkling laugh that did little to soothe his mood. In truth, he'd been a grump since he'd had to step away from the warm, soft woman wrapped in his arms. For a moment there in the forest, in the pale light of dawn, everything had been perfect. He had been able to fool himself that they could wake up like this every morning and make love before starting the day.

"Please, Sigurd," she begged, tilting her pretty little head to one side. "I told you. I always wanted to live outside, find fresh food. This is my chance."

He could not stop her. She was so excited at the prospect her eyes had gone wide as a fawn's, and just as beguiling. It would take a man with a heart of stone to deny her. "Very well. I will stand under the tree you in case you fall."

Far from looking reassured, she recoiled. "No! You will be able to see up my skirts if you do!"

He gave a growl low in his throat at the thought. "I promise I won't look up." Did she think him mad? As if he would do such thing! Even supposing he could shame himself thus, he would never be able to get the image out of his head if he ever saw the treasure hidden between her legs. Judging from the color of her mane of hair, he would unveil pure gold if he ever got the chance to undress her. The mere idea wrenched a groan out of him. "You're able to wring a newborn kitten's neck, are you not? It doesn't mean it is something you would ever considered doing."

"I..." She made a grimace, considering. "I suppose not."

"I just don't want to risk you falling to your death," he said, regretting his choice of words. Did he have to put such unpleasant images in her mind? Wring kittens' necks, really... What next? Strangling newborn babies? "The nest is very high."

This time she rolled her eyes. "I can manage on my own, thank you. Aren't you being overly cautious?"

He only shrugged. "Better that than an irresponsible fool."

Frigyth sighed in surrender. There would be no deterring Sigurd, and, in truth, it reassured her to think he would be there in case she did miss her footing. She had never climbed up a tree, after all, and even the lowest branch was too high for her to reach. He would have to lift her up. Hadn't they just decided they worked better as a team? She would get the eggs, he would ensure her safety and get her on the branch.

Perfect. Or…It would be if he understood what was required of him without her having to spell it out. But he only gave a smirk when she looked at him pointedly.

"Is there anything you want to ask me?"

The vexing man! "You know there is."

"Go ahead, then." He crossed his arms over his chest. Lord. He was intimidating when he wanted to be. And pig-headed. And impossibly handsome.

"Please, will you help me get onto the first branch?" she said, pushing the thought out of her mind.

"I thought you could manage on your own?"

She made an exasperated sound. "It's not my fault if I'm a hand shorter than you!"

"Mm. A hand. Or maybe even two." His mouth quivered.

She narrowed her eyes. He was determined to tease her? Very well. She would give as good as she got. "Of course, if you're not able, that's another question."

He snorted. "I might be too heavy for climbing flimsy branches but I am certainly strong enough to lift you a foot in the air, *birdie*. You must weigh less than the sparrow painted on your shoulder."

Oh it was a sparrow now. How ridiculous! The mark looked nothing like a bird, whatever he said, and she should know, she had looked at it often enough, deploring the way it marred her otherwise flawless skin. Still, his determination to see something cute in the mark that had plagued her life for years touched her.

"Listen, I would like to get back to the hut sometime today and I'm sure you would as well. So either tell me you're not going to lift me up or just—"

Before she could finish her sentence, he had dropped the bundle of furs and swept her into his arms. She let out a small gasp and grabbed at his neck.

"Sorry," he drawled. "I didn't mean to startle you. You're so light, it took me by surprise. A real sparrow."

"You're... impossible, you know that?" she breathed back.

A corner of his mouth lifted. "That's not what you were about to say."

No. It was not. But she would not tell him what she really thought of him. His ego hardly needed to be flattered.

"You were about to put me on the branch, I believe?"

"Oh, yes. I forgot."

Before she could blink she found herself with her legs dangling in the air. It was not easy to go from a sitting position to a standing one on the narrow branch and it was even more impossible to do it with a semblance of grace. Still, there was no choice, she would not give up now. Doing her best to preserve her modesty and dignity, Frigyth managed to right herself on her feet. At last, she was ready to climb. She bit her lip when she considered her options. The prospect, so exciting a moment ago, now seemed rather daunting.

"Just don't look down," Sigurd's deep voice was reassuring. "You'll be fine."

The encouragement was all she needed. If he believed in her, the least she could do was try. She started to climb, taking her time.

When she finally reached the nest, she found it empty.

Frigyth let out a sigh of frustration. All this effort for nothing! Then she bit her bottom lip. Perhaps it was for the best, for how exactly would she have carried the eggs down? It wasn't as if the shells were fragile, or if she needed both her hands to get down the tree... She had not thought this through, which went to show how unsuitable to this life she was.

"So?" Sigurd's voice reached her from down below.

"Nothing."

"Ah. Well, don't be too disappointed. 'Tis often the way. In town, food might be less fresh but in the wild it is not guaranteed."

Yes, he should know, he who'd had to rely on his wit and patience to feed himself as a child. Her chest felt painfully tight. She promised herself to ask him about his childhood as soon as the opportunity arose. She would not be able to contain her legendary curiosity much longer.

"I'm coming down now. Don't look!" she couldn't help but add.

"I will enjoy reminding you not to wring the poor creature's neck next time we see a stray cat in the village, and see how you feel," was the rumbled response from below. The big Dane did not like to be reminded to act honorably. She did not try to hide her smile. In the same way one couldn't help but melt in front of a big, shaggy dog, she just loved a disgruntled Sigurd.

Slowly, she started her descent, and found it even more nerve-racking than the climb. Grateful for the knowledge Sigurd was poised to break her fall in case of a problem, she picked her way down gingerly, ensuring her footing twice before allowing her weight to rest on one leg. It was slow going but eventually she reached the lowest branch, only to realize it was a lot higher than she was comfortable with.

Unsurprisingly, Sigurd was delighted by her dilemma.

"Now, shall I let you jump on your own or do you want me to catch you?"

"I..." She didn't trust herself not to fall flat on her back and expose herself as she did, or break a bone upon landing—or both. After her descent, her legs didn't quite feel steady. "Please, get me down, I don't want to twist my ankle. I hear it's painful." There. Two could play at this game.

The blue eyes flashed. "You're... impossible, you know that?"

"That's not what you wanted to say."

A corner of his mouth lifted. "Maybe, it is, maybe it isn't. You'll never know."

Oh. She might well love teasing Sigurd even more than she loved disgruntled Sigurd.

"Sit on the branch, like before," he instructed her. "It will be the easiest way." Once she was perched with her legs dangling in air, he came to stand in front of her. "Put your hands on my shoulders." His voice had gone impossibly husky. She leaned forward and braced herself against him. He placed his hands on her waist, ready to lift her up into his arms. Only he did not. For a moment, they stayed like this, gazes locked.

"Are you going to help me down?" she murmured.

Was he going to help Frigyth down, Sigurd wondered, or was he going to do what he was aching to do? If she opened her legs and he took a step forward, he could bury his face between her thighs. The branch was just at the right height for his mouth to cover her folds. The thought of licking her intimately had his shaft pulsing unbearably. He'd been hard since he'd woken up snuggled close to her, or so it seemed, and he was aching to put an end to the torture.

Before he could lose his mind, he plucked her from the branch and deposited her onto the ground gently.

"No eggs," she said, sounding breathless.

"No eggs," he repeated, sounding just as hoarse. "But at least you got to climb a tree."

For a moment, he had been perilously close to uncovering the treasure he coveted and begging her to let him pleasure her, while she sat on the branch just above him. His mouth was watering at the thought of the sweetness he would find under her skirts.

"You'll have to do without, I'm afraid."

He blinked. "What do you mean, 'do without'?" Had she known what he was thinking about? No! It would be a disaster.

"The eggs, fried with nettles and garlic."

It took him a while to understand what she was talking about. Then he sagged in relief. She'd had no idea he had been imagining himself with his head under her skirts. "It's not a problem. I'm sure you can think of something else to make, equally as tasty."

But I'm not sure I can forget the need to taste your silky sweetness so easily.

He bent down to retrieve the bundle of furs and made for the hut without another word.

Frigyth set off after Sigurd, feeling slightly dazed. What had just happened? She wasn't sure the unsteadiness in her legs was caused by the perilous descent from the tree. She felt as if she had escaped a dangerous predator intent on devouring her. Except... Except that she might not have objected to that particular beast putting his mouth on her.

The rest of the walk was accomplished in silence.

As they reached the hut, Sigurd made her halt. "Wait. I will check that the smell of fish has gone before you enter."

She smiled, touched by the attention. "I'm sure it has. It's been almost a day. It will be fine. If it hasn't, then I will just have to bake some oatcakes to cover the smell."

"I certainly won't stop you. You know they are my favorite."

He disappeared inside the hut and came back a moment later, smiling. "All clear. I'm glad I asked Wolf to open the door at dawn."

He really had thought of everything. Her heart melted. "Thank you."

"While you get settled, I'll go and see if I cannot get some birds with my sling, since we have no eggs."

Last night, a snare for the rabbit, now a sling for the birds. My, but the man was resourceful. She didn't doubt he would come back with more meat than they needed. A moment later, just as she had imagined, he came back with three medium-sized birds, already cleaned and ready for the spit.

"I will put these on while you make the griddle cakes, shall I?"

"Yes." The perfect team again. "Do you want to watch me?"

"Always."

Though it had merely been an answer to her question, he'd made that one word sound almost lewd. It was as if he had admitted to wanting to watch her... pleasure herself. "I meant as I make the dough," she specified.

"I know. Still, I would always want to watch you, birdie, whatever the circumstance."

Frigyth was certain this batch would be the worst she had ever baked. With Sigurd's gaze heavy on her, she hadn't been able to focus on what she was doing. But when he bit into an oatcake, he declared it the best yet. She tried another one and was surprised to find it more than palatable.

The afternoon passed in a blur of activity and they barely saw each other. Once they had finished a light supper of bread and cheese Sigurd came to stand in front of her. There was an expression on his face she had never seen before. In another man she might have identified it as unease, but surely the tall

Dane was not prey to such feelings? He cleared his throat and she could not fool herself any longer.

He *was* embarrassed.

"I'm afraid tomorrow I will wake up in the same state as this morning. It cannot be helped. I promise it doesn't mean anything will happen between us but I can sleep by the fire like the first night if you prefer," he said in a low voice.

She reddened, embarrassed herself. He should not feel guilty for being a man. "It's fine. Now that I know it's normal, I understand nothing untoward will happen."

No. Unfortunately it would not.

CHAPTER FOURTEEN

F rigyth was not surprised to find Sigurd already gone when she woke up in the morning, even though it was still early. She guessed he had not wanted to make her ill at ease by risking exposing her to his hardness. Such consideration warmed her. At the same time, she could not help but think back to the feel of his manhood pressed against her. What with another man might have scared her, with him had aroused her. It could have made her feel threatened or soiled, it had made her feel wanted and beautiful.

What would have happened if she had reached out to Sigurd, instead of opening her mouth to ask about his intentions? Would he have parted her legs and plunged into her? It was best to push the question out of her mind. She would never know and wondering about it would only kill her. As awful as Olaf's assault had been, she was lucky to know that being with a man was not necessarily painful or degrading. Thanks to Caedmon, she knew men could be considerate and gentle, she knew they could kiss her without demanding more, she knew her body could feel desire. That was how she had identified what she had felt when Sigurd had pressed himself against her as arousal, because she had felt something similar when her friend had slid his hard thigh between hers and rubbed her sensitive parts during a particularly daring kiss.

But once again, the similarities between the two men ended there. With Caedmon, she had felt a comforting warmth. With Sigurd, it had been a brazier. Just thinking about it made her breathing go faster. Her hand started to snake down her stomach and then landed on her soft folds. Perhaps if she rubbed she could ease the discomfort...

No.

She got up before she could make it all worse. The last thing she wanted was for Sigurd to walk in on her while she was touching herself. She would never live down the humiliation. Then a thought struck her. This was the first time since the assault that she had dared place her hands on the most intimate part of herself, or even thought of physical pleasure. Could it be that she was healing? Perhaps.

Hope swelling in her chest, she reached out for her dress.

As soon as she was dressed, she started to shell some nuts, focusing on cracking the hard shells without reducing the soft kernels to a pulp. It suddenly seemed an apt image for what was going on in her life. If she could get past the pain, push past the doubts and reluctance, she might get to reap the rewards of her efforts. Of course, she would have to expose her inner self to do that but with the right instrument, it could be achieved, in the same way that using the pliers instead of a rock allowed her to keep the nut kernels intact.

When the sun reached its zenith, Sigurd came back.

"I have a trout and some mushrooms. Do you think you can make something with it?"

She smiled. "Of course." Her mouth was already watering. "How did you get the trout? With a bow and arrow?"

He burst out laughing. "No. That would be a masterful shot

indeed. My bare hands were enough. When you know how, you can easily coax the fish into them. Wolf taught me to do it when he arrived two years ago. I wish I'd known that trick when I was growing up."

She could not resist this golden opportunity to find out more about his childhood. Only the day before she had resolved to ask about it. This seemed natural enough. And he already knew she was curious.

"Why is that?"

"Being able to catch fish that way would have been useful," he answered levelly.

"Yes, of course." It would not be as easy as she'd hoped to prize information out of him. Seeing she would have to be more direct, she went for in for the kill. "Didn't your father show you how to fish?"

If Wolf had not told her about Sigurd being orphaned, she might not have noticed anything. But he had and she did. He stiffened and the light in his eyes flickered for a moment. "No. I have no memory of him, or my mother. They died before I was four summers."

His voice was so gruff she instantly regretted insisting. Her and her wretched curiosity! It was obvious thinking about them was painful. "I'm sorry. I shouldn't have asked."

"It's all right. You didn't know."

This only made her guilt worse, because she had known, and still she'd pushed him. Unable to bear the pain in his eyes, she turned her attention to the mushrooms. While she sorted through them, Sigurd started to prepare the fish with swift precision.

Once it was gutted and clean, he lifted his head to her and said, "They drowned when their ship overturned in the fjord. Oddly, for Danes, they didn't know how to swim."

Oh, Lord.

That was why he could swim so well, why he had wanted to teach her, why he'd been so adamant she learned. He'd been desperate to save her from the same fate.

"They had gone fishing with a few other villagers, leaving me in charge of the house. I was left alone for days, wondering what had happened to them, until someone remembered they had another son."

"Another?" Frigyth thought she was about to be sick.

"They had taken my baby brother with them on the boat, as my mother was still feeding him. He was only a few months old."

Everything inside her dissolved. "Sigurd, I'm so sorry."

"No need to cry, birdie," he told her gently. "It's over now."

Was she crying? She hadn't noticed. She must be, because he wiped at her cheek, lingering over the gesture. What was this? She should be the one consoling him, after what he had told her, not the other way around.

"None of the villagers thought to welcome you under their roof? You were only four, you could not be left on your own!" This was scandalous. How could they have left a child so young to fend for himself?

He shrugged. "A few tried at first. But they were poor already and I was not the easiest of children to warm up to." Frigyth refused to believe that. No four-year-old boy was unlovable. "My wayward ways and refusal to let them cosset me did not endear me to them. I was passed around from family to family. After a while, they stopped trying, arguing I was old enough to fend for myself, anyway."

Old enough! He could not have been more than six or seven then! Frigyth was scandalized. This time she didn't cry, she just tried her best to contain her outrage.

Now she knew why Sigurd was the way he was, gruff at times. Because he couldn't be any other way, having been rejected all his life. And as if that was not enough, he'd then been called a beast by the people who should have looked after him! He'd had to fend for himself, feed himself, defend himself, deal with the death of his family on his own. He had never been able to rely on anyone.

A silence followed.

"I was not the only one having a difficult childhood," she whispered.

"No. Ironically, I spent my time wishing my parents came back, while you spent your time wanting to escape yours."

She could tell he was fighting the urge to take her into his arms and she was battling the same need. Why were they resisting? It was clearly what they needed. Before she could move, he stepped away.

"Let us start cooking this fish, shall we?" She nodded. If he thought it best to act as if nothing of importance had happened, she would do the same. "I'm starving, I left before I had anything to eat this morning."

"I've already made a few honey and nut tarts," Frigyth offered, uncovering the plate where six of them were cooling down.

He rolled his eyes in appreciation. "Ah. You're too good to me, birdie. Can I have one now?"

She couldn't help a laugh when he took one without waiting for her answer. "You're worse than a child, do you know that?"

"Am I?"

Laughter got stuck in her throat when he skewered her with a fierce look. The glint in his eyes was incendiary, and nothing like a child's. She was suddenly certain he wanted to take a bite out of her, instead of the tart he was holding in his hand. Perhaps she had been too hasty in dismissing the idea of kissing him earlier. Perhaps he wouldn't have minded.

Slowly, he lifted the tart to his mouth and groaned when he

bit into it. Frigyth almost whimpered in response. Why did it feel as if he were nibbling at her flesh?

"Do you like it?" she asked, her voice little more than a breath.

Sigurd cleared his throat before answering. The tart was delicious but he could not tell Frigyth he had bitten into it for want of something better. For a moment, he had been perilously close to drawing her into his arms and crushing his mouth onto hers. It wasn't the first, the second, or even the tenth time such an urge had overwhelmed him in the last week. Things were getting out of hand, fast. Waking up hard, and rubbing himself against Frigyth's perfect buttocks, fantasizing about feasting on the honey hidden between her legs and dreaming of kissing her at every opportunity... It would not be long before he went mad.

He chewed and forced himself to calm. "Yes, thank you, the tart is just—"

A voice coming from right outside the door interrupted him.

"Hello, is anyone here? Frigyth?"

Sigurd arched a brow at her. "Do you recognize that voice?" he asked, glancing in the direction of the call. A man, evidently, but he had no idea who that might be. Not a villager, that was for certain, but who else would call out for her here?

"Yes," she said, beaming. He frowned, getting more and more ill at ease. Who was this man who made her eyes sparkle with joy? It was not Caedmon, he knew that, at least. Just how many men did she have hankering after her?

She rushed past him to open the door and came to a skidding halt. Without seeing her face, he knew that whoever was in front of the hut was not the man she had expected to see.

"Toland? Is everything all right? Where's Dunne?"

Sigurd's whole body relaxed. She had not been excited by the prospect of seeing the *man*, rather she had hoped he would be accompanied by her sister. That was what had made her eyes sparkle, the prospect of seeing Dunne. The man was only her brother-in-law. She was clearly not interested in him, only in the news he was bringing.

"She sent me to tell you she has been delivered of the babe," Toland explained. "When I couldn't find you at the house, your neighbor told me where I could find you and even offered me a bed for the night, seeing as it was already nightfall. A most helpful woman, this Gedla."

There was a odd glint in the man's eye and Sigurd wondered if the 'helpful woman' had not joined him in the bed she had so propitiously offered. It was possible. She had certainly eyed him up shamelessly when they'd gone to town and would have welcomed him into her bed had he betrayed any interest in her. Toland might well have made the most of the not so subtle invitation. The way he was smiling was too smug by far.

Frigyth, however, was oblivious to the whole thing. She wavered on her feet. "The babe was early then! Is everything all right?"

"Well enough. It's only a girl anyway." This announcement was followed by a grimace. Sigurd tensed. The more the man spoke, the less he liked him. Not only had he most likely cheated on his wife, but he was belittling her for giving him a girl. But, once again, Frigyth didn't appear to have noticed the comment. She looked worried.

"I will need to go see her."

"Naturally. That's why I came in person, instead of merely sending word, to inform you of the birth and to take you to her. I have a horse waiting."

Frigyth was already hurrying back to the hut, but Sigurd stopped her with a hand at her elbow. He was not going to let her go anywhere alone with a man who accepted women's lewd invitations the day after his wife had given birth, disparaged her for having given him a healthy daughter, and was... He bared his teeth as if he'd just eaten a raw sloe berry. A man who was looking at Frigyth like Gedla had been looking at him the other day.

This Toland was *not* going to take her on his horse and sit her on his lap.

Over his dead body.

"'Tis too late to leave now," Sigurd growled in Frigyth's ear. "We'll go to your sister tomorrow. And I'll take you myself."

She disentangled her arm from his hold as quickly as if his touch had burnt her. Oh, his little birdie didn't like being ordered about. Well, too bad. He was not letting her out of his sight. If he'd balked at the idea of her following her friend Caedmon back to her own house, he was not going to allow a lecherous stranger to take her to a place he didn't know.

"A word with you please," she hissed. "In private. Toland, if you'll excuse us a moment."

She disappeared into the hut before he could take a breath. He smiled grimly.

His little 'wife' was about to unleash her temper on him.

A soon as the door was closed, Frigyth rounded on Sigurd. Who did he think he was, telling her what she could or could not do? This was her sister they were talking about, what did he mean by preventing her from going to see her?

"May I remind you that we are not truly married?" she exploded. "You have—"

"No, you do not need to remind me. But that Toland was likely told we were living together by your neighbor during their... discussion." There was an expression on his face she could not quite fathom. "And yet he looks at you as if he would like nothing more than to pounce on you. I don't trust him."

"Are you mad?" She recoiled. Toland pounce on her? She

was his sister-in-law! "He's not interested in me. He's married to my sister and she's just had his baby!"

Sigurd only snorted. "Yes. His baby *girl*."

"What does that have to do with anything?"

He shook his head and pinched the bridge of his nose like a man attempting to keep his temper on a tight leash. She was impressed that he even tried to do it. She already knew he was not the most patient of men. "Nevermind. I'm telling you. There's something off with that man. I am not leaving you on your own with him, and that's final."

"Please! You distrust him, you disliked Caedmon, a man who's only ever been kind to me... Will you not give me the benefit of the doubt and allow that I can decide for myself who I can trust or not?"

"It depends. Tell me, what did you think of Olaf before he jumped on you? Did you think him trustworthy? Well. We both know where that got you."

Frigyth felt all the blood drain from her face. She fell on the stool behind her, all the wind knocked from her sails. How *could* he? Sigurd had never before given her reason to believe he thought her irresponsible and naïve. He'd taken her defense, for Heavens's sake, told her she was not to be blamed in anyway for what had happened to her. And now this!

For the first time, she felt a surge of hatred for him. Did he have any idea of the pain he had just inflicted her? The blow had been so unexpected she could hardly breathe.

"I-I can't believe you would dare to even to ask... I..." She bit her lip to stop herself from crying. And then...

Then Sigurd fell to his knees in front of her. She was so stunned that, for a moment, she forgot about the pain piercing her chest.

"Frigyth. Please, *please*, forgive me. I didn't mean to suggest you had done anything wrong or were to blame in any way. I told you once, and I'll repeat it, Olaf is the only one at fault for what happened that day, not you." Sigurd ran a hand through his hair, looking genuinely contrite. "I can't believe I just said that. It's that damned temper of mine. I'm sorry, I only meant—"

"I don't want to hear your apologies," she whispered. "I care not what you think of me. I just want to see my sister, see that she's all right! Do you understand?"

She knew she sounded on the verge of panic but that was no wonder, considering she *was* on the verge of panic. She needed to see that Dunne and her babe were alive and well. And Sigurd was standing in her way. In that moment he was, if not her enemy, at least an obstacle to be vanquished.

He stood back up and nodded. "I'll take you to her now, if that's what you want. I will go ask Wolf to lend me his horse. Toland can follow us or not. I don't care. But I will not let you go on your own with him, however you may hate me for it."

She did not answer.

———

"FRIGYTH. PLEASE. TALK TO ME."

Sigurd sighed. She had not said a word since they had left the village, which was perhaps little wonder, considering what he had the gall to tell her. He'd all but accused her of being an irresponsible, naïve fool, of leading Olaf on and make it inevitable that he should lose his head and pounce on her. What had possessed him to say such cruel things? Was he mad? No wonder she was not talking to him. It was a miracle she had agreed to ride Demon with him.

Ahead on the path, Toland was leading the way on a gray rouncey that looked about to collapse under his weight. How the man had thought the poor beast would be able to carry two people was beyond him. It only confirmed his poor impression of him. In Sigurd's experience, people who did not care about injuring animals were not to be trusted with people who could not defend themselves.

Besides, he could not rid himself of the impression that the man was more interested in Frigyth than, as her brother-in-law, he ought to be.

Still, he would not speak another word about it. He had upset Frigyth once, he would not do it again. He would keep a sharp eye on Toland, but make her think he trusted her opinion. It might well be that jealousy prevented him from thinking straight where she was concerned. It wouldn't be the first time. Hadn't he made an ass of himself with Caedmon, who was obviously a good man, and intent on protecting her?

He decided to distract Frigyth, make her laugh with a ludicrous story. She might not want to answer his questions, but she would not be able to stop herself from hearing what he had to say.

"One winter when I was about ten, it rained for days on end, and the whole land became a mire. I fell into a muddy bog while out on the hunt." He twisted his lips. "I ended up so completely covered in mud it got in everywhere. In my nose, in my eyes, in my ears. I was all but deaf for a few days. I dunked myself in the sea every opportunity I got for a week afterward, in the hope of dissolving the mud in my ears. Eventually, it worked. Fortunately, as I didn't have anyone to talk to, it mattered little."

Frigyth did not answer but she stiffened in his arms. Ah. So he'd caught her attention.

Then she turned to look at him over her shoulder. But contrary to what he had hoped, she was not smiling. "This is the saddest thing I have ever heard. A child of ten, so lonely he didn't speak to people for days on end. My God."

Sigurd stared back when a tear fell down her cheek. Well.

He had not made her laugh, but he had broken through her coldness, at least. Unexpectedly, a weight lodged itself in his chest. Would she cry every time he mentioned his childhood? He hadn't meant to upset her. Perhaps with hindsight talking about it had not been the best of ideas.

"I'm sorry," he murmured. "I truly am. About... everything. Please, you have to believe me."

She bit her bottom lip. "I do."

After that, she relaxed in his arms and when they reached her sister's cottage, he was confident they had put their disagreement behind them.

CHAPTER FIFTEEN

"I don't understand how I can love this child so much," Dunne mused, her eyes fastened on the little bundle in her arms. "It is the oddest thing, because God knows I'm not in love with my husband. I would even go as far as saying that I wouldn't miss him if he decided to leave me. Sometimes I think he does. And truly, I wouldn't mind, as long as he allowed me to keep my daughter with me. It is awful of me, I know, but..."

Silence stretched into the room.

There was nothing Frigyth could say after such an extraordinary declaration. Unfortunately, she already knew all about Dunne's unhappy marriage, knew her sister didn't feel anything for her husband, which was not surprising, considering the kind of man he was. Twice her age, with a paunch and what was worse, an unfortunate tendency to selfishness and idleness, Toland could hardly have been called a catch, despite his money. And now Frigyth was wondering if she should not add lechery to a list of faults that was already as long as her arm.

She had balked at Sigurd for daring to suggest her brother-in-law was looking at her the wrong way, but since they had arrived at his house, she had been uncomfortable. The way he had brushed her hip when leading her into the house, his hand lingering longer than was necessary or even decent, on her body, had made her squirm.

She pushed the uncomfortable thought away. Even if Toland had designs on her, she had nothing to fear. Sigurd was here, and he would not let him touch as much as her little finger if she voiced any concern. As angry as she had been at him at first for insisting in coming with her, she was now grateful.

"I love her so much," Dunne said, brushing a finger along her daughter's cheek. "I do not want her to have to bear the burden of who her father is. I don't want her to ever resent the manner in which she was... imposed on me, or even wonder about it. Does that make sense?"

"Yes. It does, to me, at least."

Frigyth's mind immediately went to Olaf. What would she have felt if she had fallen with child from the horrific encounter? A soon as she asked herself the question, she knew the answer. She would have welcomed the babe, regardless. Her gaze fastened on her niece, peacefully asleep in her mother's arms, so innocent. She gave her sister's hand a squeeze. Yes, she did understand. Love was love, it was inexplicable and that was all there was to it.

"Thank you for coming so fast."

"You're welcome. What can I do for you? Tell me."

Dunne smiled sleepily. "Would you make some of your famous oatcakes? I've been craving them for months, you know. Try as I may, I just cannot make them as well as you or Mother."

Frigyth could not help a laugh. "Well, they are certainly popular!"

"Oh? Why? Who else has been asking for them?"

"Erm... Sigurd seems to like them," she said cautiously, feeling as if she were admitting to something very personal.

"Sigurd? The... tall Norseman who escorted you here?" Frigyth had the impression that Dunne had wanted to say something else to describe Sigurd, but, at the last moment, had settled on 'tall' instead. And she was right. He was tall, but he was above all... striking. Mouth-watering. "You cook for him?"

Oh, she did more than cook for him. She lived with him, she slept in his bed. She lusted after him, and most worryingly of all, she had come to care for him.

"It's a long story and you need to rest now." She had not told her sister about the role they were playing yet. When they arrived late last night Dunne had already been asleep. And this morning they had understandably talked about the little girl.

"Yes. I think I need to. Having a child is exhausting."

Frigyth took the baby who was now sound asleep and placed it into the cot while Dunne settled herself more comfortably. "I will go and make a nice broth to go with the oatcakes. You need to build up your strength after the birth."

There was no need to insist. Dunne was already half asleep thanks to the healer's potion she had drunk earlier.

"Thanks. That sounds heavenly."

"How is she faring?" Sigurd asked Frigyth when she joined him in the main room.

Toland and Dunne lived in a spacious cottage which had two rooms, a separate shed for the livestock at the back, a vegetable patch and even an orchard. If her husband had not been a condescending lecher, Frigyth's sister might have been considered to have made a good marriage.

"Well enough. She's tired, but that is to be expected."

"Of course."

"She asked for me to cook for her while she rests, so I will have a look around, see what I can find."

She looked tired herself, he noticed, which was little wonder. As she had slept in the same room as the new mother, they had not been able to sleep together last night and he knew she found it difficult to settle on her own. Or perhaps getting up several times in the night to see to the child's needs had tired her.

"These can be a start." He handed her a basket full of wizened apples he'd found at the foot of the trees in the orchard. Only someone who'd never starved in his life would have left them there to rot. They did not look like much in their present state, admittedly, but they would make a nice purée.

Frigyth gave him a brilliant smile. Obviously she agreed with him. "Thank you. I can use them for tarts. Dunne will be dead to the world for a while, I expect, she was given a sleeping potion for the pain."

"I will go see to Demon outside while you cook." Sigurd nodded meaningfully. If she thought it safe to remain alone while her brother-in-law was on the prowl, then he would not presume to know better. After all, he would not be far, and Toland's wife was just in the other room, with her newborn daughter. Surely the man would not be so foolish as to try anything in these circumstances? "Unless you need some help with the cooking?"

Her lip quivered. "From you, who by your own admission can only make lumpy dough? I don't think Dunne will thank me."

"No, probably not. Rub down Demon it is then. And when I've finished, I'll come back to peel the apples. This, at least, I can do."

With one last nod, Sigurd left the room.

"Mm. It smells wonderful in here. What are you making, lovely?"

Lovely? Frigyth stiffened when Toland sauntered into the room a moment later. How did he think this nickname appropriate for her?

"Thank you. I'm making oatcakes and apple tarts," she said quietly, stealing a glance at the door. Where was Sigurd? Surely it did not take so long to rub down a horse? All of a sudden, she wished he would come back. "I'll also be making broth," she explained. She'd thought that talking about something so mundane would help keep Toland at bay, but he only appeared more interested.

"Ah, so you can cook, as well." He shook his head as he came nearer. "It seems I really married the wrong sister."

Frigyth stiffened further and focused her attention on the ladle she was holding. How could the man be so insensitive as to tell her something like that?

Seeing she wasn't answering, Toland leaned against the table next to her. "Dunne is hopeless in the kitchen, you know. In bed, as well. She just lies there like a corpse, expecting me to do all the work." Frigyth gritted her teeth so hard it hurt. Was he expecting her to answer? She fought the urge to spit in his face. "As if all that wasn't bad enough, she's also grown fat since our wedding."

This time Frigyth couldn't remain silent. She had to defend her sister. "She's not fat. She was pregnant, that's not quite the same, I would say."

Pregnant with the child you imposed on her, you rutting maggot, she felt like shouting. Instead she carried on stirring the pot. Where *was* Sigurd? In a moment, she might well go and find him.

Toland leaned in, causing all the hairs on her arms to stand on end.

"It's you I wanted, lovely," he whispered in her ear. "I might as well tell you now."

By now, he was so near she could feel his heat and smell his unwashed body. That smell reminded her of Olaf. Bile rose in her throat. She willed herself not to recoil or shout in protest, even though a scream was bubbling in her chest. If Sigurd heard a commotion he would come rushing in and then she would have to watch as he maimed or even killed her sister's husband for daring to inconvenience her. A moment ago she had wished for his presence, now she wanted him to stay well away. With his temper being what it was, there would be no stopping him.

"All along, it was you. When I approached your father to ask for your hand last year, the fool was adamant I should marry Dunne instead. For some reason he wanted his daughters to marry in the order they were born. He insisted I got his elder daughter off his hands first. There was no budging him, so I had no choice. But it was you I wanted in my bed. I still do."

With those words he grabbed her breasts with his hairy hands.*

The scream of agony pierced Sigurd's loins.

"Frigyth!" he roared.

Why the hell had he left her alone with that bastard lurking around? Dropping the bucket of water at Demon's feet, he ran toward the house. In the main room, he found Toland rolling on the floor next to a panting Frigyth, not quite the scene he had expected to find. His heartbeat slowed down marginally.

"What happened here?"

He barely spared a glance at the man. The Saxon could be at death's door for all he cared, as long as Frigyth was all right.

"I—" she started, her eyes wide.

"She blinded me, that's what!" Toland bellowed.

Blinded him? What was the man talking about? How could have Frigyth blinded him? She was not holding any blade and there was no blood on the floor. He looked at her inquiringly. "What did you do, birdie?"

"I had no choice, he... H-he wanted to..."

Leaving the man howling on the floor, Sigurd swept her into his arms and brought her outside, where they could have a private discussion. He'd heard enough to guess what the wretched man had done and to know he'd gotten everything he deserved if she really had blinded him. Why, oh, why, had he left her alone? It was all his fault.

"Did he touch you?" he growled, placing her gently on the ground.

No answer.

So he had. And she didn't want to tell him as much because she feared what he might do. As well she might. In that moment he wanted nothing more than to unleash his fury onto the man. His nostrils flared and he glared in the direction of the hut. "I'm going to k—"

He stopped and looked back at Frigyth. She hadn't wanted him to hurt Olaf for actually raping her, so it stood to reason she wouldn't want him to kill Toland for merely touching her. Besides, it seemed she had already dealt with the issue herself. He didn't want to give her the impression he thought her incapable, because he did not. He was impressed she had managed to stop him on her own, and that when she had been petrified with fear.

He took a deep, soothing breath. It didn't help much but he knew he had to calm down or risk alienating Frigyth for good.

"He said you had blinded him?"

"H-he started to tell me how I was the woman he had always wanted. And then he..." Flushing, she glanced at her breasts, making her meaning clear. The bastard had lunged at her. White-hot rage caused Sigurd to clench his teeth. Still, he forced himself to remain impassive. Frigyth was not finished with her explanation. "He was holding me too tight, I couldn't push him away, so I did what I could... I-I was cooking broth. I threw boiling water in his face with the ladle."

"Clever girl!" She had made up for her lack of strength most efficiently. "I do hope you've blinded him," he added savagely. The bastard had actually got away with it lightly. *He* would have gelded him and not felt a moment's remorse.

Frigyth started to shiver. He forced her to sit on the bench and knelt at her feet. Then he waited for her to talk. It was obvious something was still weighing on her mind.

"It seems that you were right, and Toland intended to have his way with me before we reached his house. If you hadn't come with us I think he would have assaulted me on the way." Sigurd didn't contradict her. He didn't think he would have, he *knew* he would have. "He said he had wanted to marry me all along, only my father refused. He said all those horrid things about Dunne, that she was fat and didn't please him in bed... Oh, he's a monster, and I am a fool for wanting to see the best in people," she said on a sob. "After what happened to me, you would think I would know better!"

"No. No." He all but crushed her into his arms. "Frigyth, listen to me. Never become like me, do you hear, a jaded, unreasonable cynic. That you should still be able to trust in men after what happened to you awes me. Please. Stay your lovely, trusting, self. I won't have you any other way. Those bastards lusting after you don't deserve it. You are perfect the way you are."

She shuddered in his arms.

"What am I going to tell Dunne? She's just given birth! She won't want to hear what her husband did to me even if she doesn't love him. Oh... And I might not be the only one Toland has accosted."

Sigurd nodded but said nothing about his suspicions concerning Gedla. It would only hurt her, for very little gain. "Maybe not," he said slowly. That was as far as he would go.

Frigyth inhaled and drew back, looking mercifully calmer. "Thank you for rushing to my aid."

"Mm. It appears you didn't need me. You did a splendid job on your own." He brushed a finger along her cheek and stood back up. If he stayed at her feet he would end up kissing her. It would be a disaster, make her think he was no better than that Toland, who thought he could touch her uninvited. "Now let me go and check on the man."

He could not care less if she had truly blinded him, but if he had really lost the use of his eyes, then his wife needed to be told. Arrangements would have to be made. He didn't know whether to wish it or not.

Frigyth placed a hand on his forearm. "You promise you won't—"

"I promise."

No, he would not smash Toland's skull in. But he would most definitely threaten to do so if he *ever* dared to talk to Frigyth again about his vile urges or his intentions toward her. And if he ever touched as much as her little finger, he would rip out his eyeballs first, ensuring he was well and truly blinded this time. From what he had seen, the man was a coward, so a well-worded threat might be enough to make him soil his pants.

"Will you also check that Dunne didn't wake up during the commotion? Perhaps the potion will have been enough to keep her asleep?" Frigyth sounded hopeful.

"I will. You stay here. I'll find you something to drink while I'm there."

He found Toland sitting on the stool. The right side of his face was bright red, and blisters had started to form. Good. Sigurd could not resist. He made to strike him. The man flinched. Ah. So he could see well enough then, even if it was only with one eye. He dropped his arm but leaned in to bring his gaze level with his.

"Listen to me, you stinking maggot. I will not give you the thrashing you deserve on one condition," he hissed in his ear. "You start showing your wife and daughter the consideration they deserve and you keep your filthy hands to yourself from now on. You forget Frigyth even exists. Do I make myself clear?" The man trembled so much he did not point out that this was more than one condition. He nodded. "I will be keeping watch. In two weeks, I will be back, and if I hear any complaints from Dunne, about *anything*, then you and I will have another chat. Man to man. And you might lose more than an eye then."

CHAPTER SIXTEEN

The first part of the journey home was accomplished almost in silence. Then, out of the blue, Frigyth said one word. Or rather, one name.

"Caedmon."

Sigurd tensed and slowed Demon down to a walk. He could tell this conversation would require his full attention. "What about him?"

"I... Do you think... Now I'm wondering..." She was having difficulty wording her question. He waited, knowing she would eventually find the courage to speak out. "I trust him. But I never thought to guard myself against Toland and I know that Caedmon wants to marry me, even if I don't think he is in love with me. Do you think he would—"

Sigurd cut her off by tightening the hold on her waist. "No. That friend of yours will never be a threat to any woman, least of all to you." He made sure to speak clearly and not leave the least doubt in her mind. It was important she did not allow what had happened with Toland to taint the friendship she had with Caedmon. The man deserved better. "I've seen the way he is with you. He's a good man. You're right to trust him."

She turned to look at him over her shoulder. "I thought you hated him?"

He sighed. Had he made his feelings that obvious? "I don't hate him, exactly."

But he was jealous of him, for certain. After all, the man had given Frigyth her first kiss, had seen her grow, had protected her. In other words, he had done all the things Sigurd would have liked to do himself. But he could not tell Frigyth that, since he was not supposed to be interested in her in that way.

Still, he could not let her fear her best, and possibly her only friend, when he knew deep down the man only had her best interest at heart.

"You need not worry he will pounce on you when you least expect it. He wants to marry you, not hurt you." He also wanted to bed her, but Sigurd could not hold that against him. What man in his right mind would not? He knew Caedmon would not force her any more than he would force her himself, no matter how strong his desire for her. "He only wants to protect you. But you had better not tell him about what Toland did. He might not be as measured as I was."

Mm, actually, that was a thought, Sigurd mused... Should he have a discreet word with the Saxon when he came to check on Frigyth, let him know what had happened? Use him as his weapon of revenge? No. He fought his own battles, he was no coward hiding behind another. But more importantly, he could not do that to Frigyth. She would never forgive him if he went behind her back after he'd promised not to hurt Toland.

He realized then that she had not answered and was staring at him. He blinked. What now? What had he said?

"Did you say 'measured'?" Frigyth said after a while, shaking her head in disbelief. Sigurd really thought he was *measured* in his reactions?

"Yes." He frowned. "Why?"

"Well..." She threw her hands up in the air. Where could she start? There was nothing measured about him, not even his appearance. One glare from him and you would shake in your boots. "You swear dozens of times a day, you fight with your best friend on a weekly basis, you threatened to kill Toland and Olaf for—"

"But I haven't!" he roared, thereby showcasing the temper she was referring to. She barely refrained from rolling her eyes. "I promised you I would not and I kept my word. Of course, I would *want* to kill them for what they did! That doesn't mean I would actually do it, nor does it prove I'm unreasonable or violent! Don't try to make me the villain here, it's a normal reaction, I would say. What else could I do? How else am I suppose to react? Did you expect me to congratulate the bastards for hurting you, for attacking an innocent, unwilling woman?"

The outburst left her stunned. She hadn't meant to hurt his feelings, merely point out that he was all about fiery temper.

"Well, no, I wouldn't expect you to react any differently," she said slowly. Put like that, she could not disagree with him. "And I know you are not a villain. I was just saying you were not what anyone would call measured, unlike Caedmon."

She had always hated men who did not think before they acted, who thought nothing of what others might feel about they did. And yet... With Sigurd, it was different because that hot-headedness was not all there was to him and she knew him now. She understood why he swore, why he fought with Wolf, why had felt the need to belong to a community and build himself an intimidating reputation. And his fierceness in protecting her made her feel cherished. She realized with no small measure of shock that she wouldn't have him behaving in any other way, even if it might have made her life easier.

"Well," he grumbled, before nudging Demon back into a trot. "I'm sorry. Not everyone can be as perfect as your friend."

Oh, now she had offended him. How could she make amends? For a moment, she toyed with the idea of telling him a story from her childhood, like he had done the other day, to shake him out of his sulk, but she could not think of a single one. In the end, she just apologized.

"I'm sorry. I didn't mean to hurt you."

No answer.

"Sigurd, please, talk to me. I can't bear you being angry with me."

He sighed and she felt him relax and draw her back into his embrace. "I'm not angry with you, birdie. I know what you mean. And you're right, I'm nothing like Caedmon. I do have a temper. But—"

"No but. That is who you are, for a reason." She felt all the more guilty for making him wretched, because earlier, he had begged her to stay true to herself, told her he would not have her any other way. And now she was criticizing him for being himself with her. It wasn't fair. "Please, don't change. There is no need. I-I like you the way you are."

He stilled. "Beast and all?"

"Beast and all."

THEY ARRIVED BACK so late Frigyth was already half asleep when Sigurd brought Demon to a halt in front of the hut. He lifted her from the saddle and carried her straight to the pallet. She would have protested had she not been so exhausted.

"You need rest. You barely slept the last two nights," he told her, covering her with the furs.

"I know. Come lie with me." She had missed his presence next to her, his heat, his smell.

"I will, in a moment. I must see to Demon first and then start a fire."

"Are you not tired?"

He gave a soft snort she could not quite decipher. "Sleep, birdie. Don't worry about me."

In the morning, predictably, she slept until late. This was quickly becoming a habit, a habit she could not explain and did not like. But for some reason she slept like she had never slept before. All she remembered from last night was snuggling up to Sigurd as naturally as they had in the forest when he finally joined her on the pallet. Only this time she didn't have the excuse of being cold. Sigurd hadn't seemed to mind, closing his arms around her and keeping her close. She had been able to relax and finally give in to sleep.

When she stepped out of the hut, she found Sigurd seated on the bench, weaving a funny-shaped basket complete with lid.

"What are you making?"

He answered without raising his head, his attention focused on cutting a twig to the right dimension with his knife. "It's a creel."

A *creel*? She made a face. "You know I don't speak Norse."

This time he stopped and looked at her before bursting out laughing. "That is not Norse." She might have been embarrassed at her silly mistake if she did not find him so entrancing when he laughed. "Don't tell me I speak your language better than you do!"

"Well... Apparently you do, at least where everything connected to life in the wild is concerned."

He grunted and picked up another stick. "Yes. I expect I do."

The creel, as Sigurd had called it, was quickly taking shape. Frigyth was fascinated by the way his strong, agile fingers worked. Not a single move was wasted, every flick of his wrist had a purpose, every gesture was perfectly judged. One hand pushed, the other twisted, one pulled, the other cut. It was almost like watching the currents swirling in a river, everything flowed seamlessly under her gaze. How many times would he have done it to have achieve such expertise?

"So what is a creel?" she asked, earning herself a chuckle. She knew Sigurd liked her curiosity.

"It's a basket for holding fish. Mine is old, almost broken." He stared at her. "I expect I'll have to use it more often since you can only eat fish fresh so I need a new one."

She staggered. He was doing this for her, because he antici-pated having to see to her needs in the future. But why? They both knew she would only be at the village for another week, at the most...There really was no need for him to make such an object for her. Frigyth couldn't find the courage to point it out to him, however. The less she thought about the moment they would part ways, the better. Besides, he would find a use for it even if she didn't live with him. After all, he ate fish, too.

Soon the creel was finished. Sigurd inspected it carefully, clipped a few rebellious twigs to the right length and declared himself satisfied.

"This is very impressive. Can you weave other kinds of baskets, too?"

He nodded. "The one used to hold nuts is the last one I made." He took another twig from the pile at his feet and tested its flexibility. "Actually, Wolf has asked me to make a basket for Merewen. I'll start it now. Do you want to watch me?"

He was echoing her question from the other day. Her heart skipped a beat. Surely he had seen the way she was observing him and was only mocking her?

"Always," she murmured. "And I think you lied when you said you weren't skilled with your fingers."

"I didn't quite say that, if I recall." His voice had gone even huskier than usual. "Only that I was useless at making dough. But I know in certain circumstances I can use them to good effect. No one has ever complained about my... basket weaving skills."

Frigyth stayed very still, focusing on not betraying the fact that her body had gone liquid. "I've never heard it called that before," she breathed, knowing she was only stoking a fire that hardly needed stoking.

The corner of Sigurd's mouth curled. Why did he have to have such a sinful mouth? It made it impossible not to wish he would kiss her. "Well. Maybe I do know your language better than you do," he purred.

Should she carry on that dangerous conversation? She dearly wanted to. But then Sigurd licked his lips. It was not meant as a provocation, she could tell, but she received it as a blow to the gut anyway. Suddenly she wanted to feel that mouth on hers, and then on her neck, on her breasts and on her nipples.

And everywhere else.

Frigyth started. What was she doing, fantasizing about such forbidden things, and with this man in particular? He was not interested in her in that way! He was just teasing her because that was what he liked to do.

She stayed silent.

With a nod Sigurd focused his attention back on the twigs in his hands. In a moment, he had made a flat disk, obviously the bottom of the basket. Satisfied with the result, he put it on the ground and stood up, dwarfing her once more. Lord, *how* could she stop herself from fantasizing about this man? Physically, he was everything a woman might want.

The words were out of her mouth before she could think. "Will you tell me something in your language, then, since 'creel' is not a Norse word?"

His eyes lit up in amusement. "Why would you want to hear something you don't understand?"

"I don't know." She felt stupid for asking but all the same, she wanted to hear it. If he could not kiss her, at least let him *talk* to her!

Eyes fastened on her, he said something. The raspy sounds of the Norse language, a complete contrast to his velvety voice, were like having your back scratched when it itched, a rough gesture that brought you immense satisfaction.

"What did you say?" she breathed, slightly too late to pass as natural.

"I said I've just remembered that the geese pen needs repairing. I will see to it now."

"Oh." She flushed. She had been so certain he'd said something wicked... Never had she felt more foolish. But then again, why would he be making scandalous declarations to her, in Norse or otherwise? She really was losing control, fast.

"You sound disappointed, birdie." He crossed his arms over his chest.

"No. Only, surprised." It had sounded so erotic.

"Let me try again. See if you like this better." Eyes burning with a low flame, he said something else. Frigyth swallowed to hide her turmoil. This time... This time she was certain he had said something lewd.

"What was that?" She attempted breeziness when her heart was thumping hard. "There's a rip in your tunic? The broken pitcher needs replacing?"

He shook his head slowly.

I want to kneel at your feet and worship your body.

How many times had those words threatened to escape his lips, Sigurd wondered? Too many. Now that he had said them out loud, with luck, he might be able to rein in the urge to blurt the scandalous declaration out at the most inappropriate moment. He had finally told Frigyth what he wanted to do to her. That she hadn't understood made little difference. In fact, it was probably for the best she hadn't, for she might take fright.

"Can you say it again?" she asked, cheeks flushed. "It sounded so beautiful..."

Was she trying to kill him? Oh, well, it would be a pleasant death, at any rate. Slowly, he repeated the sentence. Then, to his shock, he saw her mouth the words, as if trying to imprint them in her mind. The idea that she was, in effect, telling him that she wanted to kneel at his feet and worship his body caused his groin to explode. If only!

"What does it mean?" she asked when she had stopped talking.

He cleared his throat and fought the urge to rearrange his hard shaft in his braies. "I cannot tell you."

"I'll ask Wolf then."

"No!" He almost shouted. The idea of her telling his friend such a lewd thing was unbearable, even if the chances of her repeating it clearly enough for him to understand were slim, and the odds of him being tempted to let her do what she has promised when he was in love with his new wife, non-existent. "He's an Icelander. I'm a Dane. Our languages are close but not that close. He won't understand you anyway."

She made a pout. "Will he not? He understands you. I've heard you two talk in Norse enough times."

Damn it, of course she had! Though it was true they didn't always use the same vocabulary and their accents differed quite significantly, the two friends had found a way to make it work. "Yes, well. It pleases us to use our native language together, so we persist, even if it is not always a good idea," he grumbled. Damn her inquisitive nature. He loved it but it could be awfully inconvenient at times. "Now if you'll excuse me, I have a geese pen that needs repairing."

Right now the idea of hammering posts into the ground held a certain appeal. If he worked hard enough all afternoon he might be able to lie next to Frigyth tonight without wanting to pound into her.

Sigurd snorted. That would never happen. Even at death's door he would want her. Hadn't he dreamed of her while he was fighting the fever, and imagined kissing her with all the intensity he was capable of? Yes, he had, and he still felt guilt over that, as if he'd stolen something from her, something he knew she didn't want to give.

He took the hammer and stormed away.

Later that evening, he decided to have a quick wash in the river before joining Frigyth in the hut. After a day of hard work, he most probably smelled. The last thing he wanted was to have her wrinkle her nose at him. Besides, a good dousing in freezing water might help cool his blood. It was certainly worth a try. Swearing under his breath, he plunged into the icy stream. Damn, what did a man have to do to try and bring his body under control? It was dark and he was half frozen by the time he made his way back to the hut.

He found Frigyth folding her clothes into a neat pile. She arched a brow when she saw his wet hair.

"I went for a wash in the river," he explained, reaching out for his comb.

"I thought you preferred to bathe in your house with warm water?"

Yes, well, that was what he usually did. But now she was in the hut, and having his bollocks frozen was exactly what he needed to be able to withstand an evening alone with her. "I prefer to eat tasty, hot food," he growled. "That doesn't mean sometimes I don't make do with what I find under a rock."

"Under a rock?" She looked aghast.

He shrugged. "Some insects and maggots can be—"

"Please." She made a face. "I don't really need to be told. And I'm very pleased to tell you, you can have tasty, if not hot, food tonight. Merewen gave me some goat's cheese in exchange for a few oatcakes. I bet you have never tried to eat it with honey and walnuts. You should find it most interesting."

She gave him a tentative smile. His heart constricted. And, damn it all, his groin instantly tightened. How was that possible? It had been shriveled out of all recognition only moments ago! He wouldn't be surprised if the woman had the power to raise the dead from their grave.

"I'm sure I will love it," he said, his voice hoarse.

Unsurprisingly, he did.

Once the meal was finished, Frigyth took her place on the furs to watch him while he carried on with the basket intended for Merewen. They talked about everything and anything. She asked a thousand questions, each more unpredictable than the last and he did his best to answer. Sigurd already knew he would remember this as one of the best evenings of his life.

Once the light of the fire had dwindled to a glow and he could not see well enough, he put his twigs away. Time to put his fingers to better use.

"Will you allow me to repay everything you have done for me?" he rasped.

"What *I* did for *you*?" Frigyth asked, eyebrows shooting up. "You were the one who offered me shelter and a way to refuse Caedmon's offer without hurting his feelings, who protected me from Toland, who saved me from drowning. I think if anyone should repay the other, it is me."

He waved her words away. It had been his pleasure to do all this.

"You tended to my ankle on that first day, you protected me from your neighbor's advances, you've been cooking and ensuring I ate like a prince for days, you looked after me during my illness and probably saved my life."

"Please, I don't need any mon—"

He stopped her with a raised hand. "No money. I don't have any to offer you, anyway. But I would like to make you feel good."

She blinked. "Good? What do you mean?"

"If you allow me, I would like to massage your feet."

He had not forgotten how good it had felt to have his skin brushed the day she had bandaged his foot, but he could tell his demand had taken her by surprise.

"I—"

"You'll like it, I promise." Without waiting for her answer, he folded his legs from under him and reached out for a fur, which he placed over his groin. Better to take his precautions now, before they started. He already knew he would get hard while he stroked her. "Lie down. Put your feet on my lap."

Frigyth did as she was told. Refusing didn't even cross her mind. The prospect of feeling Sigurd's hands on her body had her blood racing through her veins and she reasoned, probably foolishly, that in the dimmed light of the fire, she would be able to hold on to her composure better. And if she did not, at least he might not be able to see her blush.

The risks seemed minimal, and the temptation was overwhelming.

"May I take your stockings off? It will feel even better."

She nodded slowly. Once again, refusing was simply not an option. But she already knew this was going to kill her.

"Close your eyes," he instructed.

She already had.

Sigurd's skilled fingers brushed each toe in turn, he used his knuckles to knead the arch of her foot, his thumb to apply pressure on the heel and then circle the bone of her ankle slowly. It was a succession of strong kneading and featherlight caresses. Around them, the darkness was almost complete. Frigyth thought she might well have died and gone to Heaven.

All too soon, he stopped and she almost whimpered in protest. More, she needed more.

"Now the other one," he rasped.

Oh. The exquisite torture would start all over again. She couldn't wait.

"Yes," she breathed. "The other one."

CHAPTER SEVENTEEN

"Why did you bring me here?"

Brow furrowed, Sigurd looked around. They were at the edge of the lake, further down from the place where the boats were moored. Did Frigyth want to go into town? She had not hinted at it while they ate the left-over rabbit stew this morning and even if she did, he doubted she would choose to go by boat. So what were they doing here?

Frigyth took in a sharp breath, as if steeling herself for a task she found unpleasant. "You are going to teach me to swim."

He almost recoiled in shock. "Now?"

"Now."

He stared at her for a long moment then shook his head. "It's too cold." Though it was a pleasant, sunny day, hinting at the spring waiting to burst across the land, the water would be just as cold as it had been the other day, when the boat had sunk.

"It matters not. I want to learn. And I want you to be the one to teach me."

"I..." He didn't know what to say. That she'd understood

how important this was for him and trusted him with her life was enough to bring him to his knees.

Before he could move, she started to pull at the laces of her dress.

By the gods, how was he going to withstand this? His throat went dry when the dress pooled at her feet in a sigh. Her shift was incredibly thin. Too thin. Once wet it would be almost transparent, and cling to her body like a second skin. He would be able to see her breasts, her taut nipples, the curve of her hips, the triangle of curls at the top of her legs. It was going to be torture. But he could not back down now, not when she had taken the initiative and was ready to face her fears for him.

In the blink of an eye, he had stripped down to his braies. Frigyth stared at his naked chest, and what he saw in her eyes caused blood to rush to his groin. Unfortunately, it was not quite cold enough for the air to his dampen the worst of his ardor. Before she could ask why he was hard when he had clearly not just woken up, he gestured at her feet.

"You'll need to remove your shoes."

With trembling hands, she obeyed. Was she cold? Probably. Worried? Almost certainly. Aroused? Perhaps... He knew she liked his body, and he was bare-chested, after all. He shook his head. All this didn't matter right now. He was here to teach her to swim, nothing more, he had better get on with it. He waded into the water, and winced in dismay. It was too cold. He would not be able to teach her anything today, save the sensation of being immerged in water. It was the first and most important thing to get used to.

"Come here then, birdie."

Frigyth took the hand he was holding out and followed him into the lake. Her teeth started to chatter before the water even reached her waist. He opened his mouth to tell her she didn't have to do this but before he could say anything she lifted big, imploring eyes to him.

"I'm sorry. I c-can't. I'm too cold," she whispered, sounding crestfallen. "I can't feel my feet. I want to learn, I swear, only it—"

"Hush. I know." Sigurd swept her into this arms and brought her back to the shore where he cradled her a long moment, warming her against his chest. His heart was beating hard, his shaft was pulsing, his mind was all in disarray but nothing could have made him let go of her in this moment, and she seemed happy enough to let herself be held.

After a while he remembered what she'd said about her feet. He lowered her to the ground and knelt next to her. With his discarded shirt, he dried her feet, keeping his gestures matter-of-fact and his gaze averted. Last night in the hut it had been dark but now, in the sunshine, the sight was just too tempting. White, elegantly arched, with delicate toes and slender ankles, her feet were glorious.

Was there an inch of this woman that wasn't perfect? He smiled to himself when he imagined her arguing that the turnip-shaped mark on her shoulder was anything but perfect.

But... it was, because it was on her.

"I feel so silly for not even making it fully into the water," Frigyth mumbled, sounding dejected.

"I'm sorry, I should not have been so forceful the other day." If he had not been such a boor she would not have felt compelled to dunk herself in freezing water in the middle of winter to appease him. "We'll do as you said, and wait for the summer. There's no point doing anything today anyway. You need to be relaxed for this to work and it's not going to happen while you fight for body heat."

She nodded. "Did you learn in the summer then?"

"Mm, no. And the temperature of the water in Denmark is

not exactly pleasant, whatever the season. I taught myself, going everyday without fail until I could swim without thinking, until I felt as at ease in water as I did on land. It took a while, but I didn't give up."

"Oh, Sigurd, I'm so sorry."

Frigyth broke into sobs. What was happening to her? She was not usually prone to such emotional outbursts... But it seemed as if she could not stop crying every time he mentioned his childhood.

She cried for the little boy he'd been, half drowning himself in freezing water to ensure that he did not die like his parents and baby brother had died, for the youth who'd been taunted and called a beast, she cried for the grown man who had almost died a few days ago, for herself, who was developing feelings for him, for a future she wasn't sure they could have. Everything made a confused mess in her mind.

All through the tempest racking her soul, Sigurd did not say a word, he just held her, allowing her to empty the excess of emotion threatening to overwhelm her. When she finally drew away she felt better, if slightly self-conscious. She felt ridiculous, and would look even worse, with her reddened eyes and runny nose. But Sigurd handed her stockings and shoes and started to put his own back on, as if nothing untoward had happened.

"Thank you." She managed a watery smile.

"It's quite all right. Come. Let's get you back in the warmth of the hut." She accepted the hand he was holding out to her. But when she was up he didn't make any move to leave. Instead, he looked deep in her eyes. "I am humbled that you wanted to trust me, birdie. When the time comes, I hope not to disappoint you."

"You won't. But... You know I won't be here in the summer, don't you? I will be leaving in a few days."

Her chest constricted at the thought, but she could not shy

away from the fact any longer. Sigurd pursed his lips as if he did not see her point.

"Mm. Us not having to pretend to be husband and wife doesn't mean we have to stop seeing each other, don't you think? We could always meet at the lake for swimming lessons."

The weight crushing her chest lifted marginally. "Yes, I'd like that."

Seeing Sigurd again? Yes, she'd like that very much indeed.

"So you *ARE* sharing his bed, then."

Frigyth stiffened and turned to face the woman who'd just spoken. Too busy drawing water from the well, she'd not heard her approach. As soon as she saw who it was, her heart plummeted.

Edith. The lover who'd visited Sigurd the day his ankle had been injured. It seemed such a long time ago now.

"P-pardon me?" she stammered, even though it was pretty clear whose bed they were talking about.

"You're lucky," the woman added as if she had not spoken. "That man is a beast. When he gets going, nothing stops him. He barely gives you time to catch your breath. I've often thought he could satisfy two women at the same time. He might well have done so in the past. I wouldn't put it past him."

There was nothing Frigyth could answer to that. Sigurd was not sharing her bed, he had made it painfully clear he was not interested in bedding her, and he was most definitely *not* a beast. In fact, after the way he had massaged her feet the other night and held her at the lake while she cried the previous morning, she would have called him one of the most considerate people she knew.

Even so... She instinctively knew that Edith was not lying

about Sigurd being a fiery lover. They had shared a white-hot kiss while he had lain in bed with a fever. A man who could kiss like this when incapacitated would indeed be formidable when in possession of all his faculties. He might well leave his conquest for dead once he was done with her.

Being with him would be nothing like what she'd had to endure at Olaf's hands.

She stared at the bucket at her feet. More than ever she was grateful no one knew about the attack on her person. It was awkward enough being mistaken for Sigurd's lover but if Edith had known what Olaf had done to her, there was no telling what she might say, or how she would taunt her.

Seeing that she was not answering, Edith planted her fists onto her generous hips and huffed. "You're a scrawny little thing aren't you?" she sneered, eyeing her up and down. "Well. There is no accounting for taste, I suppose."

"No, there isn't," Frigyth replied, lifting the bucket. She had to get out of here before she threw the contents all over the woman's face. "Because I sure as hell have no idea why Sigurd would want to bed someone like you. And perhaps the reason he likes to keep you out of breath is because he can't bear to hear you talk."

Leaving a dumbfounded Edith behind, she made her way back to the hut. What had possessed her to say such a thing? She had never used such crude language before. She had spent too much time with Sigurd, she decided. His love for swearing was rubbing off on her. But really, the woman had it coming!

When she entered the hut, she found Sigurd crouching on the floor, rearranging the furs on the pallet. The sight of the bed only comforted her in her decision to confront him at last.

The words were out of her mouth before she could even put the bucket of water on the floor.

"Why will you not try to bed me?"

CHAPTER EIGHTEEN

I t sounded like an accusation.

Why will you not try to bed me?

Sigurd blinked. What could he say to that? He usually liked Frigyth's questions, but this time, he was at a loss. What could he answer? Certainly not the truth.

I am not trying to bed you because I know you would take fright when I unleashed the desire I feel for you. Because, though I am dying with the need for you, I cannot bear to cause you a moment's anxiety after what happened to you.

He slowly got back to his feet. What had gone into Frigyth? Why was she asking him that all of a sudden? Was it a trap?

"Is it because you favor men?" she asked before he could think of the best way to answer.

Favor men? He blinked. What the hell?

"No!" The word exploded out of his mouth. "How can you even suppose such a thing?"

The color on her cheeks made his blood roar. No, he most decidedly *did* not favor men over delicious, wide-eyed women, women who asked the most inconvenient, infuriating questions, women who made him feel for the first time as if he weren't alone in his life. If she took one look at his groin she would see that for herself.

She placed the bucket she was holding on the floor and closed her eyes to take a deep inhale. When she looked at him again her lips were trembling.

"Wolf and Merewen said..." The sentence trailed off at the furious stare he threw her.

"They told you I preferred men?" He let out one of his most colorful curses. Oh, he would make sure to tan Wolf's hide for that. Frigyth was the last woman he wanted to believe he was not worth pursuing because he would never return her advances! "What on earth possessed them to tell you such a thing?"

"They didn't. Only, I overheard them one day... Merewen was asking him if you had found yourself a new lover now that he was not sharing your bed anymore."

"Bloody hell!" Sigurd exploded.

Wolf's supposed lust for him had become a jest between the two of them, he knew. Shortly after her arrival in the village, Merewen had accused her then captor of sleeping with him, to rile him up. Since then it had become a game between them. A game he hadn't minded at first but that had just gone beyond what he was comfortable with.

He came to stand in front of Frigyth, nostrils flared. He needed to leave her in no doubt about his preferences. If he was never to satisfy his longing for her, at least let it be for the right reasons, because she didn't want him, and *not* because of a stupid misunderstanding. He had to make sure she knew that if she ever decided to make advances at him, he would not refuse her.

"Let me be clear. I do not bed men, never have, never will. I bed women."

Frigyth stared at Sigurd. There it was. Her last, fragile hope, gone up in smoke. But, of course, deep down she'd known that him being attracted to men was not the explanation for his lack of interest in her. He had bedded Edith, had he not?

"Right. You bed women. But you won't bed me."

If he didn't favor men, then there had to be something to explain his lack of interest in her, something to do with her. Perhaps Edith was right, perhaps she was too small and delicate for his tastes. It was possible. Men seemed to prefer curvaceous women.

Whatever it was, not once had Sigurd tried anything with her. When he had massaged her feet, he had not tried to slip his hand under her skirts. When he had woken up hard in the forest, it had not been because her proximity sent his blood to boiling, but only because he was a virile man and such a thing could not be helped, he had told her as much in no uncertain terms. He had kissed her with all the passion a man was capable of once, but only because he'd been unconscious and had not realized who she was at the time.

With Edith he was a beast in bed, with a warm, unknown woman already in his arms, he allowed his desires to come through, with her, he never stepped out of line. The message was clear.

Were she the last woman in the country, he still would not be interested.

"I understand."

Sigurd took a step toward her. "No, you don't, Frigyth. Not all men are despicable brutes incapable of controlling their urges." He clenched his jaw. It was not hard to guess who he was referring to. "I can feel desire for a woman and not bother her with it if I think it would embarrass, frighten or just plain not interest her."

Something—perhaps hope—surged through her. "But you do feel desire for me?"

She was poking at the beast in him by asking the question, but she had to know. Had she been wrong all along? Did he feel desire for her?

"Please, don't ask me this." Sigurd closed his eyes like a man in pain.

"Why not?"

A pause. "Because you might not like the answer."

"Oh." Her heart sank. He didn't feel any desire for her, and he didn't want to admit it because he thought she might not like to hear that the man posing as her husband, sleeping close to her night after night, didn't feel anything for her. Well, he was right. She did not like it. "I see."

He opened his eyes again. Blue, so blue. Her heart skipped a beat. "Forgive me, but you sound disappointed."

She forced a smile. She was not disappointed, more like crushed. The man who had made her feel as if she could heal after the assault she had been a victim of, had no interest in her.

She took a step back.

"It's not a problem. You like women but you don't like me... not in that way, at least." Why was she even surprised? He did not remember giving her the most decadent kiss of her life. "You're only pretending to be married to me to protect me. 'Tis no issue."

Sigurd closed the gap between them, all predatory intent and suddenly she knew. Even before he opened his mouth, she knew that she had it all wrong.

He did feel desire for her.

White-hot, scorching, devastating desire.

Her throat went dry. Oh, now she had well and truly woken the beast.

"When I said you should not ask the question, it was because I didn't think you would like to hear that I'm going out of my mind with the need to have you. I crave to prove to you that a man's touch doesn't have to be painful, to show you what your body is capable of." He leaned in to speak in her ear. "It is what I dream about day and night. Although I can control myself and ignore my own needs, it kills me to deny you the pleasure I know I could give you. There. Now you know the truth. I desired other women. With you, it's more, it's different. It's inexplicable." He shook his head as if he didn't like not understanding what he felt. "I crave you so much it kills me. And yet I don't mind not giving in to it, because I know you're not ready to hear it, and I would rather cut off my hand than cause you any distress."

Her heart flipped over in her chest. He was refraining from touching her for her sake! He was denying his urges for fear of frightening her. He did feel desire for her but he chose to forget it for fear of frightening her.

It was the last thing she had ever thought to hear, both wonderful and terrible.

"You... lied then?"

"Lied?"

"That morning in the forest, when you said it didn't mean anything that you were hard after having slept next to me."

"Well." He ran a hand through his hair. "I do wake up hard regardless of what happens at night, that much is true, but that morning I wanted to bury myself so deep inside you, you would come apart and shout my name in ecstasy. As I wish to do every moment of every day. I want to make love to you and show how it should be, not just between a man and a woman but between *you* and *me*. I know it would be explosive. The night I stroked your feet I got so aroused I left the hut once you had fallen asleep to bring about the relief I needed with my hand."

There. It could not be clearer. Frigyth could tell he was horrified to have been so blunt, so crude. But she was not horrified in the least, because he had given her the answer she wanted to hear.

He wanted her.

Even better, he was dying of desire for her.

"But I know you don't want me, you're most probably afraid of men so soon after your ordeal. I understand." He took a step back. "I know I cannot touch you."

Could he not? She wasn't so sure. And was she afraid of men? She wasn't afraid of him, at least.

"What if I did want you... What if I allowed you to touch me?" The words were little more than a whisper but in this moment everything was clear in her mind. She wanted this man, had wanted him for days, and now she was assured he shared her desire, she did not see why she should fight the attraction any longer.

For a long moment, the crackle of the flames in the fire pit was the only sound they could hear. Then Sigurd spoke.

"That's different. If you wanted me then—"

"I do."

She found herself lying on her back on the freshly made pallet in the blink of an eye. Her heart started to beat unbearably fast. How had he tumbled her to the floor without hurting her? This proof of strength, control and thoughtfulness reduced her insides to warm honey, as did the feel of his hard body atop her.

"Frigyth. Are you sure? I'm afraid once I start I—"

"I'm sure."

He swallowed hard. "Can I undress you? I'm dying to see you."

"Yes." The word was out of her mouth before she could think.

He tugged at her clothes, exposing her breasts, revealing her legs, baring her feminine folds. She could tell he would have liked to be more patient, take his time, but had been driven mad by days of unfulfilled craving. Instead of feeling used, she was flattered. His actions made it clear that he did desire her most ardently.

Once she was naked, he said something low in his throat, something she couldn't quite catch. Perhaps he had spoken in Norse. Even though she couldn't be sure, she guessed he was praising her beauty. Warmth flooded her, allowing her to ignore the cold in the hut.

"You are so damned beautiful." There he was, swearing again. She didn't mind. It only added to the urgency in his voice, made his desire for her more obvious. He shook his head, one hand hovering above her body. "I have dreamed of this moment for days but now I feel as if I have no right to touch you."

"Oh, please! I need you." She would die if he stopped now. "Touch me. Everywhere."

Forgoing the obvious choice of her breasts, he went for the place on her right hip where angry red scratches and cuts were still visible from the day she had been thrown against the rocks in the lake. He covered them with a gentle hand.

"You will have scars, I think." He sounded appalled by the prospect.

"I care not," she breathed back. And now less than ever. If he could just touch her, she would forget about her scars, the cold, her shame and everything else!

"But I do care. Nothing should mar the perfection of your body. I should have been the one thrown against the rocks that day." Slowly, he licked each and every one of the red marks, lingering over the caress. Frigyth started to squirm. Was he trying to torture her? It certainly felt like it.

A strangled cry escaped her lips and mercifully Sigurd

seemed to understand that she was on the verge of madness. He lay on his side next to her, and propped himself up onto his elbow.

What was he waiting for? How many times would she need to tell him she was desperate?

"Have I got your permission to touch you intimately?"

Oh. He was waiting for her agreement, because he knew the last man who'd taken her had done so without her permission and he didn't want to shock, hurt, or worry her.

She almost let out a sob "Yes. Please, Sigurd. Touch me."

And to make sure he didn't hesitate any more, she opened her legs.

Sigurd's hand, warm, assured and reverent, slid along her flank, smoothed over her stomach and then finally came to cup her where she needed it the most. A finger brushed her entrance and she barely refrained a cry. She could not, however, stop herself from arching her back in supplication. Yes, more, he had to give her more, or she would burst!

"You're so soft, so wet," he rasped. "Let me watch you as I give you pleasure, watch you come for me."

Come? That was a new word to her. He did have more vocabulary than her. "W-what do you mean?"

He lowered his head to whisper his answer in her ear. "I will stroke you until your body catches fire, until you feel as if you are bursting at the seams. Of course, I have never experienced the pleasure of release as a woman so I cannot be sure exactly how it will feel, but I know that it will be glorious."

Glorious. Yes, that much she had already guessed.

"Sigurd. Please, make me come." Frigyth understood the word was perhaps not one a woman should have said out loud when Sigurd's eyes flared in arousal.

"I will. Don't be scared, it will not hurt. Do you trust me?"

"Yes."

True to his word, nothing he did hurt. When he dipped his head to her breast and blew on one of her nipples, she moaned. When he licked it and then drew it into his mouth, she groaned. And when he slipped a finger past her entrance, she yelped. This was divine. Who would have thought her body was capable of such ecstasy? And thanks to Sigurd's earlier words, she knew the best was yet to come, so to speak.

Sigurd kissed and teased her breasts while his hand carried on with its daring exploration lower down her body. His tongue on her nipple was mirroring the action of his thumb on a small point at the apex of her thighs. Oh, he was skilled with his fingers, there was no doubt about it, even if he couldn't handle dough. A fire started to build inside her, stoked by the maddening caresses and the compliments he kept lavishing on her.

And then she shattered, just as he'd promised. It lasted for a long, glorious, moment. By the time he withdrew his hand she had melted into a puddle.

While she lay there, trying to catch her breath, Sigurd tore at his clothes. In an instant, he was as naked as she was, poised over her, magnificent and ready.

"Tell me how you want this, or rather tell me..." He hesitated and placed his forehead against hers. "Tell me what you don't want me to do."

His meaning was obvious. He didn't want her to be reminded of what had happened with Olaf while she was in his arms. There was such anguish in his voice that her own chest tightened.

"I trust you," she repeated. How could she not, after what he'd done to her, after the way he'd done it? "But maybe... maybe you could make sure I see you at all times?"

Sigurd let out a curse in his own language. He had gotten used to doing it in her presence, she noted, as if he allowed his true self to shine through with her. She liked it.

"You will see me, never fear. Come here, birdie. You take me."

Before she could ask any questions, he rolled onto his back and lifted her onto his lap.

"How am I supposed to take you?" she asked, bemused. "I'm not a man."

He chuckled. "No, you're a very beautiful, very desirable woman who has been sending me mad with need from the moment I saw her." His eyes darkened and he brushed a nipple with his finger. "Look at you, sitting on me. I swear I could come just looking at you."

"Don't!" she almost cried out, because she now had a fair idea of what he meant by that. "I need you inside me."

He snorted. "Don't worry. One way or another you're going to get what you want. I will not allow it to happen otherwise. Lift yourself off my lap and sit back, taking me in as you lower yourself onto me."

This sounded too tempting for her to hesitate even a moment. Slowly, she allowed him to enter her. She closed her eyes at the exquisite sensation of fullness. How was it that he did not cause her any pain when Olaf, who was not so generously endowed from what she'd seen, had seemed to skewer her?

"Oh," she said out loud. This was what her first time should have been like.

"Brace yourself against me, like so." He made her lean forward and guided her hands until they rested on his chest. Then he took hold of her hips to steady her. "Use me to find your pleasure. Grind your hips if you need to, find the rhythm you want. This is for you."

"Am I not hurting you?"

He closed his eyes. "Nothing has ever felt so damned good. Don't worry about me. You can do what you want as long as it's not hurting you."

It wasn't. As he'd said, nothing had ever felt this good. Well, except what he had just done to her. She could feel the glorious moment within her grasp once more. Heat had started to build inside her. Moved by instinct, she raised herself slowly and ground her hips as she came down. It was perfect. All her blood rushed to the point between her legs and her body started to burn. Sigurd groaned and closed one hand over her breast, telling her he had never seen a more perfect woman.

She came then.

A raw cry escaped her lips. Shocked by the intensity of the moment, she stopped moving while the part of her encircling him contracted and spasmed in release. Under her, there was a grunt and she felt Sigurd surge inside her, push into her pulsing core to prolong her pleasure. She screamed again as sparks exploded within her. Then her whole body went limp.

Sigurd growled when she collapsed on his chest. "Sweetheart, I'm going to come. You need to move."

Move? How? She didn't have the energy to go anywhere or do anything. She felt herself being lifted and deposited next to Sigurd, who wrapped his hand around his shaft and started stroking it with furious jerks of his hand.

"Frigyth. Ah!"

Her name sounded almost like a curse. A moment later he stilled, muscles corded, neck arched, fist clenched. Frigyth watched, fascinated, as he erupted in thick spurts that covered his convulsing stomach. She had never seen anything more entrancing in her life. It felt like the outward manifestation of what had just happened within her, and just as devastating.

When he'd stopped jerking he collapsed onto the furs.

Mumbling to himself, he reached for his undershirt and covered himself, then he drew her to lie against his flank. For a long moment they didn't speak, allowing their breathing to go back to normal and the heat of their bodies to mingle.

"So, how did it feel?"

"Like you said. As if I were consumed by a great fire."

"Then I'm glad."

With some effort she lifted an eyelid, because it sounded as if Sigurd was smiling and she wanted to see the happiness she had given him. Her efforts were rewarded when he bared his teeth in a brilliant smile. She nuzzled herself closer to him.

Sigurd tightened his hold over Frigyth. He was right where he wanted to be, in bed with her, with her leg draped over his thighs and her breasts pressed against his side. Finally he had fulfilled his mission and shown her pleasure. He would always remember it as the best moment of his life.

"How did it feel for you?" Frigyth's voice was tentative and her words ever so slightly slurred. He smiled to himself. She sounded like a sated woman if ever he'd heard one.

"Like never before." It wasn't a lie. Never had he lost himself in the act thus, never had he enjoyed seeing the woman in his arms come apart more. It had been more than a feast of the senses. It had been a gift for the soul.

"You know when you... came."

Oh, that word in her mouth! He would never tire of it. "What about it?"

"It looked..."

When she hesitated, he lifted his head. "What did it look like, birdie?" Had he shocked her? Disgusted her?

"As if you'd emptied every last drop in your body."

"Mm, it certainly felt like it." He was utterly drained. "I'm sorry you had to see it but I was past reasoning. All I could focus on was not to spill inside you. Did it upset you very much?"

Now that the moment had passed, he wondered if he should not have turned to the side and hidden his release from her. Yes, probably. But to his relief, she shook her head and looked him straight in the eye.

"Upset me? It was the most fascinating thing I have ever seen."

CHAPTER NINETEEN

As had become a habit, Frigyth woke up alone. But this time there was a pleasant languor in her body. Slowly, she stretched, marveling at how relaxed and happy she felt. How could it be that her two experiences of being in a man's arms were so radically different?

Olaf had hurt and humiliated her. Sigurd had given her unsuspected pleasure and put her in control. He had looked at her as if she was the most beautiful creature he had ever seen, had stroked her to ensure she reached her pleasure first, and then had reined in his own needs so she could come again. He had made sure she would not fall with child from the encounter when she had forgotten all about the risks for a moment. He had cradled her in his arms afterward, and murmured compliments in her ear while she fell asleep, sated and comfortable.

It had been nothing like the frantic couplings Edith had described, much more emotional and intimate. It had been like what she imagined Wolf and Merewen, who loved each other, might do in bed.

So what did it mean?

As she laced the front of her bodice, she tried to answer a

series of uncomfortable questions. What was between her and Sigurd? In just a few days she was supposed to leave. Did she want to? Did she have any choice? Would Sigurd agree to let her stay if she decided to carry on living here at the village? But why would she live with him? They weren't married or even involved together. Perhaps what had happened didn't mean anything to him, perhaps now that he had done what he had set out to do, namely show her the pleasure she could have in a man's arms, he would consider his mission fulfilled.

She knew that, for him, sharing a bed with a woman did not mean he wanted more. Edith was the living proof of this. He had bedded her repeatedly, passionately, and yet by all accounts he'd abandoned her without a word of apology or a second glance. Would he do the same with her? But then, why had he told her he desired her above all women? Why had he ensured they met again by the lake so he could show her how to swim?

This was an insoluble problem. She needed someone to confide in or she would go mad with all the questions jostling in her head. Before she could think better of the idea, Frigyth walked over to Wolf's hut, hoping to find Merewen on her own. She did. The Saxon woman was putting kindling into the fire pit and giggling to herself as she did.

"What's so funny?" Frigyth couldn't help but ask.

A pang of jealousy swept her. Merewen always seemed so happy, so content with her choice of husband, so in love with him... Frigyth didn't remember her mother or her sisters smiling when they gazed at their husbands, or giggle to themselves when they talked about them. Merewen always did. And it was the same with Wolf. He was devoted to his wife. The two of them were such a perfect match, it was hard not to be envious.

"Two months ago I complained to Wolf about the size of the logs he cuts for the fire. They were monstrous, far too big for me."

"Yes..." Frigyth said cautiously. That still didn't sound like a suitable explanation. What was funny about that?

"Now I'm looking forward to telling him he should actually cut them a bit bigger." Merewen shook her head at what was obviously a private joke between her and husband. "It should make for a very interesting conversation... and night."

When she winked, the pang of jealousy within Frigyth became full blown envy. Not only did they share complicity during the day, but they were hot for each other in bed. It was the perfect life. Wolf was so dependable, always helpful and attentive, able to evaluate situations and react accordingly. One could rely on him not to come back home drunk or to get himself involved in stupid brawls.

"You seem very happy with your husband," she observed.

The smile she got in return was an answer in itself. "Blissfully so."

"But..."

"But what?"

Frigyth hesitated. Would Merewen not take offence at her questions? She went for it, knowing she would never be able to contain her curiosity much longer anyway. Better to ask now in a composed manner than blurt out the comment later on. "I heard he bought you."

"He did. At a slave auction a couple of months ago. I was abducted and handed over to the slave owner by my enemy, the man who later tried to force me into marriage." A shadow passed over her friend's eyes at the memory. "Wolf paid an extravagant sum of money for me and scared me half to death when he took me away, as you can imagine. He doesn't exactly look harmless at first glance."

No, he didn't. The poor woman would have been terrified.

"I-I don't understand," Frigyth couldn't help but say. Surely being bought as a slave by a stranger didn't preclude for marital bliss? How had they managed to get past the initial hurdle?

Merewen sighed. "I'm not surprised. I was perplexed myself when I understood I was falling for him. To be attracted to a man who had bought me like cattle was... upsetting, I will not deny it."

This Frigyth could well believe. If she could be perturbed by her attraction toward Sigurd just because he didn't conform to the image of the quiet man she had always wanted to marry, she dreaded to think what Merewen would have felt as she was developing feelings for her captor.

"How did you get past it?"

"Because there was no other choice. It was either accept it or be without him. And this, I could *not* accept. In any case, it was not so difficult in the end. At first, I ranted against Wolf's high-handedness and unreasonable behavior. But then I understood what was behind it. He actually wanted to protect me, the way he had not been able to protect his first wife. So I decided to stop hankering after the life I had dreamed of and start living the one I had instead. It was the best decision I ever made." The smile was back on Merewen's lips. "And now I have a marriage that is beyond what I would have imagined. And I think... I think you understand very well what I'm trying to say."

"Yes," Frigyth murmured. "I do."

She *was* developing feelings for a man she had thought unsuitable at first, and she *was* hoping she could find a life beyond what she had imagined here at the village. But it didn't mean hers and Sigurd's story could have a happy ending. One thing was certain, things would change between them after last night. They would need to talk about what had happened, she needed to understand what he meant to do before she risked her heart.

If she decided to put aside her doubts and questions, only to find out that Sigurd had never thought anything could develop between them, she would be crushed.

"Do you think I'm beautiful?" she blurted out.

Merewen arched a brow. "Er... What are you asking me, exactly?"

"It's a silly question, I know, but I... I have never seen myself properly. I was wondering what someone would think when they saw me."

"Someone?" Merewen stole a glance over to Sigurd's hut. "Anyone, or someone in particular?"

Could this get any worse? Frigyth felt herself going crimson. "Someone in particular."

"I see. You find him impossibly attractive and you are wondering how you could possibly compete. You want to know if he sees the same thing you do when he looks at you and whether he thinks you the most compelling woman he's ever met because it would crush you to know you don't hold a particular place in his heart or even in his life."

This was so close to what she was thinking that Frigyth could not help a gasp. "How could you possibly know that?"

"Because that was what I wondered when I first met Wolf, even when I did not want to accept the desire I felt for him. I could not quite believe a man like him could be attracted to me." She shook her head as if she still wasn't sure why that might be. "But from what I've seen, you have nothing to worry about. Your Norseman finds you more than beautiful. And you are."

"Thank you." Frigyth was moved. She had come to the hut for answers and she had gotten something even better. She had gotten reassurance. She now knew it would be down to her to decide what happened between she and Sigurd, because he was ready to hear about her feelings and might even already return them.

"I will leave you now."

Merewen took her hand and gave it a squeeze. "Let me know how it goes. And if you have any questions about Sigurd, I can try to answer them. I don't know him as well as Wolf does, of course, but I know he's a good man. He was of assistance to me once..." Her voice trailed and she swallowed. "And without him, Wolf and I might not be together."

Outside, it had stopped raining. Frigyth lifted her eyes to the sky and took a deep inhale, feeling hopeful. Maybe there would be a future for her and Sigurd after all. When she brought her head back down, the air froze in her lungs.

Oh no.

This time she didn't have her back turned, so she saw Edith coming— no, *marching*— straight to her. Would the woman never leave her alone? What would it be today? Would she boast about all the things she and Sigurd had done in bed? Would she ask if she wanted to share him with her? At the same time?

Nothing would surprise her at this point.

"Good afternoon," she said, deciding it was better not to show her fear or, even worse, her jealousy. It was bad enough to feel those things, but she didn't have to make a fool of herself by letting Edith see what was on her mind. The woman would only gloat.

Edith ignored her greeting. "You can tell him I won't pine for him."

There was no prize guessing who this man was but that didn't mean Frigyth knew what to answer. As always, in front of Edith, she felt ill at ease. The woman was tall, beautiful, curvy and self-assured. In other words, she was nothing like her. Of course, this time Frigyth could at least rely on the assurance that Sigurd found her desirable too, but still, she could not help but feel at a disadvantage. She did not have the wealth of experience the other woman obviously had. In bed, Sigurd had not behaved like a beast, not ridden her until she could not breathe and, of course, he had not even alluded to the possibility of exploring the elusive 'other place'.

He had been sweet, gentle. It had been wonderful but now she was wondering if he had not found her lacking. After all, she had not done anything to please him, allowing him to do all the work and luxuriating in his touch.

Edith's smile was smugness personified, as if she had guessed what was going through Frigyth's mind.

"I'm thinking of accepting Olaf's advances if you must know. He's been after me for a while. So you can tell your precious lover that and see what he thinks."

Bile rose in Frigyth's throat. There was no way of knowing if this was true or just a way of making Sigurd jealous. It was more than possible. But just in case it was true, she had to warn the woman.

"I would stay away from Olaf if I were you."

Far from taking the hint, Edith smirked, as if she had hit her mark. "Jealous, I see? You want all the men in the village for yourself? Haven't you got enough with Sigurd? I should think he's enough for one woman, but now you want Olaf as well?"

"I don't want him!" Frigyth exploded. "I never did, but he didn't care!"

Leaving the woman dumbfounded, she rushed back to the hut—and the safety of Sigurd's arms.

CHAPTER TWENTY

Sigurd almost collided with Frigyth when she burst in through the door.

"What happened?" he asked immediately, dropping the log he was holding into the fire. She was panting hard and there was a dazed look in her eyes that scared him. Was it Olaf? Had she seen him? He'd feared this would happen! With him still lurking in the village, it was only a matter of time before the two of them met. How had he let Frigyth convince him to let the man get away with what he'd done?

It was all his fault. By not bringing Olaf to heel, he'd allowed this to happen. How could he ever forgive himself?

"What did he do to you?" If he had touched as much as her hand, promise or no promise, Sigurd would rip his heart out.

"Who?" She looked confused for a moment, then she shook her head. The dazed look in her eyes cleared somewhat, as if his mere presence calmed her. "Nothing. It's not like that."

"Then, what?" He was only marginally reassured. Something *had* happened, he was sure of it.

She took in a deep breath. "I bumped into Edith outside."

Oh, no. Sigurd clenched his fists. "What did she tell you?"

It was clear she'd been less than kind, which did not surprise him if she'd recognized Frigyth for the woman who had been in his hut the other day and was now living with him. Edith was jealous and had a mean streak about her. She could well have mocked Frigyth. Or she might have revealed all they had done in bed together and appalled or even scared her.

And this the day after she had allowed him into her bed, showing him the trust he never thought she would grant him and he wasn't sure he deserved. She might already be regretting giving in to her urges, now was not the time to be told how depraved or demanding a lover he could be! Last night he'd been careful with her, gentle, and she had allowed herself to relax and him to show her pleasure, but would she not recoil in horror if she knew what he was capable of? Not that the women he had bedded had ever been hurt or even complained, of course, but it had been different. They had been experienced, equally adventurous and, most importantly, they had never suffered at a man's hands beforehand. There had been no chance of reawakening any trauma with them.

And, if he was honest with himself, he had not worried himself overmuch about what they would think. If they found him too fierce for their tastes, then they did not welcome him back into their bed a second time. The notion did not bother him.

Now it most definitely did, because he did want this woman to welcome him in her bed again and again.

"She told me to tell you she had found herself a new lover."

Sigurd allowed himself to breathe. That was all? Edith was trying to make him jealous but he simply didn't care what she did or who she did it with. She was welcome to all the lovers she wanted. "She can do what she wants," he told Frigyth, relieved. He had feared much, much worse. "I care not. It's not as if we—"

"It's Olaf."

The hated name resounded in the hut like a clap of thunder.

Oh, but now he *did* care. He would not have any woman he knew going to a rapist, place herself in danger just to provoke him, or have anyone hurt if he could prevent it. It had been a mistake to heed his promise to Frigyth, to allow the man to get away with a mere beating from Wolf. His instinct had told him it wasn't enough and he had just been proven right. If the whole village knew what Olaf had done, Edith would not be considering going to him.

"I need to go and warn her," he said through gritted teeth. Of course, that was exactly what the woman wanted. She'd hoped he would come running as soon as he heard she was considering going to another man. She probably imagined she would lure him back into her bed once he was in her hut. Well, it mattered not what she thought. He would not risk a woman being hurt just so he could protect his pride. But he was *not* going to her to resume their affair, he would make that very clear.

"Please. Just don't tell her what..." Frigyth's face was a mask of anguish.

"I won't mention your name," he assured her. "But she needs to know the kind of man she's dealing with."

"Yes," she agreed bravely.

He almost kissed her then. Instead, he stormed out of the door.

By the time Sigurd came back to the hut, it had gone dark and Frigyth was getting quite frantic.

When the door opened and then closed behind her, she didn't move, keeping her eye on the fire she was stoking. It seemed Edith had had what she wanted after all, namely Sigurd back in her bed. A discussion to warn her about her choice of man would not have lasted all afternoon. A tryst with an indefatigable lover, on the other hand, would have.

"So you gave Edith what she was after," she murmured, remembering she had no right to be jealous. They were only pretending to be married after all, she had no claim over this man, even if they had slept together.

There was no answer. Finally she turned around—and froze in horror. Sigurd's clothes were covered in blood and his chest was heaving. Rushing to him, she saw that a large bruise was forming on his cheekbone and his lip was split. But other than that he didn't appear to be injured. So where had all the blood come from then?

"Edith?" she asked, not knowing quite what she meant. Surely the woman could not have inflicted such damage on him, even if she was furious at his defection?

"She's fine," he growled.

"So what happened?" Had he been attacked in the village? A dark glare skewered her and she knew before he opened his mouth what he would tell her. "Olaf," she said, sure of herself.

He didn't answer, didn't deny it. He had the man's blood all over him when he had promised he would not touch him and he did not even think to say anything to explain himself. Frigyth shivered as understanding dawned. He hadn't gone to Edith to warn her at all. He'd gone to Olaf to do what he'd sworn not to do. Instead of making sure Edith refused the man's advances, he had ensured her prospective lover was in no state to hurt her.

Horrified at his duplicity, Frigyth took a step back.

"But you said... you promised you wouldn't—"

"I did. And I regretted it every moment of every day," Sigurd snarled. "I hated not giving him what he deserved. But I did it, for you."

Yes, he had. Until now, obviously, when his patience had finally snapped. "So what changed?"

"If the bastard doesn't want to have his balls ripped from his body, then he should make sure he keeps them in his braies."

Dear God, he was not saying... Surely he had not *ripped Olaf's balls from his body?* Bile rose in Frigyth's throat. No, not now, she could not be sick now, she had to find out what he had done to Olaf.

"Did you...?" She could not say the words out loud.

"He's still alive, if that's what you mean." The words were little more than a bark. "Though why you might lament his death is beyond me."

Though he had not exactly answered her question, she didn't insist. She wasn't sure she was brave enough to hear what had happened to the man. It would be gruesome, the amount of blood on Sigurd's clothes made that clear.

"I had no choice but to confront him. He—"

"No choice!" she cried. "There is always a choice!" And he had made the wrong one.

The wrong one for them, because he had just proven things could not work between them. She could not live with a man who got himself involved in brawls at the drop of a hat, even for a good reason, who could not control his temper. Earlier that day she had wondered if they could have a future. It seemed that fate had made the decision for her by showing her what life would be like next to Sigurd and she could not stomach it. Literally. She was nauseous with anguish—and wretchedness.

Before they could talk about the potential significance of what had happened between them, before she could find out if he was prepared to give them a chance, she had been forced to see that she could not live with Sigurd. A man like him would never offer her the tranquil life she needed. She would always be afraid of him snapping and unleashing his temper onto an unsuspecting, perhaps even innocent man.

Day after day she would be reliving the misery of her child-hood. This was what she had tried to avoid all along, what she had hoped would not happen to her as an adult.

The death of one's parents was usually met with sorrow. But Frigyth had not been able to mourn. At her mother's death a few years ago, the overwhelming feeling had been relief on her behalf. At last, the poor woman would be free of the torment inflicted on her by her husband. At the death of her father, only a few weeks ago, the predominant feeling had been relief, again, this time for herself. It was over. She would finally be able to live her life without the threat of violence, without the constant fear of having to hear that someone who was supposed to care for her was hurt, that he had got himself into trouble.

But it was not over. The source of disquiet had merely changed origin. Instead of dreading seeing her father tumble into the house half-dead from drink, she would worry about seeing the man she lived with tumble in half-dead from his fights with dangerous men. It would be even worse, because she cared about Sigurd.

More than cared.

But she had fallen for the wrong man, one who could not offer her what she wanted. Caedmon wanted to marry her and would ensure she got the quiet life she craved but unfortunately she only saw him as a friend. Sigurd, who she definitely wanted in a deep, carnal way, was so uninterested in building a future with her that he didn't think it important to honor his promises to her.

"Why did you have to do that?" she whispered.

And ruin everything?

All pretense at calm was forgotten. Sigurd grabbed Frigyth by the shoulders, barely resisting the impulse to shake her in his fury. Had she really asked him why he'd wanted to punish a man who went around raping women?

"If you think I can live with the knowledge that someone who hurt you so badly is allowed to roam free, then you don't know me at all," he said, articulating each word carefully. "I would want to see him punished for what he did if it was with another woman. With you... With you I want to see him suffer first, I want to see him crawl, I want to see the fear in his eyes as he understands that this time he's found an opponent that is stronger than him."

"But I told you that Wolf—"

"And I warned you, I'm not like Wolf!" His vehemence scared her, he could tell, but he could not lie to her or himself any longer. He would kill for her, and without a moment's remorse if the man turned out to be such a bastard. Olaf had chosen to rape innocent women, no one had forced him to do it. If he had to pay the ultimate price for it now, then he had no one but himself to blame. Sigurd bunched his fists. "I cannot be reasonable. Not when it's about you."

Frigyth's eyes filled with tears. "Well, I can't deal with that. It frightens me."

He let her go immediately and took a step back. "You're afraid of me? You think I could hurt you?"

To his relief, she shook her head. "I'm not afraid of what you might do to me, but to others. And I cannot live like that, waiting for the next disaster. I told you I needed security, I needed calm in my life and I told you why. I can't live next to someone who thinks he can pummel people to the ground and beat them to a pulp when he pleases just because he's stronger."

He recoiled. Was that what she thought of him? "I'm not like that!"

I'm not a beast.

Not her as well. He'd thought she had seen past the cruel

nickname, past appearances. Then the glance she threw at his chest made him blanch. Because in that moment he looked exactly like a beast.

"You're hurt and covered in blood," she said slowly. "You said yourself that you weren't like Wolf, that you wanted to see your opponents crawl with fear, that you could not be reasonable."

"I only meant with you!" Couldn't she understand he could not keep a level head where she was concerned and why? Had the last few days meant nothing to her? And last night? Had she only wanted to soothe her ego, see that she could seduce him if she wanted, like Edith and others had? Had he been a fool for thinking that it could be the start of something between them?

Frigyth bit her bottom lip, obviously prey to intense emotion.

"If you can't be reasonable near me then you shouldn't be near me. I cannot bear that burden and you shouldn't be anywhere near someone who stops you from being reasonable. It's not fair on either of us."

His heart missed a beat. "What are you saying?"

"Tomorrow or the day after, Caedmon will come to ask if I want out of our supposed marriage." She paused and took a deep inhale, like a woman making a decision. A decision he wouldn't like. "I cannot go to London, I don't want to marry him so I will tell him I want to stay with you."

Though she was telling him exactly what he'd wanted to hear, Sigurd frowned. Her tone did not match her words. "But it will only be a lie to placate him. You don't mean to stay at all."

"We only pretended to live together. It was never the arrangement that I should stay."

"No. But things have changed since then, can't you see that? Bloody hell, Frigyth, we fucked last night! Or don't you remember how I made you come?" The crude words exploded out of his mouth. He regretted the outburst when he saw her pale. Damn it all, why did he have to be so crass and call what they had done 'fucking'? It had been so much more than that. But how was he supposed to stay calm when she was telling him she was leaving because she didn't trust him, because she was afraid he might one day kill a man?

It was unbearable.

Only the night before, they had made love. He'd thought he had finally broken through her resistance and he'd fallen asleep full of hope for the future. He had meant to talk to her about it, find out where they could go from there, but before they could build on it, she'd told him about Edith and Olaf. And he'd had to leave.

"Forgive me. I shouldn't have spoken like this." He knew he could be too rough for his own good. It had been the only way to survive as a child. As to the swearing, it had become an unfortunate habit. But he was not a violent man, whatever she said, he would never hurt her.

Her words suddenly came back to him.

I've lost count of the amount of times he came back home bruised and bloodied from a brawl at the tavern. My mother had to stitch his wounds time and time again, all the while enduring his foul cursing and ranting.

Damnation. She had every reason to fear she would live the same life as her mother if she stayed with him. His lip was cut, he was covered in blood, and he had just sworn at her.

This was a disaster.

"Please. You know I don't think what we did was just..." He could not repeat the word. What had possessed him to call what they had done 'fucking'? It had been nothing like that.

Frigyth nodded slowly. "I know. But it doesn't change the fact that I need to know the person I live with is not going to get embroiled into fights and come back half dead, or kill someone in a mad fit of temper, least of all on my behalf. I don't want to live like that anymore. I'm sorry."

As if all this was not hard enough to hear, at that moment, there was a knock on the door. Without opening, Sigurd knew it would be Caedmon, come back to claim Frigyth.

CHAPTER TWENTY-ONE

F rigyth froze when a deep voice called out to her from the other side of the door.

"Frigyth? Are you there?"

Oh, no! Not now! She'd thought she would have another day, maybe two to come to terms with all the latest developments. The last thing she wanted was a confrontation with her friend when her mind was in such turmoil. In the state she was in, she might well blurt out the truth and then Caedmon would take her away for sure.

"Hide!" she whispered to Sigurd, who instantly bristled.

"I'm not hiding. This is my house."

"You're..." She gestured at him wildly. "You look as if you just killed someone." Of course, that might well be what he had done. "If he sees you covered in blood, he will never accept my word that I am safe and happy here with you."

"Bloody hell." Begrudgingly, but obviously seeing the logic in what she was saying, he moved to one corner of the room.

Pasting a smile on her face, Frigyth opened the door, placing herself so as to obscure his view of the inside. Of course, Caedmon was so much taller than her that he could still see above her head. "Caedmon. I'm so sorry to keep you waiting. I was..." Not knowing how to explain the delay, she tugged at her sleeve nervously. It gave her an idea. "I was getting dressed."

"I see." He glanced behind her as if he expected to see Sigurd. His gaze fastened onto the pallet and his face darkened.

Frigyth flushed bright red when she realized she had all but admitted she had been rolling in bed with her husband. Why else would she need to get dressed so late in the afternoon?

"Anyway... Did you want anything?"

He stared at her in disbelief and she kicked herself for asking such a stupid question. As if she didn't know why he was here!

"You know why I came, Frig. I need to know you are content here, and do not wish to leave."

There was rustle and a soft rumble in the corner where Sigurd was waiting. She cleared her throat to cover it. "Yes. I am. There was no need to come see me before you left. That is," she amended quickly, "of course, I am grateful you came to say goodbye. I will miss you. I thank you for everything you've done for me and wish you all the best in your new life."

Suddenly she was crying. This man was her oldest friend, he had looked after her for years, been there to help when she needed it the most, had protected her. Despite being told of her shame, he still wanted to marry her. Despite her refusal, he was ensuring she was treated well by her husband and happy in her new life. And she had almost closed the door in his face!

What sort of a monster was she?

"There is no need to thank me. It was my pleasure to do all that." Caedmon drew her into his arms before she could protest. "I only wish I could have done more."

Another rustle reached her from the left when a kiss landed on her hair. Sigurd's patience was quickly wearing thin.

"Let's go outside," she begged, before he could launch

himself onto her friend for daring to touch her. This sort of reaction was precisely why she could not stay with him. She needed to be with a man who did not fly into a rage when a friend showed her the comfort she needed. "I need some fresh air."

The light of the moon was so bright over the frosted village that they could see almost as well as they had during the day. It was far colder than she had anticipated, though. Frigyth regretted not having taken her cloak but she dared not go back inside in case Sigurd did not allow her to get back out again.

"Must you go to London?" she blurted out. Now that she had lost the man she had fallen for, the idea of being apart from her only friend was unbearable. Once Caedmon was gone and she had left Sigurd, she would be all alone.

He gave her a sad smile. "Would you have me staying here so I am reminded every day that you refused me and married someone else?"

"I... Forgive me, I didn't mean to be cruel." She had not thought his feelings for her to be so deep. Had she wounded his heart instead of hurting his pride? She had assumed he'd only asked for her hand to protect her, but what if there was more to it? Should she not accept his offer if he did love her? At least married to Caedmon, there was no risk of seeing her husband come home bloodied and blind with rage.

As if he'd heard her musings, Sigurd chose this moment to appear through the door. Heart in her throat, she turned to face him. Thankfully he had changed into a fresh tunic and washed the blood from his chin, but his lip was still cut and the bruise on his cheeks more prominent than ever in the pale moonlight. Combined with the look of thunder on his face, it made him look positively lethal.

Caedmon did not let it worry him, even though she doubted he would have been able to hold his own against the Norseman in the event of a fight.

"Good evening," he said with his usual calm. Sigurd didn't answer. Instead, he glared at him. "I came as planned to ask Frig whether she—"

"You can ask Frigyth all you want, but not before she has covered herself up. How can you keep her outside clothed in only her thin dress? You don't want her to freeze to death, do you?" With those words he disappeared back inside the hut. A moment later, heavy fur wrapped around her. She saw Caedmon nod approvingly at the cloak Sigurd had placed over her shoulders. It was his, so much bigger than her own, enveloping her completely in warmth and wonderful masculine scent.

"You're right," Caedmon said. "It is bitterly cold tonight. I should have thought."

Sigurd grunted. Yes, he should have. Still, he could not help being impressed that the man had bothered to come back and face him at all. Such an endeavor required guts of steel. Few men would dare bait the beast in his own lair, and he should know. This proof of the man's regard for Frigyth's safety pleased him in spite of himself.

"So what have you decided?" the Saxon asked, looking at her.

Sigurd waited, willing her to say she would not leave and go to London but she refused to meet his eye.

"I'm sorry, Caedmon," she answered after a pause during which his heart threatened to give out. "My life is here. I cannot marry you."

She had not lied, he noticed, not said she wanted to stay with him, not reminded her friend that she was already married. Because she did not want to stay with him, that was why, and they were not truly married, would never be.

Everything within him collapsed. Once she left, he would be alone, once again. Only this time, it would be his own fault.

His parents had not chosen to leave him. Frigyth had, because he could not give her what she needed. It would be a hundred times worse. How was he going to survive this loss?

"Before I go, I have to ask," Caedmon said, finally looking at him. "What happened to you?"

Sigurd nodded. He'd expected the question and was even relieved to hear it. If the Saxon truly meant to ensure Frigyth's safety and happiness, he could not overlook the fact that her supposed husband looked like he'd been in a fight, since everyone knew a violent man could not be trusted not to hurt his wife.

Except he was *not* a violent man, damn it! He'd had every reason to attack Olaf, say what everyone might.

"I got into a fight with one of the villagers," he said curtly.

"The one who attacked Frig?"

Seeing as Frigyth knew the truth anyway, Sigurd didn't see any reason to lie. "Yes."

"Then I cannot say I blame you. I hope you gave him what he deserved."

Next to him, Frigyth inhaled sharply. He could tell she did not like to hear that her measured friend, as she'd called him, condoned the use of violence. He mentally thanked the Saxon for siding with him so unequivocally. Perhaps hearing from a man she trusted that Olaf had only got what he deserved would help Frigyth see that his actions had not been unreasonable or disproportionate. Sigurd straightened. He would seize this opportunity to tell her what had really happened. She seemed to think he had just gone to Olaf to kill him in cold blood knowing all along she would disapprove and yet had not cared.

It had been nothing like that.

If she were to leave him, let it be in good conscience, not on a misunderstanding. He wanted her to know he was not an unreliable, hot-headed, dangerous fool like her father had been and Caedmon, an unlikely ally, had just given him the chance to do that.

"I went to visit a friend this afternoon and found that bastard Olaf pinning her to the ground, trying to get between her legs." He heard Frigyth's gasp but he kept his eyes on the other man. Let her hear what had happened and see that she had not given him the benefit of the doubt. "Now, I will readily admit that I saw red, for it was my fault. If I had not allowed him to get away with what he'd done to Frigyth, Olaf would never have been in a position to hurt anyone else. It took all my inner strength not to rip him to shreds."

"So he lives?"

Sigurd clenched his jaw. "He lives. But he might well be wishing I'd killed him, after all. If he recovers, he will be banished from the village. My friend, Wolf, will see to it."

Caedmon nodded, as if satisfied with this answer. Then he let out a long sigh, a man knowing he'd been beaten. "I see that with you around, I have no reason to worry about Frigyth."

"You don't. I would give my life to protect her." It was not a lie. If only the stubborn woman would let him do it...

"I'm leaving tonight. I have arranged to travel with a group of merchants going to a fair on the road to London. That is why I came here slightly earlier than I meant."

Frigyth's throat was tight. This was it. Her friend was really leaving. After hearing what Olaf had done, she was more confused than ever. Sigurd had not lied, he had truly gone to Edith's house, he had not broken his promise not to punish Olaf, he had merely done what needed to be done to stop him from assaulting another woman. Why had he not told her as much earlier?

Then without warning, Caedmon engulfed her in a bear hug. She stiffened, wondering how long it would be before Sigurd ordered him to let go of his wife. But nothing happened, even when Caedmon placed a kiss on her forehead. "Be happy, Frig. You've earned it."

Tears got stuck in her throat and she relaxed into the embrace. "You, too."

"Thank you."

The deep voice behind them made her start. Sigurd was *thanking* Caedmon? She had half expected him to throw the Saxon to the ground for daring to touch her.

"What are you thanking me for?"

"For having been there for Frigyth when she grew up, for wanting to ensure her safety and happiness now."

Caedmon nodded. "And I thank you for being here now to take care of her."

Sigurd didn't answer. A moment later, they were alone. Silence, as thick and suffocating as smoke stretched between them.

"You... Why didn't you tell me what had happened at Edith's hut?"

Sigurd stared at her, his face set in granite, as if he didn't know who she was. "I tried to. You would not listen. You decided that I had just pounced on him for no reason, because I can't keep a level head. You didn't trust me, didn't give me a chance to explain that I am not a blood-thirsty beast."

Frigyth's heart plummeted. He was right. She had cut him off, when he'd said he'd had no choice but to confront Olaf, had not waited for the rest of the explanation. And in doing so she had hurt him.

"I—"

"You told me there was always a choice," he cut in ruthlessly. In the same way she had denied him the opportunity to justify himself, he would not give her the chance to apologize. It was his way of making her pay for jumping to conclusions. And perhaps she deserved it. "Well, you were right. I did choose to finally punish him, to finally make sure he would not hurt another woman and I do not regret it. I would do it all over again. He deserves nothing less." He clenched his jaw. "And now you are choosing to leave."

Yes, she was. After what had happened, she could not stay. She needed to think.

She nodded, choking on a sob. "I will leave in the morning."

CHAPTER TWENTY-TWO

"So."

Sigurd cleared his throat. Frigyth knew he had not slept a wink last night, because she hadn't either, and she had heard him twist and turn on his blanket until dawn. Of a common accord, they had not slept next to each other. Snuggled up in the furs that smelled of him, she had not tried to contain the tears flowing down her cheeks, only refraining from wiping them and drawing his attention.

He reached out to the basket holding the nuts and emptied it on the table. "Here. Take the basket. Please. You can use it to carry your clothes home."

You can have a keepsake from me.

Frigyth did not even think of refusing. She did want something to remember him by. Carefully, she placed her bundle of clothes into the intricate basket and turned to face the door. This was it, she was truly leaving.

She couldn't help it. At the last moment, she retraced her steps. Raising herself onto her tiptoes, she placed a kiss on Sigurd's bruised cheek, wishing she had the courage to kiss him full on the mouth.

"Thank you for what you—"

"Stay." The one word was little more than a rasp.

She stared at him. After the way she'd treated him, he wanted her to stay? She swallowed hard as more tears threatened to flood her cheeks. "You know I cannot."

His answer was uncompromising. She should have known he would be blunt. "You can. You just won't."

"I won't. I need time." She needed to come to terms with everything that had happened in the last two weeks. She could not allow the undeniable attraction she felt for Sigurd to muddle her judgment. Before she did anything she needed to be sure she would not regret it. At the moment, she wasn't. Sigurd made no secret of his fiery temper, did not think it a problem.

His chilling words came back to her.

I want to see him suffer first, I want to see him crawl, I want to see the fear in his eyes as he understands that this time he's found an opponent that is stronger than him. I warned you, I'm not like Wolf. I cannot be reasonable. Not when it's about you.

A man like that would get involved in scraps and brawls, it was inevitable. He would fight, and he would get hurt. She did not think she could stand it, even if he had good reasons to do it. She trusted him not to pounce on innocent people but she knew he would want to punish scoundrels. This was all very well on principle, but what did it mean for the woman sharing his life? Constant worry and possible heartache, that was what. Last night he'd come back with a split lip and a bruise. Next time it might be a slash to the stomach, or a broken nose, the time after that he might face three men at once and end up with his throat cut and his body thrown into a ditch.

It would kill her.

Better to leave now, and try to forget that she had thought, briefly, that they could have a future together.

"Goodbye, Sigurd. Perhaps we can meet again in the

summer by the lake?" Despite her best judgment she could not help but try to make this parting less final.

When Sigurd answered, the look in his eyes was incandescent. "I will hold you to that promise, birdie."

Had she made a mistake?

As she stared at the ceiling in her lonely, cold bed, Frigyth could not fight the impression that she had. Returning to an empty house after living with Sigurd had been a shock. At night she writhed in bed, in search of warmth and reassurance. In the morning, she wished she had someone to talk to. At the table she stared at the empty space in front of her, eating her oatcakes without tasting them. It had been a miserable two weeks.

Perhaps she should have accepted Caedmon's offer, left a house which only held bad memories and started a new life away from a man she could not afford to be with. Why had she refused her friend's offer of marriage? It made no sense. Caedmon was everything she wanted in a man. Calm, predictable, gentle, reliable. With him life would be...

Dull.

She shook her head, appalled by the disloyal feeling but unable to deny it. A skilled cook, Frigyth knew that salt and spice were what gave food its flavor. Spice was rare, and all the more valuable for it, but she'd had it with Sigurd. Had she thrown away what she'd had instead of savoring it? Had she been overcautious in thinking it was preferable never to risk being hurt than to live an exciting life?

She was starting to wonder.

With a resigned sigh, she got up. She would get her mind into a tangle if she started thinking like that. What was done was done, and she would see Sigurd again anyway. Spring was coming. Only this morning she had been awoken by the chirping of birds. Perhaps in a few weeks it would be warm enough to go to the lake. For now, she might as well get dressed, and try to—

The scream pierced a hole through Frigyth's body. It was the worst kind of scream, caused by pain, fear and disbelief. Before she could think, she rushed out of the house.

In front of the draper's shop, a man she recognized as one of her neighbors was beating a child who could not be more than four or five summers. Frigyth's whole body seized in horror and then she sprung into action. By the time she reached Osric, the boy had curled up into a ball and had stopped screaming, too busy trying to avoid the kicks to waste energy.

"Let go of him!" she cried, tears blinding her vision.

How dare the man attack someone so much smaller than him? How dare he hurt the poor child? She pummeled at his back in powerless rage. Though her blows clearly had little effect on the man, at least he stopped kicking at the boy to turn his ire onto her.

"This has nothing to do with you, wench! Leave!" He grabbed her hair and forced her head backward. A glint appeared in his eyes when he saw her. Arousal instantly replaced anger. "Unless you prefer I attend to you instead?"

Frigyth whimpered. "I don't."

But Osric's attention was now fully on her. Her blood curdled when she saw the smile blooming on his face. How was she going to get out of this? "Well, I might want a moment in your company," he drawled. "We could keep each other warm, you know."

"I am warm already. Just let me go."

"Oh, now, why would I do that?"

"Because if you don't I will ram my fist down your throat so far you will think your body has been turned inside out."

The calm, deep voice suddenly cut through the tension. Osric swiveled around to reveal a scowling Sigurd standing in the middle of the road. Frigyth's body instantly relaxed. She was safe. If he was here, nothing would happen to her.

"Who the hell are you?" Osric did not look best pleased at the interruption.

"At the moment, no one of importance, but if you don't let go of the woman immediately, I will become your worst nightmare."

"Will you now?"

The vile man released her hair so he could straighten to his full height and went to plant himself in front of Sigurd. He could almost stare at him straight in the eye and he was twice as heavy. But Sigurd was younger, leaner, fitter, and he was not drunk. There would be no contest. If he could hold his own against a man like Wolf, a Saxon in his cups didn't stand a chance.

Frigyth ran to the little boy who had scrambled back onto his knees and held him tight against her, shielding him from the inevitable confrontation. He was trembling but mercifully, there didn't appear to be any broken bones. Maybe she had reached them just in time.

"What the hell was that about?" Sigurd growled, lowering his face to glare at the man. Not only had he hurt a child, but he had then wanted to assault Frigyth. When he'd come hurtling round the corner, alerted by the screams, his heart had almost seized in his chest. Seeing his little birdie with her hair in the man's fist and his face hovering over hers had been enough to turn his stomach.

"The woman presumed to dictate how I can treat my own son," the man spat, as if that would justify anything.

It did not.

Sigurd stole a glance toward the little boy who was hiding in

Frigyth's skirts. He certainly didn't seem worried about what would happen to his father when he was confronted with an angry Norseman. That told him more than he needed about the kind of relationship the two of them enjoyed.

"Perhaps it was time someone presumed to tell you. In my experience, children are not afraid of their parents unless they have reason to be."

He remembered Frigyth's story about her drunk father. She would have seen the man mistreat his son and had not been able to stay away. He shook his head. Her heart was in the right place but what was she doing, confronting a man as wide and as opinionated as a bull? Didn't she have any sense of self-preservation?

Well, he was here now. No one was touching her as long as he breathed.

"Elwyn is my son," the man repeated, his words slurred. Unsurprisingly, he stank of drink.

"Then treat him as such, not as your dog."

"You haven't even seen anything. You don't know me."

"No, but I know her. And whatever she objects to, I object to."

"Is it a fight you want then?"

Yes. Sigurd was itching to show the man how pleasurable it was to have someone stronger than him kick at him. But he could not, not in front of Frigyth, who was looking at them with huge, worried eyes and the boy who, though he had hidden his face away, would be able to hear everything. He would not act like the blood-thirsty beast she took him for.

She had left him because she thought he could not control his temper. The first thing she saw of him after a fortnight mulling over her decision could not be him hacking at a man and leaving him for dead, no matter what he had done to his son and would have done to her had he not intervened. There would be no hope of convincing her he was not a savage after that.

"Go and put your head in a bucket of iced water. It might knock some sense back into you. I don't fight with maggots such as you."

The man reddened at the insult. "Maggot?"

"Maggot."

"I'll show you who's a maggot, you bloody Norseman!"

With those words, the Saxon threw the first punch.

Frigyth stared at the scene in incomprehension. What was Sigurd doing? Why wasn't he fighting back?

When Osric had swung his arm she had expected him to be flat on his back before he could even touch his opponent. But not only had the fist connected with Sigurd's jaw, it had even cut his lip. And Sigurd had done nothing. Nor had he retaliated when a kick to the leg had caused him to stumble back. Why? Frigyth's heart sank to the bottom of her stomach when understanding dawned. The wretched man was not fighting because of her. He was going to get himself killed to prove to her he wasn't a thoughtless brute, and perhaps even to himself that he was not a beast.

A kick to the gut had him double forward. Still he did not react, instead coughing violently. Nausea threatened to overwhelm her. Was she going to have to watch him being killed in front of her?

"Sigurd!" she all but screamed. "Fight him, damn you! Give the bastard what he deserves for hurting innocent children!"

She hadn't been able to do it, but if one man was able to make Osric pay, it was her tall Dane.

Sigurd turned to her and straightened his back, all of a sudden a different man. Eyes ablaze, he nodded once and unleashed his fury onto the man facing him.

As she had suspected, there was no contest. Now that he

was assured of her approval, Sigurd was like a man possessed. She had a suspicion that even Wolf would not have been able to withstand the unrelenting assault. Osric, who was not half as skilled or strong as the Icelander, didn't stand a chance. The blows were calculated to force him to defend himself and deny him all opportunity to attack, to incapacitate him without actually killing him.

All too soon, it was over. Osric lay on the ground, not bleeding but not moving either. Sigurd did not even appear out of breath.

"Let's go back inside," he said, nodding at the people who had started to assemble, drawn in by the prospect of a good spectacle. Disgust churned in Frigyth's gut. They were keen to see two men kill each other but where had they been when Elwyn had needed help?

Nowhere.

"Yes."

Heart thumping hard in her chest, she gathered the small boy in her arms and led the way to her house. Once the door was closed, she found she could not look Sigurd in the eye. Bruised and bloodied, bristling with ill-contained fury, he was just too intense. After a prolonged absence, she needed time to adjust to his presence.

"Let me get some linens to clean your wounds," she murmured, lowering a limp Elwyn onto a stool.

In the little room where she slept, she tried to calm the fierce beating of her heart. Only that morning she had been thinking that she might not be able to wait until the summer to see Sigurd again. And now, as in an answer to her prayers, he was here. Why? Did it matter? Was she ready to face him? She wasn't sure.

Cursing herself for her lack of courage, she grabbed one of her old shifts and started to shred it into ribbons.

By the time she came back into the main room, Elwyn had fallen asleep at the table. Sigurd gave her a wry smile and picked him up gently. "He's about to fall on his backside. Is there anywhere I can lay him down?"

She gestured to the room she had just left. "Put him in there, in my bed. He will sleep with me tonight. I doubt his father will be in a state to look after him anyway."

Something flashed in Sigurd's blue eyes. Amusement? Desire? "Replacing me with a puny boy, are you, birdie?"

Her breath caught in her throat. The intimate tone of voice, the use of his special nickname... Was he trying to confuse her further? If so, it was working.

"Yes. At least I should have room to breathe with him next to me."

He grunted, as she'd fully expected. How wonderful it was to tease him and see him respond! "You never complained when I lay next to you, as I recall."

No, she had not. Because nothing had felt more wonderful that having his big body next to her. Mercifully, he did not seem to require an answer and disappeared into the room she'd indicated with Elwyn in his arms. When he came back into the main room, Frigyth had to fight the wave of emotion flooding her chest. How she had missed him!

"Let's get you cleaned, shall we? Sit down."

When she started examining the cut on his lip and the bruise on his jaw, fury erupted within her. What would have happened if she had not spoken out when she did? Would Osric's next blow have killed him?

It was not impossible.

"You stupid, stupid man!" she cried out, landing a smack on his incredibly hard chest. And then another one for good measure. "You scared me senseless out there, you know that!"

He looked nonplussed. "But that's why I didn't want to fight him. Because I didn't want you to be scared of me."

"I don't mean it like that!" She stared at him in incredulity. "I mean that I was scared for you. You could have died. That foul man was beating the life out of you and you did nothing, you big lout!"

"I didn't want you to think—"

She roared. Oh, had there ever been a more exasperating man? "Sigurd. Sometimes violence is the only option, especially with someone who doesn't understand any other argument, with someone who is trying to kill you. Even I can see that."

He took her hand in his before she could hit him again. "If it's any consolation, I wouldn't have let him kill me. I think I would have eventually sent him sprawling to the ground. There's only so much a man can take, you know."

"Well, next time, make sure you send him sprawling *before* he makes you bleed, do you hear?"

They stared at each other a long moment, then she started to dab at his chin with the wet cloth. Placed where she was, his head was lower than hers, almost level with her breasts. Was he thinking the same thing as she was? Of how he had suckled her the night he had made love to her? Heat spread through her chest at the memory, before settling in the place between her legs.

Frigyth chided herself. Now was not the time to think about such things, with a small child asleep in the next room, and Sigurd injured.

"Here we are again, you taking care of me." He sounded wistful.

"And once again, you came to my rescue."

She swallowed hard. What would have happened if he had not arrived when he had didn't bear thinking about. As soon as Osric had seized her, she had frozen in panic, remembering the way Olaf had immobilized her before lifting her skirts. With her body not responding, she would never have managed to stop him.

Then a thought struck her.

"What are you doing here, Sigurd?" She had not thought it odd when he'd appeared, such had been her relief, but it was odd. He didn't live here.

"I heard the little boy's screams. I thought to help him. I had no idea I would find you in the hands of the brute."

"No, of course..." She paused, absorbing the information. That was all very well, but to hear the screams, he would have had to be in town already, and not far from her house. It was still quite early. Either he had left the village long before dawn or—

She shook her head, refusing to think about the alternatives. She could not afford to hope he had come to see her, and she refused to even entertain the possibility he had spent the night with another woman.

"What possessed you to challenge the man?" Sigurd asked her, shaking his head in disapproval once she had finished cleaning his chin.

"What else could I do? I heard Elwyn's screams as I was getting dressed. Should I have left him to face his father alone?" She bunched her fists.

He sighed. "No, of course, not. But you cannot put yourself in such danger."

"Why not? What is it to you?"

The silence that followed the question almost vibrated with Sigurd's indignation. "What is it to me if you get hurt?" he said in a low rumble. "How can you ask me this? After what..."

His voice trailed off.

After what happened to you. After what happened between us.

The words never passed his lips but she understood his

meaning all the same. At least he had not called it 'fucking' today.

She shook her head, ashamed of herself. "I'm sorry. I should never have said that. I've not been feeling myself these last few days." That was an understatement, but it was already too damning for comfort. Why had she told Sigurd as much? Before he could comment, she added, "Will you go back to the village now?"

"Yes. I only came last night to meet with a group of Danish merchants about to go back home. I slept with them at the camp last night."

Oh. He had not come to town to be with a woman, then. She could not help the wave of relief washing though her. "Will you not... stay here tonight?"

Irritation veiled Sigurd's eyes and he shot to his feet. "I can walk fine. Osric hardly crippled me."

"Of course, I know that. I didn't—"

"Frigyth." He skewered her with the force of his stare. "If I stay here tonight, neither of us will sleep."

Her whole body went liquid at the words. "You mean..." She could not say it, not when he was towering over her and looking at her so intently.

"If I stay here I will take you all night, again and again, until you can't move and I can't breathe." Never had any declaration of intent been clearer. It was as if he thought that, now she had left him, he had nothing to lose by being himself and letting his baser feelings show.

She almost threw herself in his arms there and then, but he took a step back before she could.

"And I don't think you'd want that," Sigurd added. "You cannot deal with this side of me."

Couldn't she?

Though she had told him as much only a few days ago,

suddenly she wanted nothing more than to have him take her until neither of them could move or breathe, and to hell with everything else, with what she was supposed to want.

Why did she feel this way? Sigurd had never looked more forbidding, more dangerous than he did in this instant, with his eyes ablaze, his cheek bruised and his lip cut, the image of the fierce, indomitable warrior. She should be wary of such a man, yet she was lusting after him. She should be horrified at the violence he was capable of, yet she was not because he'd unleashed it for a good cause. He'd only defended himself against Osric, who had thrown the first punch when nothing obliged him. The foul man had deserved nothing more than a good thrashing after his mistreating of an innocent child.

As for Olaf, who'd been beaten the other day... He should have known better than to assault women. Not just once, but twice. That she knew, at least. But perhaps she and Edith were not the only ones to have suffered at his hands...

She remained rooted to the spot, staring at Sigurd, unable to speak, unable to think. He brushed a light finger over her cheek and clenched his jaw.

"I will leave you now. Goodbye, birdie."

As soon as the door was closed, Frigyth rushed to the table. There was barely enough time to seize the basin she had used to dip the linen strips in before she was sick.

Panting heavily, Frigyth sat on the stool. Everything was unraveling fast, like a painstakingly-woven tapestry being destroyed by a mischievous child in the midst of a tantrum. She would have to do something about it if she wanted something of her to be left once fate had decided to move on to her next victim.

CHAPTER TWENTY-THREE

"Wolf. I have found your wife's attacker."

Had he not been friends with him, Sigurd might well have taken fright when the big Icelander turned to face him. There was such lethal determination in the blue eyes that he feared he had just signed Osric's death warrant.

Well, too bad if he had. He could not bring himself to regret it.

On the way back from town, to try and distract himself from thoughts of Frigyth writhing under him in ecstasy, Sigurd had tried to remember where he had seen the man before. Then when he'd seen Merewen in the vegetable patch outside the hut, it had come back to him. Frigyth's neighbor was the man he'd prized off of her two months ago when she had tried to get back home. Without his intervention, Merewen would have been raped. That day the man had taken advantage of Sigurd making sure she was all right to escape. He would not be so lucky a second time.

They had not been able to find him until now because he'd

hadn't had a proper look at his face but he remembered his bulk, his fetid smell, his foul words.

We could keep each other warm.

The same words he'd told the two women, women who had not wanted him. Oh, it was him, he was sure of it.

And so, by revealing Osric's identity to his friend, he would give him the opportunity to take his revenge on the man who'd hurt his wife. If Sigurd was not allowed to defend a woman who was only pretending to be married to him from men who raped her, he would damn well make sure Wolf could punish the bastard who had attacked Merewen, who was actually married to him. It was the least he could do. Justice had to be done.

"Who's the bastard?"

"One of Frigyth's neighbors in town, a man called Osric. I went to see her today and walked in on him beating his son and assaulting Frigyth for trying to defend the child."

"I see he almost got the better of you." Wolf nodded at his bruised cheek.

"That's only because I didn't want to..." Sigurd shook his head. It mattered not what Wolf thought. He had nothing to prove to anyone.

"Will you take me there?"

"We can leave right now. Though I'm not sure he will have gained back consciousness. He was drunk as well."

"Let's hope for his sake he never does." Wolf's voice was grim. "Because once I get my hands on him he might well wish he had died in the fight."

Just then, Merewen appeared, a bunch of weeds in her hand. She smiled when she saw her husband and Sigurd found himself wishing he had a woman—Frigyth—smiling at him like that. Then she looked at him and the smile wavered. "What happened to you, Sigurd?"

He shrugged. "Nothing. A disagreement with one of the Dane merchants in town."

"Worry not, little one, Sigurd can take care of himself." Wolf answered with a commendable effort at nonchalance. He gave her a swift, but passion-filled kiss. "Go back inside, it's getting cold. I have something to do this evening. I might be late getting back."

His wife was not fooled. Sigurd could tell she had guessed Wolf was going on a punitive expedition. Nevertheless, as she knew the role Wolf played in the community, she didn't raise any objections or make any comment.

A moment later, the two men were running toward the lake.

As she left Milburg's house, Frigyth let in a long shuddering breath. What she had come to suspect had been confirmed by the old healer.

Wrapping her cloak around her, she slowly picked her way over the snow-covered ground. What would she do now? How would she raise this child when she was on her own and her feelings for the father were of such a problematic nature? Tears started to fall down her cheeks and she didn't try to wipe them away. How could this have happened? She had hoped and hoped to be mistaken but in the end, she'd had to face facts.

She was with child.

In truth, it explained a lot. Her tiredness, her unusual sensitivity, her susceptibility to smells besides salted fish, her tender breasts. Milburg had explained it all to her as gently as she could, explained why she had not realized it sooner. The old woman, who had been the one delivering her, and a confidante over the years, had not missed how shocking the news was to her. She had given her a hug and told her it would be all right.

Frigyth could not help a bitter laugh. Would it really? How?

She came to an abrupt halt at the end of her road. A crowd had gathered in front of her house. As she drew nearer she was able to hear what was being said.

"It was only a question of time before he died anyway."

"Aye..." A woman sighed. "Pity. Such a fine, strong man."

Her jealous husband huffed. "A whole lot of good that did him, if he was a drunkard! You're better off sparring with me, wife. I have no problem raising my... sword for you!"

The men laughed at the crude jest. A shiver ran down Frigyth's spine. Were they talking about Osric? A strong drunkard... Yes, it could well be. But if they did, that meant he was dead. How? Had he died of the injuries inflicted by Sigurd the day before? They hadn't seemed so severe to her.

"What happened?" she asked the woman standing nearest to her.

"Osric was found dead in his house this morning."

"How did he die?" Frigyth didn't even bother pretending to be surprised or sorry.

"No one rightly knows. He was found lying in a pool of blood, baring the traces of a recent fight."

Oh Lord, *had* Sigurd killed the man? He'd been still alive when they'd left him the day before, she was sure of it, but... Had Sigurd gone back to him after leaving her house? And then another thought wiped all questions from her mind.

Elwyn!

Where was the little boy? When he had woken up from his nap the day before, he had insisted on going back home, refusing her offer of shelter for the night. Frigyth had not been able to stop him. But if his father was dead, what would he do? Frigyth knew his mother had died birthing him. He was now alone, he would be scared, he would be hungry and cold in the snow, he needed her! She looked around in despair.

"Has anyone seen his son? Elwyn?"

Everyone shook their heads. "When Wigmund found Osric, he was on his own. There was no sign of the boy. He will have fled upon discovering his father dead, I'm thinking."

"Fled?" To where? She had to get to him. But how? Frigyth stilled. One person might be able to help her.

She took the road to the Norsemen village at a run.

"PLEASE, I NEED YOUR HELP."

Wolf was the man of the situation. He was kind and helpful, he knew everyone in the area. There weren't many people who were not indebted to him. If anyone could find out Elwyn's whereabouts, it was him.

He lowered his axe and frowned at her. "Frigyth? What are you doing here? Have you walked all the way from town in this snow?" He looked incredulous.

"Nevermind that. I found out today that my neighbor Osric is dead, and I—"

"I know."

There was such hatred in those two words that she gasped when understanding dawned. "You... You killed him?"

She could scarce believe what she was saying but how else would he know? The news of the man's death could not have traveled to the village so fast. The only way Wolf would know that Osric had died was if he had killed him himself. But why would he do such a thing? They didn't know each other. Had Sigurd reported what he had done to her? Perhaps. But why would he care?

Before she could start panicking, the Icelander shook his head. "Come inside, you need to get warm."

"What I need is to understand."

"You will. Come."

A moment later Frigyth was seated by the fire, a cup of warmed ale in her hand. Wolf was prowling around the hut like a beast in a cage. Merewen was nowhere to be seen. Frigyth waited, fighting nausea, already knowing she wouldn't like what she was about to hear.

"Yesterday Sigurd told me Osric had attacked you."

Oh, Lord. Her blood ran cold in her veins. "Is that why you went into town? To avenge me? There was no need. Sigurd already—"

"No. I wanted to avenge my wife."

Frigyth blinked. "Merewen?" This was the last thing she had expected to hear.

Wolf bared his teeth in a snarl. "The day you met her here at the hut, she was bruised, you will recall."

Yes, she did recall. One doesn't forget something like that. She had guessed at the time Wolf had helped her escape a man intent on hurting her. And that man had been Osric? "I-I do remember," she stammered.

"He attacked her one day while she was visiting town but mercifully Sigurd arrived before the bastard could..." He paused, the blue in his eyes swirling with fury. "Anyway, he saved her and brought her back to me. I will forever be in his debt for what he did." Frigyth waited. She still didn't see what that had to do with anything. "Yesterday he told me about what happened with you and the man's son in the street. He also told me he'd recognized your neighbor for the man who'd attacked Merewen that day. Well, of course, I had to go find him."

To kill him.

The words were left unsaid but she could not mistake his meaning. She whimpered and almost dropped her cup of ale. "You k—"

"I did not kill him. Though I might well have had I not

found him already lying in a pool of blood." His voice was as hard as the blade of his axe.

"So then he died of the injuries inflicted by Sigurd." How would she live with that idea?

But again Wolf shook his head. "No. Sigurd told me he had merely incapacitated him. I believe him. He is more than capable of doing so and he would have no reason for lying to me."

She nodded. She had thought as much, but still the fact remained. Someone had killed Osric. If not one of the two Norsemen, then who?

"No one killed him," Wolf said, answering the silent question. "It was an accident in the end. He was drunk, he staggered and fell, hitting his temple on the corner of the table."

"You saw this?"

"No. His son did, just moments before we reached the house. He told us what happened. There was nothing we could—"

"Elwyn!" Frigyth cried, bolting out of the chair. That was why she had come! The rest could wait. "Where is he? I have to find him."

"Calm down. He's with Sigurd."

She fell back down on the chair as relief swept through her. If he was with the Dane, the boy was safe.

It was all too much. She looked at Wolf—and promptly burst into sobs. After a moment, Wolf crouched down in front of her, his attitude almost paternal.

"Sigurd is my friend and a good man. Not only did he save my wife from assault that day in town but he was the one who allowed me to see the mistake I'd made when I didn't want to listen to my instinct. He was the one who discovered the identity of the enemy who was after her. Without him, I would most likely have lost Merewen." He clenched his jaw like a man remembering something painful. "I owe him more than you can know. So although I will never be able to repay him for what he did, I will at least try to help him, even if it means revealing his secret."

"Secret?" Frigyth's heart started beating unbearably hard in her chest.

Wolf sighed. "The man's in love with you. Has been from the start, I think. He almost knocked me unconscious when I suggested once he only wanted to get between your legs." He winced, clearly ashamed of himself. "Forgive me for the crudeness, I had drunk too much that day and was aching from Merewen's disappearance. Anyway, that was before you came to the village and lived with him for two weeks. If he was smitten then, I cannot imagine how he feels now that you spent so much time together. I can only say he would never have done his best to spare Olaf if he didn't love you. Not that he cannot control himself, but he would have every reason to flatten the man. If he'd not been trying to spare your feelings because he's in love with you, he would not have thought about it twice."

"He did say he could not be reasonable where I was concerned," she said, almost to herself.

"I'm not surprised. I feel exactly the same where my wife is concerned. Why, I did consider killing this Osric in cold blood, something I would never have done otherwise. That is how I know Sigurd loves you, truly and deeply even if he doesn't realize it himself, even if it pains him to admit it." Wolf paused and Frigyth knew what he would ask her next. "What about you? Do you feel anything for him?"

Her bottom lip started to tremble. Feelings. Oh she had *feelings* for this man, feelings she had tried to suppress, feelings she could never admit to anyone else. Of course, she had feelings for Sigurd, how could she not? He had helped her, sheltered her, made her laugh, taken care of her, saved her life. He was the man who had reconciled her with her body, made her see she was not irreparably damaged.

Tears threatened to overwhelm her once more. With a great effort she contained them. "Even if I did, it would not—"

"Do you?"

"It doesn't matter because—"

"Yes. It is all that matters. Do you return his feelings?" Wolf was relentless.

Frigyth shook her head. She would have to spell out what the problem was. He would never allow her to go without admitting what she felt. Heart in her throat, she lifted her head.

"I'm with child."

The Icelander froze for a moment, then a smile bloomed on his face. "Well then, that's even better. I told you that Sigurd was orphaned at a young age, and never knew his parents. He craves a family. He will be overjoyed to welcome this child."

"You don't understand," she breathed, looking at her clenched fists. "The child... It's not Sigurd's."

CHAPTER TWENTY-FOUR

"**F**rigyth is here. She's come to see Elwyn."

Sigurd watched as Wolf approached, flanked by Frigyth. He did his best not to betray the fact that his heart had burst out of his chest at the sight of her but shock had almost floored him. He had been so certain he would never see her again, not in the village at least... But here she was, looking more beautiful than ever, even if it was clear she had cried. Of course, she would have worried herself sick about Elwyn. How had he not thought she would think about the boy when she found out about Osric's death?

"He's sleeping inside," he said, loath to see her so distraught. "Helga gave him a soothing draught earlier. The poor child needed peace and quiet after the horrors of the last few days."

Wolf nodded. "I'll leave you two to it. Merewen is waiting for me."

His friend threw him a look Sigurd could not quite interpret before turning away. It was almost as if he was warning him about something, or ordering him not to do anything foolish. Was he worried he would hurt Frigyth? Surely not!

Pushing the uncomfortable idea out of his mind, he drew

nearer to Frigyth. Though she was wearing a cloak, she looked frozen to the bone. Well, she would be, if she had come all the way from town in the snow. He fought the urge to lift her into his arms and bring her inside, where he could remove her sodden shoes and massage her numb feet. He did, however, take off his cloak to wrap it around her. She nodded her thanks and for a moment looked about to start crying again. His heart constricted. He *never* wanted to see her cry again.

He wanted to see her laugh, smile, scowl, pant in pleasure, look at him the way Merewen looked at Wolf. The last few weeks without her had been the worst of his already miserable life. He had been on his own before, terribly lonely, and it had been hard, but it had never threatened to extinguish the fire burning inside him. Being without Frigyth, though, had almost destroyed him. He felt like a hollow shell, without hope, without needs, without joy.

In that moment, his decision was made. Frigyth had not come to see him, rather to inquire about the boy, but it made little difference. She was here now and he would not let her leave again. He would do whatever it took to convince her that she didn't want to live all alone in an empty house that reminded her of her unhappy childhood but stay here with him and the little boy who needed a mother. He would beg, he would make a fool of himself, pretend to fall ill again, break his arm, use what she felt for Elwyn to sway her if need be. Nothing would be beneath him.

As long as she stayed with him.

"You know about Osric then," he said softly.

"Yes. Thank you for taking care of Elwyn."

"Please. It was the least I could do. He's alone in the world now. And what is he going to do, young as he is?" He clenched his jaw. Looking after the little boy might allow him to put the pain of his past behind. He would do for Elwyn what no one had been able to do for him. "If he agrees, I will be his father."

"Then he's a lucky boy."

Frigyth looked at Sigurd, so dependable, so determined to do the right thing and her heart melted. Elwyn would be happy here, with a father showing him all he knew and loving him more than Osric ever could. What she wouldn't give to have Sigurd look after her also! How had she ever thought this man would not be able to give her what she needed, thought he could make her life anything other than more beautiful?

Because now that he was in front of her, it was clear as crystal in her mind. He *would* give her what she needed, he already had. She had nothing to fear. Life with him would be exciting, finally worth living.

Merewen's words came back to her.

I understood what was behind it. He actually wanted to protect me.

That was what was driving Sigurd as well, had driven him from the start. He wanted to protect her. According to Wolf, he'd been in love with her from the moment they'd met. It sounded hard to believe but it had to be true, because it explained everything. The only time Sigurd had allowed his rage to burst through had been for her. As he'd said, he couldn't keep a level head where she was concerned. Other than that, he was nothing like the beast he had been likened to. He had kept his word not to hurt Olaf, he had found it easy to control himself in front of a man who was actually hitting him, he had then done his best not to kill or even maim him, ensuring he only incapacitated him. All the while he had put her wishes and needs ahead of his own preferences.

And in return... She had accused him of being a blood-thirsty savage, incapable of giving her what she thought she wanted. She had left him, even when he had asked her to stay.

She had not trusted he could be the man she needed. She had forsaken him.

What a stupid, stupid fool she'd been!

How would he forgive her for the pain she had caused him? Why should he? She was ready to beg him to keep her but what if it was too late and she had hurt him too deeply? What if he did love her but could not deal with knowing that she was carrying another man's child? What would she do then, alone in her empty house populated by troublesome ghosts? Where would she go if she ever found the courage to leave? So many questions she didn't have the answer to.

A wave of nausea threatened to overwhelm her. It must have shown because Sigurd placed a hand on her shoulder, concern etched on his face.

"You're not well, are you, birdie. What's the matter? You've gone all pale." She wasn't surprised, she felt about to be sick. "Perhaps I can help. Would you like to tell me?"

"I-I don't know how to..."

"Do you want to try?"

She did, but where could she start? There were so many things she needed to atone for, so many things she wanted to get off her chest! That she regretted leaving him, that she had come to realize she was in love with him and was finally ready to accept him for what he was. That old Milburg had confirmed this morning what she had dreaded to hear all along. That she didn't know how to deal with it all. That she wasn't sure what she would do if he turned away from her.

"I'm pregnant," she sobbed, collapsing onto the bench behind her.

Thunder fell at Sigurd's feet.

Frigyth was *pregnant*? But... How could she know so soon? They had slept together less than a month ago, surely it was too early to tell. And how could she even be carrying his child when he had taken care to spill outside her body? He distinctively remembered, because it had cost him every ounce of control to do so. For a long moment he stared at her in incomprehension. This didn't make any sense, he must have misheard her. He pinched the bridge of his nose, trying to understand.

Then she closed her eyes and said one word. The one word he had hoped never to hear again in her mouth.

"Olaf."

The silence that stretched between them was as thick as the snow falling from the leaden skies.

"You mean he assaulted you again when you stayed at the village?"

His voice was lethal, sharp as a blade. He already knew that if Frigyth said yes, he would track the man down and kill him. There would be no stopping him this time. True to his word, Wolf had banished the raping bastard from the village as soon as the healer had declared him out of mortal danger, but that would not protect him. He might have a few days head start but if Frigyth told him now that Olaf had touched her again, Sigurd would find him and he would kill him. It would be a slow, agonizing death, and he would enjoy every moment of it.

After all, he was a beast, wasn't he?

But she shook her head slowly, as if she didn't understand herself what she was about to say. "No. It was f-from that first time..."

From that first rape? But...

"I thought you'd told Wolf you weren't to have Olaf's child?" The day they had met she had come to tell the Icelander she wasn't with child. So what did that mean? Had she lied to appease Wolf? Surely not!

"I did believe he hadn't made me with child, but evidently I was mistaken." She buried her face in her hands and started sobbing again. "I bled a few days after the attack, and thought my courses had come. I did not pay much attention, did not see it was not the s-same flow as usual, that it s-stopped that same day. I was just so relieved, so glad to be able to put the whole thing behind me... But now it's been over two months and n-nothing! I'm nauseous, and it's not just when I smell salted fish, it's every morning, all the time. My body feels different. Oh, I'm pregnant, I just know it, and old Milburg confirmed it earlier."

Sigurd fell to his knees in front of her so he could crush her into his arms. Not knowing what to say, he let her cry her heart out against his chest, wishing he could make all her pain disappear. Rage was racing through his veins. That bastard Olaf had not only taken her innocence, hurt and frightened her, he had also imposed his child onto her.

Once she had calmed down he drew back to look at her straight in the eye. "The child—"

She cut him off with a fierce look. "I love it. No matter who his father is, *I* am its mother. Nothing can take that away from me." She shook her head, as if trying to make sense of her feelings. "I can't explain it. It just is that way. Please don't judge me."

"I don't judge you. I think you are the strongest, most amazing woman I've ever met, loving a babe imposed on you in such a way." Slowly, he lifted her chin, and leaned in, barely stopping before their lips touched. "Listen to me, Frigyth. I once pretended to be your husband. Now I want to marry you in truth."

Her lovely velvet eyes fluttered. "You do? Why?"

Why?

He smiled to himself. Of course, his little birdie would ask why. When did she not? But this question was easy to answer.

"Because I loved every moment of living with you, of seeing you laugh, of having you take care of me, of answering your endless questions, of eating your food, of making you cry out in pleasure. I loved... you." He took in a deep breath. There would never be a better moment to tell her the whole truth. He'd meant to take it slowly, but things had been turned on their heads by her revelation. "I love you, birdie, have loved you from the moment I saw you in the village looking for Wolf's hut, I think. And now I want you to be my wife. I warned you, remember? I warned you when you started living with me and made those amazing oatcakes. If you treat me so well, I will never want to let you go. Well, I don't. Please stay, and marry me."

She swallowed hard. Unlike what he had hoped, she did not fall into his arms, and declare her undying love for him. But she didn't recoil either. He waited, fists clenched to stop himself from reaching out to her.

"You know I... I do not come on my own?" Fresh tears filled her eyes.

"I do. But neither do I now." He glanced toward the hut where Elwyn was still sleeping. "As my wife, you will become his mother. Is that something you would be prepared to do?"

"Yes, of course." A tear fell on her cheeks. He wiped it away. "But it's not the same and you know it."

No, it wasn't. But it made no difference. He placed a gentle hand on her stomach and felt it harder than it had been the night they had made love. His heart leapt and he realized it would be easy to love this child, because it was hers, and she was the woman he loved.

"If you are brave enough, generous enough to love a child imposed on you by a—" He clenched his jaw to stop himself from uttering all the thoughts going through his head. Now was not the time for the beast to scare her away. "Then I am certainly brave enough to help you. You started to live in the hut less than a month after the attack and you were there for one night two weeks before that, when I twisted my ankle. If you want, we can tell everyone this child is mine, conceived in the days you lived with me as my supposed wife, or even on that first night. It might make people think you surrendered your favors easily but perhaps you would prefer that to them knowing what happened to you?"

Olaf and he shared similar looks, as did all the Norsemen in the village. Passing off a blond, blue-eyed babe as his would be easy and would not raise anyone's suspicion. Frigyth made a face he interpreted as unease.

"If you don't, and you prefer not to hide the real father's identity, it's no problem," he murmured in her ear. "It's your decision, birdie. Either way, I will be there to raise it with you."

"You would do that? Have everyone know you welcomed a child you did not father under your roof?"

"I would do whatever makes you more comfortable. Allowing me to be the father this baby needs will be the best gift I've ever received. You know why. It will help me put behind the hurt caused by my parents' absence. Together we will give Elwyn and this innocent babe the childhood neither of us had. They will be loved, they will be looked after, they will never worry about where their next meal comes from or whether they will be hurt when their father staggers back home drunk. They will be happy. As will we."

"Oh, Sigurd." Frigyth hiccupped. "Then yes, I will marry you. I will raise this child with you, as your son or daughter. And, in time, I will give you others, children of your own blood. I love you, too. I have loved you from the moment you scowled at me for looking after your ankle."

Sigurd's heart leapt. She loved him? Could he allow himself to hope?

It was not certain, because he still wasn't sure he would be able to act reasonably. If he could not control his tongue in her presence, what hope did he have of controlling his temper? He knew he was not the most patient of men, and even less so where she was concerned. If anyone ever looked at Frigyth the wrong way or hinted at what they wanted to do to her, he would want to rip them to shreds. It was inevitable.

Was she ready to accept that?

The silence was too long for Frigyth's liking. Was Sigurd having second thoughts? No, not now, it would be too cruel! She had just declared her love for him, he had just admitted to loving her as well, they had agreed to get married and raise Elwyn and the child she was carrying together. She had expected—hoped even—he would sweep her into his arms and seal the moment with a scorching kiss.

Instead, he was looking at her with bunched fists and glittering eyes. What was going on?

Finally he spoke, his voice raw. "You would trust me not to cause you any distress? You know how uncontrollable I can be and I know you need security and calm after what you had to endure. I'd understand if you thought life with me would be—"

"No! I trust you!" she cut in before he could say another word. Why had she ever told him such a thing, made him fear he was like her father, incapable of making her happy, of being a family man? This man was a loving protector to the core. The only distress he could cause her would be to refuse her now, after the best declaration of love she could have dreamed of. "I know you have a temper, I know you swear, but I care not. I wouldn't have you any different, because that man is the man I fell in love with."

"You say that now. But what if one day I—"

"Sigurd, you might think you cannot control yourself, but I know you can. I have seen you fight with Wolf without either of you getting hurt, I've seen you refuse to fight a man who was attacking you. You are capable of control. You promised me you wouldn't punish Olaf, even though you were dying to do it, and you didn't."

"Until I did."

"Yes, because he was assaulting another woman under your nose, remember!" she cried out. "Do you think I would have preferred you to walk away? No, I wouldn't. I am not worried about being with a man who will pummel innocents to the ground, rather I feel lucky to be marrying a man who can defend me and my family if need be. Besides, now that you are looking after Elwyn, I know you won't be doing anything that might get you stupidly killed."

"No, I won't."

Sigurd stilled as if he'd just realized she was right. Now that he had a family, responsibilities, people who relied on him, he would be able to keep his worst excesses in check, because it was not just about him anymore. Elwyn, she and the little life she was carrying all needed him. She knew in her heart he would not jeopardize the happiness they brought him for people who did not deserve his time and energy.

He lifted his face to the skies and inhaled sharply, like a man finally at peace. The beast in him had been soothed, it was no longer to be feared, rather accepted as an ally when needed.

"Will you kiss me, my love?" he asked, taking her hands in his. He had never looked more intense, more handsome. The woman in her quivered. "I've been dying to taste your lips for weeks."

"You already have," she whispered, making him frown.

"What do you mean? We've never kissed. Surely I would remember something like that?"

Frigyth hesitated. Should she tell him the truth? Yes. They could not start their marriage on a lie. "One night when you lay abed with fever, I... I kissed you. I know I shouldn't have but I couldn't resist and we—"

Sigurd cut her embarrassed explanations short by drawing her into his arms.

"You mean that kiss was real?" He sounded full of awe. "I've been obsessing about it for weeks, you know. I've even felt guilty about it, thinking I had somehow taken advantage of you, by doing in my imagination things you would never agree to in real life."

"It was real." Frigyth reddened. More than real. "But if you don't believe me, come and see for yourself."

He didn't need any more incentive. His lips landed on hers, reverent, gentle at first, then when she moaned and pressed herself tighter against him, the kiss became incandescent, just as fiery as she remembered. Except this time they were both fully aware of what was happening, except she knew this kiss would be the first of many, except this time there was no holding back.

When they finally drew back, Sigurd was smiling and so was she.

"Oh yes," he said in a rasp. "It was real."

CHAPTER TWENTY-FIVE

S igurd and Frigyth married three days later, in a Norse ceremony. They would have married the day after they had exchanged their first real kiss, but Frigyth had wanted her sister Dunne to attend so they had postponed it while they waited for her to arrive. Unfortunately, Birgit lived too far away to be notified. A message would have taken weeks to reach her and there would be no guarantee she could travel anyway.

Around them, nature was in full bloom, preparing for spring. The sun was making the last sprinklings of snow in the ditches sparkle, the trees had started to unfurl their leaves, birds were chirping away happily, snowdrops and crocuses surrounded the village huts in cheerful clumps.

Frigyth was wearing her dress of soft green wool. Merewen had helped adjust it to accommodate her thickening waist. For a reason neither of them could explain, her stomach had expanded almost overnight. In her hair, they had woven a few of the early spring blooms. Without asking anyone or looking at her reflection on a puddle, Frigyth knew she looked beautiful.

Dressed in a new tunic of blue wool, Elwyn was bursting with pride, pride she shared a hundred fold.

With a smile, she took his hand and led him to the middle of the village where her groom was waiting for them. Her breath caught in her chest when she saw him. His hair had been braided in a complex hairstyle that somehow made him look even more masculine, but it was the look in his eyes when he saw her that made her go weak in the knees.

Sigurd looked as if he could have devoured her on the spot.

Trembling with anticipation, she took her place next to him.

After the ceremony Wolf and Merewen were the first to offer their congratulations to the newlywed couple.

"Thank you. Now, I hope not to hear teasing about my supposed preference for men ever again," Sigurd growled in the direction of his friend. Frigyth had to bite her lip to stop the laughter from escaping. How had she even entertained the possibility of this man bedding other men?

"Oh, I assure you, it was never meant as a tease for *you*," Merewen piped up, giving her husband's arm a squeeze. "I only wanted to rankle Wolf."

Wolf sighed. "Yes. Don't I know it. You're nothing but trouble, wife, have been from the start. I should have fled as fast as my legs could carry me that day." But the fire in his eyes belied the words. Never had a reprimand sounded more like a loving compliment. Frigyth smiled, thinking that now she had found her own fierce, protective Norseman. Didn't she love it when he complained about how nosy or stubborn she was?

"We will take Elwyn fishing today and keep him with us tonight," Merewen said, ruffling the little boy's hair affectionately. "I think he will like that and it will give the newlyweds a little time to themselves."

Frigyth went red to the roots of her hair when her friend winked at her with ill-concealed mirth.

Sigurd was less easily embarrassed. "Thank you. That's the most thoughtful present you could have gotten us. We'll make sure to use it well."

With those words, he whisked her away back to the hut, carrying her like a marauder fleeing with his prize.

"Impatient, husband?" she quipped, wrapping her arms around his neck.

"No. Desperate. Ravenous. Frantic." As if he thought that wasn't enough to do justice to his feelings, he added a few Norse words to the list.

My. This was promising.

The door of the hut was kicked open with such force she knew he would have to repair it the following day. The man was clearly demented with need. But once he'd deposited her on the floor, unlike what she had imagined, he didn't tumble her onto the furs. Instead, he stared at her a long moment, hunger, pride, and love shining in his eyes. Frigyth's heart melted at the same time as her insides convulsed.

"Today I married the most beautiful, the most loving, the most incredible woman I have ever met."

"And I married the most handsome, the most caring, the most perfect man I have ever seen."

He drew her into his arms and brushed a finger along her jaw, causing her to shiver. "What now, I wonder?"

Of a common accord, they had agreed to wait until after their marriage to make love. It hadn't been easy, but they had resisted the temptation. Elwyn's innocent presence in the hut had helped, of course...

"Now, we go to bed, husband," Frigyth purred, pressing herself against Sigurd's hard body. This would be explosive, and she couldn't wait. "But before we do... I do have one question."

His mouth quivered. "Inevitably."

"What did you tell me in Norse that day?" she asked in a breath.

Sigurd did not need her to explain. He seemed to understand exactly what day—and what sentence—she was referring to. "I want to kneel at your feet and worship your body," he said slowly, his eyes fastened onto her. "I did then, and I still do."

There was such intent in his voice she flushed all the way down to her toes. "I knew it was something like that. There was that light in your eyes... and that bulge in your hose. Much like now."

He groaned when she placed her hand over his straining manhood. Lord, he was almost worryingly hard. How could he not be in pain with his body so taut?

"Frigyth. I swear you're trying to kill me."

"Oh, no, I'm not, for you would be of no use to me dead." She gave a light squeeze, enjoying the look of agony on his face. How thrilling to know she could affect him so. "Tell me, now we are married, will you unleash the beast?"

"The beast?" Sigurd arched a brow but she had been dying to say those words to him and there would never be a better time. They were married, he knew she loved and trusted him. In time she might even pluck up the courage to ask him about the 'other place' that had been haunting her mind.

"In bed. I would like you to behave like you would with any other woman, one who was not afraid of what men can do." She placed a swift kiss on his mouth. "I understand why you held back the day you took me to bed and I thank you for it but I am not afraid of anything you might do. I trust you."

Sigurd shook his head slowly, before trailing a finger over her lips. She barely resisted the urge to draw it into her mouth and suck. This man would make her do the most scandalous things. "I will not behave like a beast, not with you, not with the woman I love, with my wife, with the mother of my children."

"Well, not a beast, but... Please, be yourself, without fear of hurting or shocking me," she begged. "You know what I mean. Take me. All night, again and again, until I can't move and you can't breathe."

He recognized the words he had told her the other day in her house and his eyes caught fire. "Your wish is my command. Whatever you need, I'll do. Whatever you want, I'll make sure you get it."

Her throat constricted. "I love you, you know that?"

"I love you, too. And I'm going to show you how much. But first, I'll need to undress you, wife."

Wife. Hearing that word in his mouth sent shivers all the way down her spine.

"How did you know I wanted to hear you call me that?" she asked as he lowered first one sleeve of her dress then the other. While Merewen had helped her transform her old dress into a gown fit for a wedding, she had fantasized about the moment Sigurd would peel it off of her body.

The moment had finally come and it was as deliciously arousing as she had imagined.

"How did I know you would enjoy being reminded you're mine?" Sigurd smiled and kissed the mark on the shoulder he had just revealed. "Mm, a little bird told me."

"You're not being serious!" she gasped.

"No. With you the last thing I want to be is serious."

A kiss landed on her shoulder, then another on her collarbone, and then a third one on her throat. Slowly, he started to reveal the rest of her, keeping his mouth on her skin at all times. Once she was naked and panting in front of him, he took a step back to look at her. Her heart almost failed her. Right now she could not think of a more apt name for him than 'beast.' The light in his eyes was wild, the hunger in his gaze would have worried her coming from anyone else. As it came from the man she loved and desired above all others, it heated her blood to an alarming degree.

"Sigurd, please," she whispered, not quite knowing what she was begging for.

"You once said you couldn't think of many things that could bring me to my knees." She nodded, confused. Why was he talking about his now? "I'll show you what can. You."

Frigyth's heart jumped in her throat when he dropped down to his knees in front of her. "What are you—" The rest of the sentence got lost in a croak when Sigurd palmed her buttocks almost roughly to bring her sex to his waiting mouth. He inhaled deeply and let out a feral growl.

"Mm. Mine."

There was such intensity in that one word that she almost collapsed.

"You..." she squealed. "Sigurd, wait!"

"No. I can't wait any longer," he said in a deep rumble. "I've been waiting to do this for weeks. I told you in Norse, I told you in your language, now I'm going to *do* it."

"But you— Oh. *Oh!*" Frigyth lost the ability to talk and the will to protest when a warm, deliciously wicked tongue licked along her intimate seam. "Ah, bloody hell," she whimpered, rolling her head back.

"Who's swearing now, I wonder?" Sigurd sounded wild. "Open your legs wider. Brace yourself on the table. Put your leg on my shoulder. Now. Let me devour you." The instructions were issued in a raspy voice that frayed the few nerve endings that had not already been burnt to a crisp by his scandalous actions.

Doing as she was told, Frigyth leaned against the table and allowed Sigurd to open her up to his daring exploration. When he speared his tongue inside her she had no choice but to sink her fingers into his hair to bring him closer.

What he was doing was so intimate, so delicious, it was such a proof of love that she did not know whether to laugh, cry, moan, beg him to stop or simply stand still and let him bring her to the pinnacle of pleasure. In the end, she had no choice. The moment he slipped one finger inside her, she dissolved in a rush of blinding heat.

For a moment, Sigurd wondered how he was going to get undressed without bringing about his own release. After tasting Frigyth's pleasure, he feared the merest friction over his shaft might make him erupt.

He stood up, licking his lips where her delicious taste lingered.

"Forgive me. I need to take you now." He could not bear to waste time removing his tunic, he could not wait until they reached the pallet. He had to have her now. "You wanted the beast, and you are going to get him."

"Yes!"

With those words, he lifted her onto the table and came to stand between her spread legs. He knew she would be ready, considering what he had just been doing. Like a man possessed, he tore at his braies and slid inside her with one mighty thrust. Yes! Once he was buried to the hilt in her soaked flesh, he stilled, willing himself not to come. Knowing this woman was his, knowing he had just made her explode in pleasure, knowing that this time he would not have to withdraw when he reached his own climax, everything conspired to bring him perilously close to that moment.

"Sigurd, please, move!" Frigyth whimpered, grinding her hips.

"If I move, I'll come," he said through gritted teeth, fighting against the urge to do just that. Damn, the heat of her!

"Yes, and so will I. Please, I'm so close. I need you."

What remained of his control shattered. He started to pump

inside her, bringing his hand to the place where their bodies were joined. He knew it wouldn't be long before he burst, and he had to make sure she reached her pleasure as well. Fortunately, after his earlier attention, she would be sensitive. Using his thumb to circle her nub with almost savage intent, he rubbed her into surrender.

"Ah, like that, yesss," she squealed when her body started to convulse around him, hurtling him into the best release of his life.

Head thrown back, Sigurd erupted before she even finished the word.

For a moment, the world stilled around them. Then slowly, he came back to reality. This had been earth-shattering. And yet it was just the beginning. They had a whole life of this ahead of them.

He couldn't wait.

"Don't think this is over, my love. I've got more to give you," he breathed in her ear. Despite his mind-blowing climax, he was still hard inside her. He flexed his hips to illustrate his point, driving into her. She moaned in response. "But this time I'm going to lie you down and kiss every inch of your delectable body."

"And I, yours. I mean to show you that you are not the only one who can be brought to his knees."

The mere thought had his manhood jerk in anticipation. Oh, he would enjoy watching her devour him.

"Well, birdie, I'm sure that can be arranged. We have the whole night ahead of us. And then our whole life."

"I want a sister!"

Sigurd smiled at Elwyn. "Don't you like having a brother?" He glanced at the babe asleep in his arms. Aged eight months, little Eirik had stolen his heart, as he'd predicted he would. He loved him as much as he loved his eldest son, even though neither boys were of his blood. But the orphan he'd been knew that love, not blood, was all that mattered in the end.

The boy shrugged. "Oh, I do love him, but he doesn't do much, does he?"

This time Sigurd laughed out loud and placed the babe in the cot he had made from the branch he'd broken the day he'd met Frigyth. He had felt silly going back to the oak to see if it was still on the ground and even more silly bringing it back to the hut a few days after their wedding. But when Frigyth had started crying at the sight, he'd not felt silly at all, rather like the luckiest man in the world. He had a perfect wife and a perfect family.

"Eirik doesn't do much at the moment, but wait until he starts walking! Then you'll wish he had never left his cot. And a sister would do even less than him, you know, until she grew up, at least," he pointed out, lifting Elwyn into his arms.

The child's face fell. "Oh. Then I want a big sister."

Sigurd laughed some more. He had not planned to adopt an older girl, but who knew? He was ready to welcome more children under his roof, whether he had fathered them or not.

"What's so funny?" Frigyth entered the hut, a pile of clean clothes in her arms.

"Elwyn is telling me he wants a sister."

"Is he?" She placed the clothes on the table. Something flashed in her eyes, causing him to frown. He'd expected her to laugh at Elwyn's demand. "Well, sweetheart, you might well get one in the autumn."

Sigurd almost dropped his son at the sudden announcement. "You..." The words got stuck in his throat. Then Frigyth placed a hand over her stomach and smiled.

"Or it could be another baby brother. I can't promise anything. We'll just have to wait and see."

Elwyn started to wriggle so much that Sigurd had no choice but to put him back down. "Can I go tell Arne?" he asked excitedly. "He will be so jealous! He told me the other day he was fed up of being on his own!"

"Of course."

As soon as their son had shot through the door, Sigurd drew his wife into his arms. She was crying and, in truth, he felt blurry-eyed himself.

"You're pregnant!"

She gave him a smile through her tears. "Don't tell me you didn't see it coming! You bed me often enough to have noticed I haven't bled in two months."

"I..." He'd been hoping to hear she was going to give him another child, but... He shook his head. How had he been so remiss as to not see something like this? "Forgive me, but I feel as if I'm going to faint." His legs felt barely able to support him. Of course, he would never have admitted as much to anyone other than his wife, but over the months she had seen him in various positions of vulnerability. With her, he could be himself, both beast and lamb.

"If that's the case, then I think you should lie down."

"I'll be fine." There was a limit to how much he was prepared to admit.

"Sigurd. Lie down. Now." Frigyth's eyes were ablaze. He went instantly harder than stone. "Before I make you."

Oh, she didn't need to make such threats. He was only too happy to be ridden by his beautiful wife. He knew from experience that she was wild when she was with child and would not be satisfied until she couldn't move and he couldn't breathe.

"Bolt the door," he ordered, already removing his tunic. If she wanted him flat on his back, he would not deny her.

"I will. And then, *beast*... Then you're all mine."

Next Read
Wooing the Devil
Read about Rune and Eowyn's story

ABOUT THE AUTHOR

As far back as I remember, I have been attracted to the Middle Ages, to knights in shining armour and their ladies in spectacular dresses. Now I get to write about them, I feel like the luckiest woman in the world. Being French and married to a Brit makes each book I write extra special, as our countries share a long and sometimes painful past. But in the end, in life as well as in fiction, love conquers all!

I have published several medieval romances under my own name, including series, and also have a pen name, Judith Falcon, for spicier projects, still in historical romance.

Feel free to check my books out on virginiemarconato.com and judithfalcon.com

ALSO BY VIRGINIE MARCONATO

The Noble Norsemen

Taming the Wolf

Soothing the Beast

Wooing the Devil

Baiting the Bear